MOMMY SAID

Barbara Evans

Published by Winn Publications, Melbourne, Florida, winnpublications.com

Interior & Cover Design: Arilia Winn

MOMMY SAID

DEDICATION

To my daughter, Chrae.

CHAPTER ONE

Crawled up in a corner that use to be her bedroom, Macy tried and tried to get up but she couldn't.

"I'm so cold" she kept saying.

Her head was spinning and the smell of the urine that saturated her clothes was making her sick. She was humiliated and broken.

"Mommy is that you," Macy cried out.

Macy began to crawl across the floor. She managed to find her secret place where she kept her innermost thoughts; she assumed that no one else knew. Trying to stand up once again, she managed to get to the chair.

"So, this is how it all ends," she thought.

Slowly standing on the chair, she wipes the tears and vomit that covered a face that beauty could still not deny. A quote that her Mommy would say comes to mind but she cannot remember all of the words.

"It doesn't matter anyway," she thought. Slipping her head through the noose, she felt her body slip away.

"Mommy you said, you said………

One year later.

Darkness, total darkness. It was a mystery to her and fear gripped her very soul but the presence of evil she did not feel. How did she get here? She did not know. Even her name was past recollection. Maybe she was dead and stuck in the afterlife waiting to cross over to meet her maker in heaven or in hell! The unknown made her cry. My God who am I!

She was exhausted from thinking and trying to figure things out. How long must she endure this insanity? How long was she in this state of being? Her brain, her body, her spirit needed rest. A peaceful calm came over her and she felt her body starting to relax. Slowly she drifted to a place of rest. Later on, she would worry, later on she would try to figure it all out but for now she needed to rest. As she drifted off, she heard an unfamiliar voice softly speaking to her, *peace be still* it said; *peace be still.*

She slept and then she awoke with the sound of voices around her. Unlike the one before, the voices were deep like a thousand men but she wasn't even sure of that. She tried desperately to understand the words that were being said but everything was distorted and scrambled up in her head. She became frustrated. What's the use, I'm done, she thought but a world of darkness and the inability to move she couldn't accept. So, she tried again and again to move her fingers, her hands and her legs; determination at full force but nothing happened. This is how Helen Keller must have felt; unable to communicate; needing and wanting to speak but to no avail. It was like being on an emotional roller coaster. Sometimes she felt so strong and confident that a change would come but other times she felt weak and defeated. She tried to focus but it was like a thousand things going through her mind and still nothing made sense. She longed to hear the voices again; it didn't matter if they were coming from heaven or hell, they kept her company. She heard a voice say a name. The first time it was so faint that she couldn't make out what it said: Mrs. something. My God I felt that, she thought. She felt someone or something around her. She began to feel different, stronger with a mindset of conquering the world. Don't you give up, you fight, the softer voice said. Power was in those words. She heard a voice say a name again. This time it was low but clear, Mrs. Robinson was her name.

She wanted to let them know that she was alive. She tried to move her hand, but she couldn't. She didn't want to give up so she tried again. It was the most frustrating thing that she had ever experienced. Exhaustion overcame her and she fell fast asleep.

CHAPTER TWO

Doctor Emanuel Cartwright, the finest specimen of a man and every woman's dream of what one should be. Tall, brown and handsome with a smile that made you want to wet your pants. He was a Harvard graduate and finished second in his class and even though his career started a little late, he never regretted the hard work and the long hours he put in to become the doctor that he became. Looking back no one could have imagined the fork in his road.

Emanuel got out of his car and the November wind blew a wet breeze that made his skin feel like rubber.

"Damn its cold out here," he said as he headed to the nursing home entrance.

"Good morning, Dr. Cartwright" the receptionist said with a smile.

"Good morning," Emanuel smiled back.

"Oh, by the way, I was told to give this to you first thing."

"Thanks, Patricia, right?" Emanuel asked, looking at her badge.

"You are correct." And she handed him the file.

"Thank you, Patricia," Emanuel said showing those beautiful white teeth again.

"You're very welcome but you can call me Patty anytime," she said using her flirtatious tone of voice.

"Ok, I will keep that in mind." Emanuel responded. "Not bad, not bad at all," he said under his breath as he turned the corner.

Emanuel entered his office and closed the door. The thought of Patty and his sudden arousal was a reminder that he had not been on a date in weeks. He was also reminded to never mix business with pleasure which almost got him into trouble at his last job. Too much drama and he didn't want to deal with that type of mess again; it just wasn't worth it. His schedule was crazy and his position at Silver Care Nursing Home left him barely any time to date let alone time to be in a committed relationship. So, Emanuel found himself being satisfied by the comfort of casual sex with female acquaintances who were more than willing to give him sexual healing. So, for now, that is what was working for him. Emanuel pulled himself a cup of coffee. The aroma and the caffeine always put him right into work mode so while he enjoyed his coffee, he opened the file in front of him and became acquainted with his new patient.

"Wow" Emanuel said while reading the information in the file notes and noticing how strikingly beautiful his patient was. A photograph of her was placed in the file; one that was obviously taken before her accident.

"Tina Robinson, thirty-six- year-old African American female, married has one daughter."

Emanuel continued to read slowly.

"Significant brain swelling due to severe head trauma; contusion to the face, broken tibia, ruptured spleen; has been in coma for 10 years".

Emanuel slowly turned the pages to the police report.

"Icy road conditions, hit pole. "Wow this is messed up." Emanuel whispered.

He closed the file, drank the last of his coffee and prepared to meet his first patient of the day. Emanuel entered Mrs. Robinson's room and placed her chart on the table, he stood in awe at how very attractive she was. He had never seen anything like it before, especially with a patient in this condition. From her beautiful brown skin to her long light brown hair that really complimented her beauty. Her slightly high cheek bones and her full lips reminded him of a black Angelina Jolie. Emanuel began to check her vitals. He took his fingers and gently opened her eye lids which displayed the most beautiful eyes that he had ever seen; light brown with a tint of green. No sign of movement was visible. After examining her, he noted her chart. So sad he thought. Her condition wasn't good and the chances of her coming out of the coma were very slim but looking at her, he thought in a hopeful kind of way, miracles do happen.

"It's not over until it's over." he said softly.

Emanuel walked toward the window to pull the string that opened the blinds. Automatically the sunshine illuminated the room with an assortment of colors giving it a warm, pleasant atmosphere.

"Mrs. Robinson, does that feel better?" He asked, turning toward his patient.

Caught in his thoughts, Emanuel did not notice when Mrs. Moss entered the room. Mrs. Moss was one of the nosiest people that worked at the nursing home and she knew everybody's business and some. She was short, petite and hair full of gray and she wore glasses that hung down on her nose. In her hands, she carried a beautiful bouquet of flowers.

"Hi there" she said putting the flowers down on the table.

Emanuel turned around swiftly.

"Hi how are you?" Emanuel asked. "Does she get flowers often?"

"They come once a month like clockwork; from the time she arrived about ten years ago," smiled Mrs. Moss.

"From her husband I'm assuming?" He asked.

"No sir, her best friend Cynthia."

"Oh, ok now what about her husband; does he come to see her often?"

Emanuel asked looking back at Mrs. Robinson.

"Heck no, never saw the man." "I don't recall him ever being here. Her sister comes maybe once a month and she gets to crying every time she comes." "So emotional every time," she said and she shook her head. "After all this time you think," Mrs. Moss stopped talking.

"Are you new here?" She asked standing with her hands on her hips.

Emanuel thought she was about to get testy with him.

"Yes, I'm Doctor Cartwright and I was just assigned as Mrs. Robinson's doctor a couple of days ago." Emanuel explained.

"Oh, ok well I have to get going; I have my rounds to do and oh by the way, I'm Mrs. Moss from the Hospitality Department."

"Nice to meet you Mrs. Moss" Emanuel said.

"Hmm, hmm" Mrs. Moss replied, pushing her glasses up on her face, and walking out of the room. Emanuel turned around to face Mrs. Robinson again.

"I'm going to take good care of you, Mrs. Robinson, you hear me." Emanuel said taking her hand and gently squeezing it. "I will talk to you again tomorrow, ok."

Emanuel's last patient of the day was a round, fat burly woman named Joyce Hull. She was one of his most challenging patients. It took every ounce of strength for him to remain calm and civil toward her. She was as nasty as they come and thought everyone owed her something. No one at the place liked her and the nurses dreaded even going near her. The Lord himself probably wouldn't want to know her and Emanuel chuckled at the thought and took a deep breath and entered her room.

CHAPTER THREE

It was getting late and Emanuel could feel the effects of the day slowly taking over his body. He didn't feel like taking the 45- minute drive home so he opts to stay at the nursing home for the night. He was glad that he kept extra clothes and toilettes in his car and was on his way to get them. He loved his life but it was nights like this that he wished he had a wife to go home to. Emanuel approached his car and the freezing night air bit into his body. He hurriedly opened the trunk and removed his overnight bag and headed back to his office. Not paying attention he bumped right into Patricia coming around the corner.

"Hey I'm so sorry; me and my clumsy self," Emanuel said apologizing.

Patricia was looking good. Her hair was down and she was obviously dress and ready for the club.

"You look nice" Emanuel commented.

"Thank you and what are you still doing here?" Patricia asked.

"I don't feel like taking the drive home so I figure I'd stay here for the night."

Wow, she thought to herself looking at Emanuel from head to toe.

"So, would you like some company later?" she asked flirtatiously.

Trick question he was thinking and of course he couldn't say no.

"Yes, you can stop in," He said never taking his eyes off her while he opened the door to his office.

"Good, I will see you later than." Patricia said walking away smiling knowing good and well that her husband would raise hell if she stayed out any later than what she had already told him but who wants to stay home on a Friday night. Yes, she had promised her husband that she would be right home but tonight she had other plans and it would be well worth the trouble.

Emanuel just couldn't say no and be done with it. He took off his shoes and grabbed a towel out of his bag and headed straight to the shower.

"Me and my big mouth, damn," he said.

Emanuel removed his clothes exposing a well-proportioned body with perfect tone and just enough muscle; a body of an ancient Greek warrior. The time spent at the gym and his daily 5- mile runs had definitely paid off. Emanuel turned on the water to the shower and stepped in. The room was freezing cold but his thoughts of Miss Patty soon sent his body temperature soaring. His mind was already imagining what his plan was for her. I hope she's ready for one hell of a night he thought, and his body was already set and ready to go.

He ran and ran but in spite of the terror in his heart and the pain in his limbs, Emanuel still tried to get to the safe house but something was holding him back, pulling him down. It was like a weight had been placed on his legs. He looked back and hundreds were chasing him; Machetes in their hands lashing out at him. Some were throwing them. Then Emanuel felt something hit his back. He looked down. His legs were gone but still he ran.

Emanuel jumped up. His heart was pounding and his body was drenched with sweat. He was startled at first until he realized that it was all a dream; a dream that he knew all too well. He glanced at his clock. It was 4:45 am and everything was slowly coming back. He realized that after he had taken a shower, he got dressed and laid down and thought that he would be awaken by Miss Patty but it looked like Miss Patty had stood him up; his body was already feeling the disappointment. So, without hesitation, Emanuel got up and prepared for his morning rounds. He didn't feel like running never did after having one of those dreams but the thought of having Ms. Hull as his first patient, quickly changed his mind, and besides, running always seemed to clear his thoughts and this morning he needed just that. He needed his thoughts cleared and focused on his patients and not pondering on his own personal issues.

Mrs. Robinson could see a little light peeking through but other than that she was still in total darkness. She thought she seen an image standing before her and she tried and tried to open her eyes but she couldn't. She tried to move but she still couldn't. Refusing to give up, the voice was nudging at her and convincing her to try again. So, she did. With all her might, she tried to move her hand. Nothing happened so she tried again. The third time she did it. She tried moving her arms, and then her legs. She tried to put her hand in front of her but something was holding it back. She could feel the fabric under her so she pulled at it. With all the strength she had, she pulled and she kicked which left her totally exhausted but to somebody, she hoped that she got her point across. Then miraculously, the scales from her eyes were removed and the darkest had been lifted. Everything was still distorted like a picture out of focus but Mrs. Robinson was able to distinguish where she might be. As she scanned the room with her eyes, she guessed that maybe she was in a hospital. New questions of her condition came to mind. Just how bad was she? Was she sick with an incurable disease that in time, she would succumb to; or was it something that in time, she would eventually get better? Other than that strange sensation that she was feeling, she wasn't in any pain and she did not feel sick. Maybe that was a good sign and she hoped for the latter. She heard a voice and turned her head in that direction, then she felt a touch. *My God*, she thought.

Emanuel had finished his run for the morning. His body was feeling good and a quick shower would do the trick. In fifteen minutes, he was on the floor heading to the Grinch's room when he heard his name called over the intercom to report to room 526. As he approached the room, he expected the worse when he seen several attendants and staff members standing outside Mrs. Robinson's room. Mrs. Reeves, the head nurse, met him at the door.

"Dr. Cartwright, Tina Robinson has come out of the coma!"

A sign of relief came over Emanuel as he made his way to Mrs. Robinson's bedside to check her vitals.

"Mrs. Robinson, I'm Doctor Cartwright, can you squeeze my hand if you can hear me."

She laid there with her eyes opened trying her best to respond to the voice verbally but she could not speak.

"*Yes, I can hear you,*" she tried to say and squeezed his hand.

"If you understand what I'm saying can you squeeze my hand again?" Emanuel asked her.

"*Yes, damn it. I understand what you're saying.*" She wanted to say, and she squeezed his hand again.

"Good," Emanuel said.

"Mrs. Robinson, I just want you to know that we are going to take good care of you ok." Emanuel reassured her with a pat on the hand.

"Please have her prep for a scat scan as soon as possible." Emanuel told the nurse.

Tina's heart was beating so fast and with her vision still blurry, she could not identify the face with the voice that was talking to her. She closed her eyes hoping that would help but it didn't. Images were scarring around her and she felt her body being moved.

CHAPTER FOUR

"Oh yes baby please don't stop." "Oh yes please don't." Brock moaned loudly. Brock was always loud when that alcohol got in him and the only thing that Diane could do was lay there and wish that it would be over soon. She couldn't believe that once again she had allowed this low life to touch her.

Diane's attitude had been a little different minutes before when she allowed herself to be seduced by her husband. She should have known better than to look at that movie "The Original Sin" which left her feeling aroused and wanting. She knew that having sex with her husband was not a sin but looking back at the other things that she had allowed him to do were. The memories taunted her even though she knew that God had forgiven her.

She couldn't deny that the sex was good with Brock; it always had been but after she reached her sexual peak, she was done with him and all she wanted him to do was get the hell up off of her before reality set in. Just the thought was enough to make her want to throw up and the way he grinned at her let her know exactly what he was thinking. Oh, how she hated him.

Brock opened his eyes as he released himself from his wife. Looking down at her he could see the disgust written all over her face. His smirking grin had let her know that he had won this round. He too, couldn't deny that the sex was still good. The old woman still had it in her and she still looked good too even though she had gained a couple of pounds. Thinking back, way back, he remembered loving this woman. They had made so many plans together but her damn insecurities ruined their relationship and his life. They were both in college and had mapped their future out point to point and it looked good but she had to up and get pregnant to try and keep him. She just didn't realize that she already had him. After she got pregnant, they both dropped out of college and her parents hounded her so bad that he felt that he had no choice but to marry her. He hated her parents; always comparing Diane to Tina to the point that Diane developed a terrible complex. He hated to admit that Tina was a beautiful piece of a woman with her bougie ass self and Diane envied her. He never forgave his wife for trapping him and proved it every chance he got by his repeated infidelities and Brock sniggered at the thought. He knew that she no longer loved him and vice versa but every now and then she would succumb to her sexual needs especially when he was a little tipsy; for some reason that always seemed to turn her on. No words were said between them and he lifted himself from her and went in the bathroom to take a shower. Diane was left alone to struggle with her hateful thoughts and she asked God for forgiveness, got up and started getting ready for work.

Brock showered and put on a pair of boxing shorts and an undershirt, and made his way into the kitchen to make himself a cup of coffee. Hopefully that would help sober him up, he was thinking. He reached for his favorite cup that was always placed in the right side of the cabinet. His little girl had brought it for him during her trip to Disney, but oh he thought; she wasn't a little girl anymore. The phone rang and Brock lazily walked over to answer it.

"Yeah," Brock answered.

"Hello this is Dr. Cartwright from Silver Care Nursing Home." "Can I speak with Diane Casey please?"

"This is her husband, what is it?" He asked.

"Your wife is listed as the contact person to notify if there were any changes in her sister's condition."

"Hold on, Diane"! Brock practically screamed.

Diane had just come into the kitchen and wondered why Brock was screaming her name.

"Who is it?" Diane asked softly while getting a glass out of the cabinet and eventually taking the phone from him.

"Doctor somebody" Brock said unconcerned.

"Hello" Diane answered.

As she listened to the voice on the other end, Diane's facial expression exhibit shocking revelations from words that she was obviously not ready to hear and the glass that she held fell spontaneously to the floor.

"Thanks for calling, thank you," Diane said as she slowly hung up the phone.

"She came out of it," She whispered.

"Who came out of what?" Brock asked.

"Ting came out of the coma." Diane responded.

"Isn't that some shit, so I guess the bitch will live after all uh?" Brock said in a loud nasty tone.

"What's going on "? Brook asked when she heard the commotion in the kitchen.

The expression on her mother's face let her know that something was dreadfully wrong and she also knew that when her parents were in the same room anything could happen. Diane stooped to the floor to pick up some of the scattered pieces of glass.

"Get me the broom please," Diane asked looking up at her daughter.

Brook noticed her mother shaking and walked briskly away to get the broom. Diane stood up and her eyes met her husband's.

"Oh God, she cried out as she ran out of the kitchen almost running into Brook.

"What the hell is going on?" Brook asked and she looked to her father for answers.

"Your Auntie came out of the coma," he told her.

A scowl came over Brooks face and she began to sweep up the broken glass not saying another word.

Diane sat on the bed and cried. Every bad memory seemed to jump out at her all at once. She had made some terrible mistakes in her life and just wished that she had someone to talk to that would not judge her; but she had no one; no one except God.

"Lord, Jesus please help me through this," Diane said rocking back and forth.

She sat quietly and finally regained her composure, picked up the phone and called her job to let her supervisor know that she was not coming in.

Mommy said, "Life has its way of knocking you down when you least expect it.

"Mommy that is the truth," Diane thought.

CHAPTER FIVE

Emanuel had got to work extra early and was still hyped after being interviewed for a local news station. His patient had made the headlines and he was over anxious to get the day started. No run for him this morning. Instead, he made his way right to room 526.

"Good morning Mrs. Robinson, how are you this morning?" Emanuel asked.

She managed to share a smile and Emanuel began to check her vitals. First checking her reflexes and then looking into her eyes.

"Mrs. Robinson, can you follow the light please." He asked.

She followed Emanuel's lead looking directly at the light; Left to right, right to left, up and down and then she looked directly in his eyes. He sat down beside the bed and began noting her chart and as he gazed up, he knew that her eyes were trying to say something.

"Where is my baby," she tried to say but the words would not come. Emanuel put the chart down and took her hand into his.

"Is it ok for me to call you Tina?" "Do you mine," Emanuel asked.

"No, I don't mine," she wanted to say but instead shook her head yes. *"His teeth are beautiful and so is his smile." "This man is gorgeous,"* she thought as she gazed into his eyes once again.

"You are doing great. We still have to run some more tests and I assure you that with time you will get better and better every day." "Your husband will be here to see you in a couple of days, ok?

"Husband?" She silently questioned and Emanuel noticed the frown.

"I know you probably have a thousand questions and I will be here to answer them all, ok" Emanuel reassured her.

She began to breathe rapidly. *"Husband, who is my husband,"* she thought. She closed her eyes thinking maybe a face would give her a hint as to who he was and what he looked like but nothing came to her. She never thought about the father of her child until then.

Diane went over to the dresser drawer to get her black address book. She had not heard from Tony since Macy's memorial service and she hoped that his number had not changed. Tony had moved to another state one year after Tina's accident because he just couldn't handle seeing his wife in that state and the doctors were not very encouraging either. He probably like everyone else, never imagined Tina coming out of the coma; not after all these years. Diane knew that she had to tell him the news.

"Yes, can I speak with Tony Robinson please?" Diane asked, still shaking as she held the phone in her hand.

"Whose, calling please?," asked the person on the other end.

"This is his sister-in-law Diane."

"One moment please."

"Thank you," Diane responded.

"Yes" Tony answered.

"Hi Tony" Diane replied nervously.

"Hey how are you Diane?" "What's going on?" Tony asked knowing that it had to be something concerning Tina.

"Tony" Diane paused. "I have some good news." "Ting uh, is awake, she came out of the coma and she's doing ok under the circumstances."

A few seconds of silence came between them as Tony tried to comprehend what Diane had just told him.

"What"! He said in disbelief.

"Yes, the doctor called." Diane went on to explain.

"I don't" believe it" Tony mumbled massaging his head as if a headache was coming on.

"I know." Diane said her voice cracking.

I'll call you back ok, I'll call back." Tony managed to say before hanging the phone up.

Diane put the phone down and walked over to the bedroom window.

"Lord please forgive us" she whispered.

Diane was beginning to sound like a broken record. She couldn't keep up with how many times that she had asked God to forgive her. She was dealing with the guilt of her own selfish thoughts. What should have been some fantastic news was now becoming a nightmare. Was she imagining what she had just heard or did she hear the disappointment in Tony's voice? A flood of tears settled down on her face and Diane picked up the phone again to call her siblings and hoped that after 10 years the grudge that they had toward their baby sister would now be gone.

Mommy said, "You can't change the past, life happens."

"Mommy I know, I know," Diane whispered.

CHAPTER SIX

Tony booked a flight out of Chicago on a Tuesday morning. The weather was clear but cold and Thanksgiving was fast approaching. He hated the month of November because this time ten years ago, his life had changed forever.

It wasn't hard trying to convince Shelia that there was a medical convention that he had to attend in Atlanta. He went on business trips periodically and she would accompany him most of the time, that is, before their son was born. As Tony sat in his window seat, his mind wondered around a thousand things all at the same time. What in the world was he going to do? He thought of the night Macy was conceived and how happy he and Tina were. He closed his eyes and played with the memories of what they had once shared.

They had met in college and to him it was love at first sight. She was the most beautiful girl in the world and her eyes were unlike anything he had ever seen. One of his college buddies told him "Man don't look her in her eyes or she'll have you hooked," and he was right. She had the smoothest, prettiest skin that was the color of a pecan. Her hair was light brown with natural gold highlights and she always wore it straight back. Her face should have been on a cover of a magazine, she could have been a model but Tina always thought that her behind was way too big. Tony sat up straight in his seat and shook his head. She was gorgeous.

Even though Tina didn't like him in the beginning, Tony went out of his way to get her and he got her. She was highly motivated, thanks to her parents, and her self-confidence was often mistaken for conceitedness. She would do anything for you and would give you her heart if you needed it more. She had a sweet spirit with a low tolerance for bullshit and she would let you know it. He had proposed to her right out of college and she said yes.

It took them five years to establish their careers. He with his private practice in dentistry and her a bank investor. They had moved into their dream home and were making plans to start a family right away. It was a marriage made in heaven. Tina could cook, clean, she could do anything. After Macy was born, she took an extended medical leave and stayed home the first year to take care of her. He had insisted that he didn't want strangers taking care of his baby but when the year was up, Tina went back to work and Macy was in the care of a nanny highly recommended by a neighbor who lived around the corner. Jessie Stewart was incredible with Macy and Macy fell in love with her. They got along so well that Jessie agreed to move in to make it easier for them. And they sure did have the room; four bedrooms, three upstairs and one downstairs. It all worked out perfectly. He and Tina both wanted more children at least three, but as Macy got older their schedules became more hectic and as their careers blew up, their marriage grew apart and it was then that Tony had an affair with some chick he met at a conference. He thought that he was being ever so careful but Tina became suspicious and hired a private investigator. She later forgave him accepting half the blame for his infidelity because she knew that she was not there for him. This made both of them realize that in order for their marriage to work, some serious changes had to be made. So, they agreed to cut their work load down so that they could start spending some quality time together; and it worked. They were acting like newlyweds and falling in love with each other all over again. Everything was going well. A perfect little family; living in a perfect house with a perfect little girl. Then it happened, the accident. Tony had got home first that night and had just heated up dinner so that everything would be ready when Tina got home. Jessie had taken the day off to handle some personal business. When Tony answered the phone, it was brief and precise. Get to the hospital right away. No words could describe what Tony had witnessed. That could not be his wife. He barely had time to kiss her before she was taken to the operating room. He was told that she may not make it through the surgery but she did. She just never woke up. Not for ten whole years.

"Sir, can I get you something to drink?" "Sir, the flight attendant asked.

"Oh sorry, no thank you" Tony said.

Laying his head back against the seat, Tony closed his eyes again and memories of Macy came to mind. God, he loved his little girl and never forgave himself for leaving her. He just couldn't handle things; couldn't stand the pressure and wanted a fresh new start. He blamed him-self for the way Macy turned out and he often questioned if she would have turned out differently if he had taken her with him. He had given up on Tina ever recovering and had stopped going to see her once they transferred her to Silver Care so he turned everything over to Diane. He sent money home to Diane to take care of Macy so she didn't want for anything neither did Diane and her family. But the harsh reality was that Macy didn't need just his money, she needed him to be a father to her and he wasn't. So many times, he wanted to go back but his cowardliness kept him away and what made the present situation even more complicated was that Sheila knew nothing of his past. It was just too painful so he chose to put everything behind him. He had accepted the fact that Tina would never survive and would eventually succumb to her injuries and now his past was finally catching up with him and he had no plan whatsoever.

***

"Ting," Diane called out to her sister in a low voice.

It took every ounce of strength Diane had to go and see her sister. The room was bright and warm and the atmosphere seemed so different. A fresh bouquet of flowers, as always, sat on the table beside the bed, the aroma smelled so wonderful.

Emanuel had prepared Diane of what to expect and she was amazed that Tina was still beautiful as ever. Diane walked closer to the bed and the tears began to come. Tina opened her eyes when she heard her name called and turned her head to see who it was. As Tina's eyes began to focus, the figure looked something like her.

"Wait a minute, Debbie or Diane is it?" Tina wanted to ask.

"This is amazing"; "I can't believe your back," "I'm your sister Diane"; "Do you understand what I'm saying?"

Tina nodded her head yes and Diane became so overwhelmed with her emotions that she turned her back to Tina so that she wouldn't see her fall apart.

"Oh God what have I done" Diane said and hurriedly ran out the room.

Tina laid there confused.

"Wow I expected a kiss or a hug or something," she thought and turned her head back to its original position and went to sleep.

CHAPTER SEVEN

Tony pulled up at the nursing home two hours later in a black 2009 Lexus that he had rented for the day. Surprisingly Pastor Peterson, the one who had married him and Tina, was standing in the parking lot. Tony had not seen him since Macy's memorial service and he knew that the Pastor would want an explanation as to why he left so suddenly that day and why he was not answering his calls. Tony had purposely avoided him at the service and got away as quickly as he could and flew back to Chicago. The man had a way of seeing right through you and could sense something a mile away. Tony knew that it was no way to avoid him now. Dressed in a pair of black pants and a grey and black sweater, Tony got out of the car and grabbed his black overcoat off of the seat. He put his coat on and locked the car and headed for the entrance. It felt like the coldest day of the year and Tony rushed as fast as he could but not before running into Pastor Peterson.

"Good to see you my friend." Pastor Peterson said.

"How are you sir?" Tony asked.

"Good, good."

The two embraced and anxiety began to creep in Tony and he questioned his motives of why he never talked to Pastor Peterson about his situation. It was plain to him now. It was the guilt. In the past, there were times that he had confided in him, especially when he and Tina had gone through a period of distress in their marriage. Pastor Peterson was so supportive of them both and he didn't take sides even though Tina was like a daughter to him. Would he be supportive of him now, he wondered?

"It's cold out here let's go inside shall we," Pastor Peterson said and they walked quickly to the entrance.

The facility was all decorated for the upcoming holiday with colorful fall colors that gave the place a warm reception. Patricia was seated behind the desk and glanced up when she heard the chimes ringing. It was her idea to hang them up so that she could get a heads up when someone was coming through the door. She had a habit of shopping online while she was working and the chimes gave her time enough to get off the computer. Glancing at her face in her hand mirror, Patricia double checked her make-up to make sure that the bruises were still covered. She tried to conceal them the best she could and she hoped that she would not see Emanuel until they were completely gone. She had not even done anything this time to deserve it but her husband thought otherwise. Yes, she had the bruises but she had given him a busted lip that required stitches. She knew that one day someone was going to get seriously hurt and it didn't necessarily mean her. She had learned how to fight back no matter how big or small her opponent was and she thanked her three older brothers for that.

"Hi can I help you?" Patricia asked, putting the mirror away.

"Yes, I'm Tony Robinson and I have a 2 o'clock appointment with Doctor Cartwright."

Patricia began to check Emanuel's schedule log to verify the appointment.

"Ok, Dr. Cartwright will meet with you in the main conference room; "Go straight down this hallway to the end to conference room 236; it will be on your left." Patricia said smiling all the while admiring the man who stood before her.

"Oh, you will need these." Patricia said giving Tony the visitor passes.

"Thanks" he said turning to Pastor Peterson and handing him a pass.

"I really would like for you to be present when I meet with the doctor, if that's ok with you?" Tony said.

"Ok, I can do that" Pastor Peterson responded.

Tony turned to face Patricia.

"Thanks again." He said to her.

"You're welcome" Patricia smiled.

Tony felt as if his legs were going to collapse under his feet. Get a hold of yourself he kept thinking but to no avail; he knew that it was going to be a long day. Tony opened the door and took the first seat that he came to. He slowly pulled at his sweater thinking that maybe it would give him some relief of the sudden heat that cradled his body. Pastor Peterson noticed the nervous state of his dear friend and thought that it was acceptable behavior stemming from not knowing what to expect from his wife or was it, he thought. As he gazed at Tony, he couldn't stop himself from wondering why Tony would want to avoid him at Macy's memorial service and not even accepting his calls which he thought was a bit strange. So many questions he wanted to ask him but now just wasn't the time.

Patricia looked up just in time to see Emanuel and their eyes met for a moment and she felt a stream of embarrassment take over her.

"God, I hope he hasn't heard anything and please Lord don't let him see these bruises," Patricia thought.

"Well hello Miss Patty" Emanuel said giving her a pleasant stare.

"Hello Doctor Cartwright. Your visitors are here and sorry about the other night, rain check?" She asked, getting up quickly so that she could turn her bruised face away from him.

"Oh, good they're right on time, and yes rain check for sure" Emanuel said walking toward the conference room.

Patricia was so relieved that he didn't stop and try to talk to her and she pulled the chair back and slouched down in it.

One thing Emanuel couldn't stand was a man who beat up on women.

"Yeah, there will be a rain check for sure Miss Patty but not your rain check," he thought and he opened the door to the conference room.

"Hi I'm Doctor Cartwright" he said introducing himself and extending his hand to Tony and then to Pastor Peterson.

Tony and Pastor Peterson stood. As the three men became acquainted with each other, Emanuel noticed Tony's nervousness and knew that it had to be a bitter-sweet moment for him; happy that his wife was given a second chance at life but then again, a whole lot can happen in a man's life in a span of 10 years.

"Please have a seat" Emanuel suggested. "Can I get the two of you something to drink?" He asked.

"No thank you," Pastor Peterson responded and Tony nodded his head in agreement.

The three of them took their seats and Emanuel begin to address the issue.

"Mr. Robinson because of the doctor/patient confidentiality I would like to speak with you alone and then we can have Pastor Peterson join us in a few minutes if that's ok with you." Emanuel asked.

"Pastor Peterson is a very close friend of the family so whatever you want to discuss with me it's ok to discuss in front of him." Tony said.

Tony knew that wasn't the real truth. He just didn't want to deal with the situation by himself.

"Very well I do understand," Emanuel said.

Emanuel opened Tina's file and began to share his thoughts and concerns regarding what the next steps were to ensure the continuing progress of his patient's condition and what her long term and short- term effects were by being in a coma for so long.

"You must be elated Emanuel said looking up at Tony." "Your wife is showing signs of progress every day." "She understands what you're saying to her; just how much she understands and remembers we won't know until further tests are done." "This is a very good sign because usually patients don't come back after this long period of time, and if they do, they're usually in a vegetation state and expire shortly after." "Your wife is not showing any permanent brain damage." "We doubled checked and it's quite amazing."

"So, what does this all mean in the long run?" Tony asked.

"Well,," Emanuel paused for a few seconds. "If she continues to show signs of progress and with the excellent medical treatment that we will continue to provide for her including intense physical therapy, voice therapy, there's no reason why your wife can't lead a normal life; "Of course she will have to learn to talk and walk again but it can be done; someone was definitely watching over her." He spoke.

"Yes indeed," smiled Pastor Peterson.

"The recovery depends on the patient and every patient is different." "She will need a tremendous amount of support from her family." Emanuel explained in an encouraging tone "and she is trying to pronounce words already as a matter of fact, she has been mumbling the name Macy."

Emanuel looked up in time to see Tony sweating profusely.

"Are you sure you don't want something to drink?" He asked.

"No, I'm ok," Tony said sitting with his chin in his hand.

"I did speak with Mrs. Casey, and she informed me that her niece had died but she never gave a name or any details." "Is there something that I need to know that would affect your wife's recovery?"

Tony looked at Pastor Peterson and then back to Emanuel.

"Our daughter committed suicide last year; she was 20 years old."

"I am sorry to hear that." Emanuel said looking at Tony. "You have my condolences."

"So let me get this straight, ok she's been in a coma for ten whole years, there's no brain damage and you're saying that she could get right up out that bed and lead a normal life, right?" Tony asked sarcastically.

Tony's tone of voice caught Emanuel by surprise. It wasn't the tone that you would expect from a loving husband who was desperately waiting to meet his wife again.

"Mr. Robinson, amazingly in your wife's case when she came out of the coma there was minimum brain impairment and we can't explain why." "Your wife has beaten all odds and that's a good thing." "I'm saying that given the proper medical treatment and therapy, your wife can lead a normal life." It may take a couple of years for a full recovery, but it's possible," Emanuel explained

Tony got up from the seat and walked over to the window realizing that he had just made a fool of himself.

"Sorry I just." Tony paused.

"I know this is a lot to deal with and I do understand." Emanuel said as he went on to explain in detail, the tests and therapy that his wife would need.

"I think I covered everything." "Mr. Robinson do you have any questions, concerns?" Emanuel asked.

"No" Tony lied.

"Pastor Peterson?" Emanuel asked.

"No doctor I have no questions."

"So, Mr. Robinson are you ready to meet your wife again?" He asked him.

"Yes, I'm ready," Tony lied again.

CHAPTER EIGHT

The walk to Tina's room was even more nerve wrecking than the sit down with Doctor Cartwright. Tony could feel the sweat dripping down the sides of his face and he felt compel to spill his guts out onto the floor. "*Will she recognize me,*" he asked himself. He could no longer deny the fact that he just wasn't ready for this reunion, not now and probably not ever. The guilt was written all over him.

Emanuel entered the room first and greeted Tina with a warm and contiguous smile and she returned the same. He gently reached out for her hand.

"Hey, how are you?" Emanuel asked.

Tina met his eyes and nodded yes in response.

"Good because I have some people here that want to meet you again." Emanuel said stepping aside so that Tina could see the people behind him.

"Tina, this is your husband Tony."

Emanuel gave Tina sometime to absorb what he had just said to her and he could tell by her facial expression, that she did not recognize her husband.

"*I don't know this man,*" she thought feeling frustrated and confused.

Tony could not believe his eyes. "*My God,*" he thought. It seemed like time had rewind itself back ten years and the Tina that he knew and once loved was sitting there before him. She looked good.

"Tony, maybe it would be a good idea if you talked to your wife alone first," Pastor Peterson suggested.

"No, its ok please stay," urged Tony.

Emanuel shot a quick glance at Mr. Robinson and sensed that he was scared to death to be left alone with his wife. The reaction didn't surprise Emanuel at all. To him, Mr. Robinson seemed weird throughout the whole meeting. Tony got a little closer to the bed not knowing if he should kiss her or not so he extended his hand to her.

"Hi," Tony managed to say.

Tina took his hand and shyly looked at him but could not remember anything.

"Wow I have good taste in men," Tina thought. She closed her eyes thinking maybe something would come to her but again nothing did.

"And this is your good friend Pastor Peterson." Emanuel inquired.

"Hi Tina, I married you and Tony." He said proudly.

Tina looked at Tony than to Pastor Peterson and then back to Emanuel. Her breathing became intense and she closed her eyes once again this time nodding no in frustration.

"It's ok; it will take time." "Hey you're doing great; just relax ok. Emanuel ordered.

Tina relaxed.

"I'm going to excuse myself so you folks can get reacquainted." "I will see you later ok?" Emanuel looked at Tina.

"I hope so," Tina thought smiling at him.

Pastor Peterson pulled up a chair and sat next to Tina. He began to share stories about their friendship and his demeanor made Tina smile.

"He seems like a nice person for sure," Tina thought.

Pastor Peterson's blabbering made Tony uneasy and Tina glanced at him every now and then as Pastor Peterson went on and on about their marriage. She had to admit that the tall, brown skin, guy that was her husband was fine but she had no recollection of ever being with him or married to him. That was not good, Tina thought. He was not friendly at all and Tina could sense that he was very uncomfortable maybe with her or with what Pastor Peterson was saying. She had never given any thought as to what her husband had been doing for ten years. As fine as he was, she wasn't that naïve to think that he was sitting home alone in a corner waiting for her to come back.

With all the blabbering Pastor Peterson was doing, never once had he mentioned her baby girl. Tina longed to hold her, to smell her and to rub her fingers through her pigtails. Tina looked at Tony again and noticed tears in his eyes.

"Macy," Tina mumbled.

"Did I just say that, did I?" She asked herself. Tina couldn't believe that the words had come out of her mouth. Pastor Peterson looked at Tony; Tony looked back at him; either one not knowing what to say and how to say it. Tony wiped his eyes. *"This is just too much,"* he thought.

"I uh christened your baby girl Macy"; "A beautiful baby indeed."

"Where is she?" Tina heard herself ask and once again couldn't believe that she had said it.

Tina was aware that she had just spoken but the voice that came out of her mouth didn't sound like her own.

"Let me go and find Doctor Cartwright." Tony suggested and cowardly hurried out of the room.

Pastor Peterson had to think quickly to draw Tina's attention away from her daughter so with no help from Tony, he pushed the button on the side of Tina's bed to alert the nurse and within seconds two were standing on the side of Tina's bed making so much fuss about her talking that he was able to slip out of the room. There he found Tony outside the door pacing back and forth apparently struggling with the situation at hand. Pastor Peterson sensed that it was something else going on with him, something deep that was tearing him apart.

After discussing the situation with Doctor Cartwright, Tony and Pastor Peterson managed to return to Tina's room to quickly say their good-byes and they hoped that she would have forgotten the question that they could not answer. Not yet anyway.

The cold November air hit Tony in the face like a knife. This was one of the worse days of his life; to sit there and look at his wife and know that he had another life, other responsibilities.

"*What in the hell do I do now*?" He kept asking himself.

Pastor Peterson sees Tony's distress and addresses it.

"Tony I'm here for you if you need me to be." Pastor Peterson said with his voice catching Tony off guard.

Tony stopped walking and turned to face Pastor Peterson needing desperately to share what was on his mind.

"You don't know how many years I prayed to God to let my wife come back to me." "I just couldn't handle seeing her like that so I moved away and tried to forget about her." "I left Macy because she reminded me so much of Tina and it was just too painful." He paused for a few seconds. "I live with my girlfriend in Chicago and we have a son together."

Pastor Peterson placed his hand on Tony's shoulder.

"Please don't judge me." Tony said.

"That's not for me to do my son." "I will pray that God directs you and that he gives you inner peace."

Tony started to walk away.

"Tony," Pastor Peterson called out.

"God will forgive you but you have to learn to forgive yourself."

"Thanks Pastor," Tony said walking away feeling relieved and a little better from how he felt before.

CHAPTER NINE

Tina looked out the window and could tell that it was going to be a scorer. The weatherman had forecast temperatures in the 90's all week, but today the humility was going to make it feel like over 100 degrees. Two years had passed and she was so very proud of herself. Her motor skills had improved tremendously, she was talking better, she no longer needed the aid of a walker but was using a cane and her memory would come in bits and pieces. What she didn't know one day she would remember the next day and then there was Doctor Cartwright. Just the thought of him made her blush and Tina confessed that she liked the man a lot. He seemed to look better every time she saw him and his smile. The man had a million-dollar smile that made a sensation run up and down her spine. Tina felt that she was getting a little too close to him and in an odd kind of way, she felt that he was getting a little too close to her or was it just an act of kindness between a doctor and his patient. *"Oh God,"* Tina thought it was so hard to tell. No use dwelling on it. The man was gorgeous and probably had a wife and a couple of kids running around the house. Still memorized by her thoughts, Tina didn't hear the door open and she jumped at the sound of his voice.

"How is my favorite patient?" Emanuel asked.

Tina's countenance lit up like a little girl that had just won a prize for good behavior.

"Good" she said embarrassed by her thoughts.

"Well good because I have some good news."

Emanuel walked over to her close enough that their bodies were touching each other. He lifted her chin with his hand.

"He's doing it again," she thought. He was close enough to kiss her and Tina wanted him to.

"What is it?

"You're getting out of here in a couple of days." He told her.

"Am I going home?" She asked.

"No not yet but I'm recommending North York, a rehabilitation center not too far from here." "I'll tell you more about it later because you have some visitors that can't wait to see you."

Emanuel walked over to the door and to Tina's surprise, Pastor Peterson, his wife and her best friend Cynthia, were standing there. Cynthia couldn't help but get emotional and tears of joy soon followed and the most amazing part of the reunion was that Tina remembered them.

"It's good to see you all" Tina said as she embraced them one by one with tears flowing and emotions high.

"So how are you feeling Ting?" Cynthia asked.

"I feel pretty good.

"You look so beautiful" Mrs. Peterson said.

"Thank you, you know I'm getting stronger every day and the people here are wonderful but I can't wait to go home; I can't wait to see Macy."

A brief silence went through the air and Cynthia hurriedly changed the subject.

"Girl I can't wait for us to go shopping, that's what I'm talking about."

"What the hell," Tina wanted to say. For the hundredth time, she noticed the reaction of everyone's face when Macy's name was mentioned and wondered what it was all about. Before she could say something, Cynthia had her arm around her heading for the sofa.

"Girl let's sit down because I have a whole lot to tell you; ten years of gossip." Laughter filled the room as they sat down to talk, laugh and to cry.

"Ok so while you're getting your gossip on, Pastor Peterson and I will be right over here." Doctor Cartwright said.

"Ok good because he may not want to hear some thangs." Cynthia said waving her hand.

The ladies began to chit-chat and Cynthia watched in amazement while her best friend sat in front of her laughing like old times. So, while the ladies were deep in their conversations, Doctor Cartwright and Pastor Peterson walked to the other side of the room both affected by what they had just heard.

"Did you hear what she said?" Pastor Peterson asked Doctor Cartwright.

"Yes, I heard what she said and that's why I wanted to talk to you." "Tina believes that her daughter is still alive and she remembers her the way she was before the accident, as a little girl." She's starting to mention her a little more often, but then other times when questioned, it's like she doesn't even remember having a child. "I think it's time that we talk about her daughter and by her being more comfortable around you I thought it would be best if you told her instead of her husband." "I have already talked to Mr. Robinson and he's ok with it."

"Do you think she can handle that?" Pastor Peterson asked.

"Well," Doctor Cartwright paused; it is a delicate situation but she's a very strong and determined woman." "I think she can handle it."

"Yes, I will talk to her"

"Good" Doctor Cartwright said shaking his head in approval.

Tina laid on her bed exhausted from all the excitement from earlier in the day. It was great seeing her friends again especially Cynthia who

Tina had no trouble remembering but with Mrs. Peterson, she remembered certain events only after Mrs. Peterson would go into details.

Barely able to keep her eyes open, Tina thought about the good news of her release from the nursing home. In three months, she could be at home getting her life back to some order and she smiled at the thought but the smile that she worn on her face was abrupt by the thought of never seeing Doctor Cartwright again. Not his face, his smile or not to hear his voice. Doctor Cartwright had made it clear to her that he would stop in to check on her and it was the way that he said it that made butterflies float in her stomach. *"Ok that's enough,"* Tina thought and with a vision of Doctor Cartwright's face imprinted on her mind, Tina closed her eyes and fell fast asleep.

CHAPTER TEN

Diane picked up a wet towel off the bathroom floor and tossed it in the laundry basket. "It seems like I just can't keep this place clean" Diane said under her breath. "It would be nice to get some help around here sometimes." "Right where they have stuff that's right where they leave it" she said bending down again to pick up a pair of sweat pants that obviously belonged to her husband. Shaking her head in disgust Diane headed for Brock's room.

"I won't be washing these; that's for sure." She said out loud.

She and Brock had not slept in the same bed in years. Not after she found out he had cheated on her and more than once. Diane pushed the door open to throw the pants on the bed and smelled the alcohol before she seen him. There Brock was stretched out on the bed masturbating and purposely leaving himself exposed knowing that it would piss her off even more.

"My God man don't you have any shame?" She asked. "It could have been your daughter walking in here, you know."

"It would have served her right if she didn't knock and that goes for you too." "If I had a wife taking care of business, I wouldn't need to do this; but that's ok I'm trading you in anyway." Brock said loud and sluggishly. Disgusted, Diane turned to leave the room. "*Look at you, who would want you,* she wanted to say to him but that would have only added fire to the flame.

"You will be doing me a favor trust me; and I hope whoever she is, she has her own place." Diane said storming out of the room and slamming the door behind her.

"Lord why do I put up with this?" Diane whispered.

She knew that she could make it without him. Her position as business manager for a software firm paid pretty good money so the chump change that he was giving her for the bills wasn't even necessary. He could keep his money as far as she was concerned. The house and everything else were already in her name. He didn't have nothing thanks to his bad credit and God knows what else he was out there doing. To think that she once loved him made her want to puke, what was she thinking?

Oh, she remembered the crazy things that she did for that man all in the name of love. Right before she got pregnant with Brook, Diane remembered working her tail off to help pay his rent while he laid up with some hoochie momma. She should have seen the red flags way back than but like any other young, insecure girl, she didn't want to believe it. After they were practically forced to get married, she had money taken out of her check to help pay for his loans and even used the money that Tony sent home for Macy to put toward his bills too but when she found out that he was out there cheating on her still, all money ceased. It wasn't too long before all of his little nasty habits started coming out of the wood work and she found herself caught up in his mess. Diane found herself engaging in things that she had sworn she would never do just to satisfy her husband. The part that made her sick was that she enjoyed the very thing that she was against. One night early in their marriage, Brock asked her what was her sexual fantasy and she jokingly told him that she wanted to have a threesome not realizing that she was opening up a fire that had long been settling in his spirit. Shortly after that, Brock brought all kinds of people and things into their bedroom. Only when the sexual acts were over did Diane find herself full of guilt and shame even though Brock would try to convince her that it was nothing wrong with what they were doing. She disliked the man for what he made her become and she felt that she was as guilty as he was.

That was then and Diane could honestly say that she was a changed person trying to live and do right. She knew that she could only think about leaving Brock for the secrets that they shared bind them together and Brock never let her forget it. Secrets that weighed heavy on her mind.

The disgusting images of her and Brock suddenly caught her off guard and Diane could taste the bitterness in her gut and she made it to the bathroom just in time.

Mommy said, "Don't be a fool for no man." Diane realized that she already was and had been for a long time.

***

"Beautiful day, isn't it?" Tina asked.

"Yes, it is," Pastor Peterson said as they walked slowly through the gardens at North York.

Tina had been there for exactly three months and she loved the place. She called it her home before going home. The garden was beautiful with the assortment of flowers lined up along the sides of the walkway. Tina marveled at the sound of the birds chirping, singing to their own tune and she loved the smell of fresh flowers.

"Tina, Pastor Peterson said breaking the silence; "I want to talk to you about something."

"Sure, what is it?" Tina asked looking at him.

"Let's grab this bench right here shall we, the view here is nice." Pastor Peterson suggested.

"Sure," and Tina gave him a quick smile.

Pastor Peterson took Tina's hand preparing her for what he was about to say. Tina saw the concerned look on his face and wondered what would transpire next.

"There is really no easy way to say what I'm about to tell you Tina, I want you to be strong because God brought you back to us for a reason."

"Ok just say it, please," Tina insisted giving him a fake smile.

"Tina it's about Macy."

"What about Macy?" She asked.

"Macy had a very difficult time dealing with, I guess you can say, the pressures of life; she committed suicide over two years ago."

"Suicide?" Tina repeated.

Pastor Peterson's lips were moving but Tina did not hear a word. All that was registering was suicide.

"How can that happen?!" She heard herself screaming.

"Tina, I know that this is very difficult for you but please listen to me." He pleaded with her.

"No, I don't want to hear this!" "How can a little girl do such a thing"! Tina screamed.

"How?" Tina asked screaming.

"Tina my dear, Macy wasn't a little girl she was 20 years old."

"What, no"! "That's crazy"! Tina yelled putting her hands over her ears trying to block out the words that Pastor Peterson was saying while visions of her little girl played in her head; Macy running and turning to face her, her smile. Tina began to shake viciously, her eyes rolled back into her head and then her body went limp.

CHAPTER ELEVEN

A week had gone by since Tina's conversation with Pastor Peterson and she found herself in a state of deep depression. Nothing seemed to matter anymore. She didn't want to talk and she had no appetite to eat. Her daughter had given her something to look forward to and now all she could think about was that her little girl had obviously grown up to be a troubled young woman and it had hit her hard. How could this happen she asked herself over and over again. Nothing made sense to her. She needed answers but at the same time she questioned her sanity.

Was she strong enough to handle the truth without falling apart again? The thought of it scared her. She obviously needed time to heal mentally and emotionally.

Doctor Cartwright tried to prepare himself as he walked toward Tina's room. He had been away on a medical conference when he got the called about her relapse. She had been doing so well but the emotional trauma had caused a seizure and now she was in a very fragile state. He had his doubts about whether or not it was too much for Tina to handle but what was done was done and there was no need dwelling on it. He just hoped that her mind would not be so far gone that he could not bring her back. Hopefully, he would be able to help her come out of it.

"How is she?" Doctor Cartwright asked approaching the nurse.

"Well, she has not spoken and barely eaten in over a week. "A lot of crying, she's really hurting and we may have to find other means of getting her to eat as soon as possible." Dr. Winston explained.

"Ok" Emanuel said. He took a deep breath before entering her room.

"How's my favorite patient?" Doctor Cartwright asked in his most cheery tone of voice.

She did not respond to the sound of his voice nor did she make an attempt to acknowledge his presence. She peered out the window as if in another world and that's exactly how she was probably feeling. *"This is not good,"* he thought. As he got closer to her, he noticed that her skin was pale and those eyes that use to shine where now dimmed, red and swollen.

"Tina," he called softly.

Doctor Cartwright could now see the tear stains left on Tina's face. Her hurt was now hurting him. He pulled a chair close to the bed and sat down.

"I'm so sorry Tina but I want you to listen to me, he said taking her hand. You have come too far to just let yourself go." "All of your progress is going right out the window and I know that you don't want that to happen do you?" He asked her.

Tina said nothing. The voice sound familiar but she managed to tune it out. She couldn't say anything. "Maybe whoever it is will go away," she thought but the more she tried to tune the voice out, the more persisted and loud the voice became.

"You don't want that to happen now do you?" He asked her again. Tina still did not respond.

Emanuel got up from the chair and put the rail down and sat beside her on the bed.

"Tina, please talk to me!" He said raising his voice a bit and taking both of her arms pulling her closer to him.

The desperation in the voice and the gentle force that pulled her to him made Tina turn toward him. Her eyes meant his and she witnessed the look of genuine concern overshadowing his face. He took one hand removing the tears that flowed freely down her cheeks. Tina managed to nod her head no; she didn't have the strength to speak.

"Good that's what I wanted to see." He said pulling her to him.

There was no longer a need for words. Tina began crying as if she would never stop. Having Macy is what kept her going, she's what gave her a reason to want to live and now she was gone; she hurt so badly. Tina held on to him. She could feel his strong embrace and somehow, she knew that she would be ok.

Tina had cried herself to mere exhaustion and as Doctor Cartwright laid her frail body back on the bed, he too, knew that she would be ok.

"She has to be," he whispered and gently kissed her forehead and left the room feeling very optimistic.

Four years had pasted and amazingly Tina had fully recovered. She couldn't believe the image that stared back at her in the mirror. She had pushed and pushed herself sometimes to the point of total exhaustion but never once complained. Sometimes she felt as though her body couldn't take it anymore and just when she felt like giving up, she somehow found the strength to do it all over again. It had paid off. Rehab was no joke. Her body looked good and she felt fabulous. She was already making plans to take some refresher courses in banking investment since she was told that she had did so well in the field so her plan was to venture out on her own and start her own little business as a consultant. Doctor Stevens had given her a clean bill of health but advised her not to take on too much too soon to eliminate the possibility of any stress related problems. He wanted to make sure that she adjusted well-being that she had been out of the work force for some time but from the looks of it, Tina seemed to be ready physically and mentally.

Tina still had no memory of Tony and he showed no indication or interest in being married to her so filing for divorce was not a problem. Besides, from what she had heard, he had already moved on with his life so she made it easier for him; she set him free. Diane helped her find a little apartment not far from where she lived and with the money that she had invested, which Tony never touched, helped to buy what she needed to make her place a home. The face in the mirror now scowled at the one thing that haunted her; the death of her daughter. She was still too afraid to ask questions for fear of losing control again. She had relapsed once and she had no intentions of letting that happen again. Pushing those dark thoughts out of her mind, Tina replaced them with thoughts of expectations of things to come and it made her smile.

"Not bad, not bad at all," Tina said in a low voice as she watched the face that stared back at her in the mirror.

CHAPTER TWELVE

Diane couldn't put it off any longer and decided to start making plans to give her sister a welcome back dinner party. Getting reacquainted with her old friends and colleagues would do Tina good. Diane sat down at the kitchen table and she found herself thinking back to happier times. A long way from what it was now but she hoped that after ten years, she could bring her family back together again. Just maybe they would be able to put their differences aside for a couple of hours. Diane picked up the phone and called Thomas first. Thomas was the more sensitive one of the two brothers. He and Tina were inseparable when they were younger and the best of friends well into their adulthood but one slip of the tongue had destroyed their relationship.

"Yeah," Thomas answered.

"Hey Thomas," Diane said with caution. "Is this a good time?" Diane asked hearing the irritation in his voice.

"No, but what's up?

"Listen I'm having a little get together for Tina and some of her friends at The Peach Club and it would be nice if you would."

"I don't think that's a good idea," Thomas said cutting her off in mid-sentence.

"Why, she's your sister Thomas" Diane said trying to stay calm.

"I know that but I don't want to hear it right now; later, I have to go." Thomas said slamming the phone down.

Diane sat at the table and shook her head with disappointment.

"Well one down and one to go." She said nervously dialing Robert's number.

Robert was one of those people who didn't give a damn about nobody except himself. Diane knew that it was going to be a slim chance of getting a return call from him if he didn't answer his phone. He was probably sitting there looking at the phone ring and just for spite not answering it. Finally, his voice message came on and Diane took a deep breath and then left a message explaining the event and hoped that he would return her call-in spite of.

Diane calmly placed the phone down. "Lord I'm doing my part you can handle the rest because I can't; I have enough on my own plate already" Diane whispered.

Brook had just walked into the kitchen after hearing her mother's conversation on the phone. Diane looked up in time to see her chuckling in a sneaky kind of way and wondered what that was all about. Brook seemed to look more like that trifling husband of hers very day; had even inherited his nasty attitude too. That girl sure did keep her on her knees.

Brook was very attractive, smart and built like a high fashion model but she had a mouth that would put the average sailor to shame. That mouth kept her in trouble and the fact that she was spoiled made her even worse. God help whoever got in her way.

"I can't believe that after all this time he still blames Tina for that mess with his wife." Diane said more so talking to herself.

Brook let out a soft giggle and bit into an apple that she had just got off the table. Diane looked up at her.

"What is so funny?" Diane asked.

"Nothing mother" Brook said nonchalantly.

Brook knew that her mother would shit bricks if she ever found out that it was, she who had told her uncle's wife about his affair. She will never know by me telling her, Brook thought smiling to herself.

Diane got up from the table and walked over to the window. Once again, she was plagued by images of her putting Macy in the closet. The episodes were happening more frequently and she was becoming even more depressed.

Mommy said, "Let go and let God."

"Mommy I'm trying," Diane whispered.

Once again Thomas had let his temper get the best of him. He poured out his frustrations on his sister and that wasn't right; she was only trying to get everyone together. He wanted to call her back but it just wasn't a good time. He loved his baby sister and the night of her accident would always haunt him and he carried the guilt around for ten years; the things that he said to her had broken his heart; telling her that he never wanted to see or hear from her again and he almost got his wish. It was his precious baby sister that caused his wife to leave him and it had been hard letting it go.

Thomas tried to relax but how could he. He had just got off the phone with his estranged wife who was once again threatened him with a divorce. After all of the years that they had been married, he knew she would only bring up a divorce when she got mad and wanted to piss him off. He had other important things to concentrate on and that was raising his twin sons who were the only people that made sense in his life. He loved them with every beat of his heart and was planning on making his home their permanent home too. Seeing them one half of the year wasn't enough and he almost had their mother convinced in letting them move in with him. Thomas had just picked up the phone to call Diane back when the doorbell rang and to his surprise, he was served with divorce papers. *Mommy said, "For every one step you take forward, life will knock you back ten."* "Damn Mommy," Tommy mumbled.

CHAPTER THIRTEEN

Dressed in a black lace evening gown, Tina was a picture of perfection. She had gone the whole nine yards in preparing for her dinner party.

Hair and makeup done, manicure, pedicure and anything else that she had thought of to make the evening unforgettable. After leaving the nail salon, she had gone straight to the boutique to pick up her dress. They had promised to have the alterations done by four and that had been perfect timing for her to go home, take a bubble bath and relax before her big event. Now she was walking to her car looking fabulous.

"Hey Miss Tina, you look pretty." Ashley from the neighborhood yelled out.

"Thank you, baby," Tina replied back to her.

Tina was so glad that she only had to drive a short distance to get to Diane's house. She was so excited but scared all at the same time; not knowing what to expect or who she would remember or wouldn't remember. She had seen very few people since her recovery and she wondered how people would perceive her. Tina turned on the radio so that the music would relax her and a song was playing that reminded her of Doctor Cartwright. It was so weird and she surprisingly began singing the words to the song.

"Sho Nuff Must Be Luv, oh yeah, its heavenly with you."

Tina felt good and hoped that the evening would go well and she smiled with thoughts of Doctor Cartwright. The man stayed on her mind often and she couldn't deny the fact that his attractiveness was very addictive. She liked him and she had convinced herself that his feelings must be mutual too because he called her on a daily basis keeping it professional though;

but sometimes it seemed like he wanted to say more.

"Sipping soda in the corner café, just passin" happy hours away, --with you making all of my dreams come true and it Sho Nuff Must be Luv." "All right now." Tina sang.

Tina parked in front of Diane's house and after the song ended, she turned off the ignition. She admired the landscaping that Diane had done; everything was so nice and neat but too bad everything didn't seem nice in her home. Diane never had much to say about her family and on more than one occasion Tina had sensed a terrible vibe coming from that husband of hers. Something just didn't seem right in that household but Tina never mentioned it. She just tried to be as friendly as possible but that didn't seem to work.

Tina got out of the car and as she neared the door, a flashback of her and Tony talking and laughing stopped her in her steps. It seemed so real like it was just happening and it was the first time that she had envisioned her with Tony like this; it was like a movie playing certain clips. The doctors had told her that it would happen and that it was supposed to be a part of her memory processing. It was a bit scary.

"Hey, I didn't know you were out here, look at you." Diane said, when she opened the door and found Tina standing there.

"Oh, I just got here," Tina said still startled.

The two embraced and Diane was speechless at how beautiful Tina looked.

"Girl you look stunning." Diane said taking a step back so she could really get a full view of her baby sister.

"God is truly wonderful," Diane thought as she stood there looking at her sister. There was a time that she would have been green with envy by her sister's beauty but God had delivered her from that. She no longer hated her sister.

"Are you ready; where are Robert and Thomas?" Tina asked.

Diane hesitated at first not really knowing what to say.

"Ting they're not coming I'm sorry."

"What do you mean they're not coming, what's going on Diane?"

"Well Robert never got back to me and Thomas had a prior commitment that's work related" Diane lied.

"What did I do to them Diane?" Tina asked.

"Hey don't worry about it ok?" "Tonight, is your night." Diane said trying to keep Tina's spirit up.

"Well guess what?" Tina said to her.

"What?" Diane asked.

"I'm going to put this out of my mind for now and I'm going to enjoy myself the best way that I know how."

"Good girl, you could always do that."

"Do what?" Tina asked looking at her.

"Put up this iron shield when you're hurting; like nothing can ever get to you." "You're a lot like Daddy you know; I'm sorry Ting" Diane said.

"Mother isn't it time to go?" Brook asked coming out on the porch not realizing that her aunt was there.

"Hi Brook how are you sweetie?"

Tina walked toward her to give her a hug but Brook walked in the other direction to avoid her touch. Diane shot Brook a warning glance and chose not to acknowledge what had just happened. It would have only given Brook the opportunity to really show her ugly side.

"Ting you ready?" Diane asked.

"Yes, I'm ready.

The three got in Diane's car and headed for the party.

"*You don't get nowhere by being nasty to people,*" Tina heard a voice say and she shook her head in agreement.

CHAPTER FOURTEEN

The Skylight Ballroom was beautiful. The ceiling was a 30ft high by 40ft glass dome with chandeliers hanging from each corner of the room and the floor was made entirely of marble. On each table were long glass vases that held white lilies, Tina's favorite flower. Everyone looked so nice; the women dressed in their evening gowns and the guys in their tux enjoying an hour of Hors D'oeuvres, consisting of some of Tina's favorites; meatballs with cabernet sauce, scallops wrapped in bacon and stuffed mushrooms.

It was a large turnout probably based on the curiosity of some. The guest couldn't help but whisper and wondered if Tina was going to look the same as they had remembered her; beautiful and sophisticated with a charming spirit. As Cynthia looked around the room, she couldn't help but wanting to give herself a pat on the back; everything was beautiful. She and Diane had done a wonderful job getting things together but she was still curious as to why Diane had asked for her help with planning the dinner. They were not the best of buddies because Cynthia was well aware of how Diane really felt about her sister. On more than one occasion, she had warned Tina about it but Tina didn't want to believe it. Maybe things were changing.

"Ok can I have everyone's attention please?" Cynthia asked speaking into the microphone.

The conversations ceased and the room became a desolate space.

"It's time to re-introduce my friend." "It has truly been a long time coming and Tina we all missed you so much and we love you still; please let's stand and give a warm welcome back to the most beautiful person in the world who happens to be my best friend, Ms. Tina Robinson, welcome back girl."

Everyone stood and the applauses began as Tina walked out onto the floor.

"Oh my God she looks fantastic," someone shouted.

The emotions took over and it was truly an amazing moment.

"I love you girl," Cynthia said as she gave Tina a kiss and handed her the microphone.

"Wow this is beautiful," Tina said. "Thank you everyone, thank you."

Tina waved her hand for everyone to sit and the room became silent once again.

"First I just want to thank God for allowing me to be here this evening." "This is so beautiful and I cannot find the words to express how I feel right now." "Cyn and Diane, thank you so much for putting this all together." "Everyone, thank you for coming out and sharing this special occasion with me." "I promise to come around to each of you to say hi." "So, on that note I'm going to take my seat because it's time to eat." Tina said emotionally.

Everyone applauded once again and Tina was escorted to her table where Diane, Brook, Pastor Peterson and his wife were waiting. Diane smiled as Tina walked toward their table and even though other family members were present, Diane thought of how perfect it would have been if Robert and Thomas were there.

Tina gave the dinner five stars plus some. Fresh spinach salad was followed by a serving of orange sorbet and the guest were given the choice of Lobster Tail, Flounder with Crab Imperial, Stuffed breast of chicken or Prime Rib which were all served with a baked potato and glazed, mixed vegetables. To complete the meal, a slice of vanilla bean cheese cake topped with a strawberry sauce was served which was sure to satisfy everyone's sweet tooth. The guest was entertained with soft music by Kenny G, whom just happened to be one of Tina's favorite musicians. After dinner, as Tina promised, she graciously catered to her guest re-introducing herself with

Cynthia right beside her. She laughed at some of the stories told to her and a couple of people she actually remembered.

While Tina was getting reacquainted with her guest, Diane had her hands full trying to keep Brook under control. She was acting up as usual and it smelled like she had been drinking. When Pastor Peterson and his wife left the table, Diane was determined to get her under control before she embarrassed not only herself but the rest of the family. Diane knew that she could and would if given the opportunity.

"Look, you're not going to embarrass me in front of Tina's friends; won't you act like a lady," Diane whispered to her.

"A lady mother really coming from you?" "I didn't want to come here in the first place" Brook said raising her voice.

Brook got up to leave but Diane pulled her back.

"You sit your ass down now!" Diane demanded and Brook took her seat.

Brook knew by her mother's tone of voice that she was not one to play with. Brook was furious but she did not want to make her mother any angrier than what she already was so to occupy her time, she took her cell phone out and dialed Antoine's number. Again, his phone went right into his voice mail. She hated when he wouldn't answer his phone especially when she knew that he was purposely avoiding her calls. Antoine had been on a guilt trip ever since Macy's death and he wanted to keep everything on the down low but Brook didn't seem to understand that or she just didn't want to understand. She wanted so bad to flaunt their relationship to prove a point but she couldn't see that it was going to make her look like the bad guy. The one thing that Brook knew for sure was that if her mother ever found out that she was seeing Antoine, she would never hear the end of it especially now since she was supposed to be so holier than thou.

"Damn, she just won't quit," Antoine said after seeing numerous calls from Brook.

He just didn't want to talk to her, not now or ever but he didn't know how to tell her. He felt so stupid for not standing up for himself and that's why he despised her now. He had allowed himself to get caught up with how good the sex was. The girl was wild in bed and he had to admit that she did things to him that he didn't know was possible. I guess he could say that she had opened his nose up real wide. As time passed, it didn't matter how good the sex was especially when she slipped and told him during one of their wild nights that she had set his stupid ass up purposely to hurt Macy; she hated Macy. As far as he was concerned, it wasn't even a relationship but Brook called it one so that's what it was. He allowed himself to get caught up in a no-win situation and now he wondered what in the world was he going to do about it.

Doctor Cartwright entered the room and all eyes were on him. The ladies couldn't help but steal a glance of him when their partners were not looking. He looked sharp in his black tux, looking ever so handsome and his cool, calm and collect demeanor made him every woman's dream; he was definitely a sight to see. His eyes scanned every corner of the room until he found her. He had never witnessed such beauty before. Catching a glimpse of her from the side, Doctor Cartwright was filled with much admiration for his favorite patient. She was absolutely stunning!

He had called Tina every week after she was released from the center. There were no doubts about his feelings for her; they were real and he knew what he wanted. He had been feeling her for some time now and even though he kept it professional, she had to know how he felt about her. Yes, he had female friends that he kicked it with from time to time but that was the extent of it; having casual sex wasn't filling the void any more, he wanted more and Tina weighed heavy on his mind. Doctor Cartwright walked toward her just as she was making her way to another table.

"Wow, look at my favorite patient."

Tina turned around slowly when she heard that voice; it had to be him, she thought. Then their eyes met and it felt like her insides were turning to

Jell-O.

"Oh, my goodness you're here." "I didn't know that you were coming." *"Thank you, Cynthia Diane, Jesus, she said to herself." And he's alone, she thought and then she smiled."*

"You know I would not have missed this for anything"

"How are you Mrs. Robinson?" He asked.

Then at that moment she knew for sure. It wasn't just the look on his face but it was the look in his eyes. She had been right. He liked her and he liked her a lot.

"I'm fine." She spoke.

"Yes, you are." He said to her.

Tina exposed a smiled and Doctor Cartwright walked closer to her and planted a kiss on her forehead.

"Uh oh I love this song" he said looking at her. "Would you like to dance?" He asked her.

"I would love to." She said.

Doctor Cartwright led her out onto the dance floor gently placing one arm around her waist and taking her hand in his; both hearts were pounding. He had waited so long for an opportunity to hold her like this. He knew that Tina was the "it" in his life, because she felt so damn good in his arms.

This fine man had Tina's head spinning and she felt as if she was floating on air. *"Boy, does he smell good,"* Tina thought as Doctor Cartwright pressed his chin up against her temple.

"It's simple, I love it, having you near me, having you here."

Doctor Cartwright stared at her.

Our conversations, outrageous you smile, then I smile then I say ooohhh-this is getting personal, personal, personal let's stay for a while, and play, girl lets make this a moment.

Tina stared at him.

Giving you the best of me, Amazing, amazing oh having you close to me, Amazing, outrageous give your best to me.

Doctor Cartwright placed his chin on Tina's forehead again and held her closer to him.

Good morning it's breakfast, lost track of time but-we had a ball, let's catch a movie, then dinner, tonight's the night we'll just unwind and stay, hey let's stay personal let's stay for a while and play, such a beautiful moment.

As the song ended, they stared at each other, either one wanting the moment to end.

"Hey do you want to go out on the balcony so we can talk?" Doctor Cartwright suggested.

"Lead the way" she said so he took her by the hand and escorted her from the room.

It was a perfect night. The air was warm and the sky was clear occupying a thousand stars.

"It's beautiful out here" Tina commented.

"Yes, it is." He agreed.

With his back against the railing, Doctor Cartwright turned to face her and hoped that what he was about to say would initiate a positive response.

"You don't know how much I tried to keep my distance from you being that you were my patient but as you can see it's not working." He said looking serious.

The last time that Tina had seen him this serious was when she had relapsed at the center.

"I look at you and think back when I first seen you lying in that bed in a coma." "I would have never imagined that you would be standing here, right here right now." "I know the struggle was hard for you at times but in spite of all of it, you didn't give up."

"I almost did" Tina said to him."

"Yes, but you didn't." "You were stronger than what you thought you were and you were determined to get your life back and you did that." "You are a strong, intelligent, beautiful black my kind of woman, that I would love to have in my life." Doctor Cartwright said smiling.

"So…what are you saying?" Tina asked.

Doctor Cartwright put his head down and smiled and then lifted his head up looking straight in her eyes.

"I really would like to get to know you even better if that's ok with you." He answered her.

Tina could no longer hide her feelings that she had for him and she knew that it showed.

"Really?" Tina asked smiling.

 He nodded yes.

"Well, I would like to get to know you better too." She responded.

"Good, and one more thing that I would like to ask of you, if you don't mind, that is." He spoke.

"And what is that," Tina asked.

"Can you call me Emanuel" he laughed.

"Ok Emanuel, I like that."

"Good"

Emanuel knew that it was the perfect moment so he leaned in and gave Tina a gentle kiss on the lips; a kiss that was sure to seal their past, present and future; a new beginning indeed.

CHAPTER FIFTEEN

Diane stood outside of her house and embraced the warm early morning breeze. She loved the Japanese Maples and the Bellflower Dahlias that blossomed beautifully against her house. Her hard work had finally paid off and now she could reap the rewards; it was breathtaking. Tina loved it too and she always complemented her on how nice the yard looked and she, for once, had to agree.

After admiring the scenery, Diane walked toward the garage. She was still feeling pretty good especially since the dinner party that she had given Tina a couple of months ago. Thinking back, it had turned out very well in spite of her daughter's rude behavior. Diane couldn't understand why she didn't have a boyfriend tugging after her which would surely occupy some of her time. God bless the one who took on that responsibility and Diane chuckled at the thought. As she pushed the button to open the garage, Diane noticed that Brock's car was not there.

"He must be laying up with one of his women," she mumbled getting the sprinklers out of the garage.

The thought disgusted her and she pushed the button again to close the garage door. Diane took one final look around the yard and concluded that her work was done so she took off her gloves and headed inside only to find a sink full of dirty dishes that had been sitting for days. She had been so busy lately that she didn't have time to do much house work so today would be the day to get caught up. As she picked up a glass, a flashback of a fight Macy had with Brock robbed her of her thoughts and without thinking Diane squeezed the glass so hard that it broke sending pieces of fragments into her skin.

"Jesus" Diane said aloud.

The water turned red and she quickly grabbed a towel and tied it around her hand. The cut was deep and Diane knew from the look of it that she would definitely need stitches. How was she supposed to deal with this she wondered, realizing that her nightmares were coming to life again and tormenting her very thoughts. Overwhelmed, Diane broke down and wept.

Brook laid restlessly across her bed. Sleep would not come so once again she witnessed sunrise come in. She could hear someone moving around downstairs and she would bet that it would most likely be her mother. Then her thoughts drifted to Antoine and she wondered what he could be doing and why his calls were becoming less and less. Not talking to him was driving her crazy and she knew that if she didn't nip this thing in the bud, she would surely lose him. Brook leaned over the nightstand and turned the radio on allowing the music to ease some of the tension. In anticipation, she picked up her cell phone and called Antoine and once again the only sound that she heard was a familiar voice message asking to leave a message.

"That figures, call me if it's not too much trouble for you."

Brook threw the phone down and got up off the bed and opened the closet door. There hidden beneath a blanket was a bottle of whiskey.

"This will work." She said and she took a long swallow straight from the bottle.

***

"*Ok it's one o'clock so where is she,*" Tina thought as she paced back and forth. She was meeting Diane at the mall for lunch but Diane was almost a half hour late. Just as Tina was about to call her, Diane came walking through the parking lot.

"Hey you, I was just about to call you." Tina said reaching out to give her sister a hug.

"Hey what happened?" Tina asked reaching out for Diane's hand.

"Oh, it's nothing; I cut myself on a piece of glass while I was washing dishes" and she quickly changed the subject.

"So, how's everything?" Diane asked looking away from Tina.

"Everything is good."

"And how is Emanuel?" Diane asked turning to Tina.

"We are officially dating." "It's been what, three and a half months now".

"Well, I'm happy for you girl, truly I am." Diane said sincerely. "It sure feels good to play hooky; I need to do this more often." Diane said as they walked into the mall.

"Hooky?" Tina said frowning.

"Girl it means staying home from work for no reason at all" Diane explained.

"I knew that." Tina said and they both started to laugh.

After two hours of shopping, Tina and Diane headed for their favorite fast-food restaurant. For lunch Tina ordered a cheeseburger with lettuce and tomato, French fries, coleslaw and a large soda. She was basically eating what she wanted and could still manage to maintain her weight. Diane on the other hand was just the opposite. The more stressful her life became, the more she ate so she opts for a garden salad and a diet coke. Tina had noticed the weight gain but chose not to mention it because Diane seemed to be so self-conscience of it. Suddenly an argument between Diane and a man; a woman scolding her about her weight and Diane becoming very emotional flashed before her. Once again Tina was startled.

"Wow" Tina said.

"What's the matter?" Diane asked noticing the strange look on Tina's face.

"It's nothing really oh did I mention that I'm thinking about moving out of the condo and going back to the house" Tina said in between bites of food.

Diane stopped eating and looked at her.

"Why would you want to do that?" "I thought that you were thinking about selling the house?" "Don't you think that it will be a little too much for you?" Diane asked with an attitude.

"Well, I was thinking about selling it but I quess I've had a change of heart. I'm going to give it a try and if it's too much, then I'll sell it but I have to at least try." Tina explained.

"Well, I think that it will be a little too much but you do what you want." Diane said defensively.

Tina noticed how tense Diane had become so she let it go and changed the subject. She was thinking that lately she was letting a lot of things go and she was really getting tired of it.

"I got this" Diane said taking the check to the front desk.

"Ok my treat next time and I will see you again soon call me, ok?"

"Ok I sure will" Diane replied. And they gave each other a hug and went their separate ways.

Diane walked back across the parking lot to get to her car and thought about how nasty she had just acted toward her sister. She sure hoped that the old Diane wasn't coming out of the woodwork again. She wanted her sister to be happy because she deserved it but the fact of the matter was that if Tina moved back into her house sooner or later, she was going to asked her to come over and Diane just didn't know if she could ever go back in that house again. It was just too many bad memories.

Tina was about to walk to her car when she heard her phone ring, and not paying attention, she ran right into a man walking toward her.

"Oh, I'm so sorry"! Tina said apologizing as she looked up into the eyes of a very handsome man.

The man stared at her in an odd kind of way and his facial expression led Tina to believe that maybe he knew her. She even sensed that he wanted to say something to her but he didn't. Weird, she thought.

"No problem." He said and slowly walked away.

The man was shocked and turned around and watched Tina walk away. The woman was fine as hell and looked just like someone that he knew. "Damn"! He thought.

"Hey"! Tina said in the phone still a little startled at the man that had just passed her.

"Hey what are you doing babe?" Emanuel asked. "Is something wrong?" He asked hearing the distraction in her voice.

"No no I'm ok" she said and smiled.

"So, what are you doing?" He asked again.

"Well, I'm just leaving the Mall and I'm about to head home."

"Ok, well I was thinking, would you like to go out tomorrow night, maybe have dinner and see a movie?"

"I would love to what time?"

"Maybe around 7:00." "Does that sound good?"

"Yes," she agreed.

"Ok I will call you sometime tomorrow to confirm, ok?"

"Ok."

"Bye now." Emanuel said not really wanting to hang up.

"Hey, never say bye just say I will see you later."

"Ok, I will see you later, better?" Emanuel asked.

"Much better" Tina replied.

CHAPTER SIXTEEN

Emanuel sat up in his bed. His breathing was fast and erratic and his body dripped with sweat. *"Calm down,"* he told himself, it's just another dream. Emanuel took a deep breath and got up to take a shower thinking maybe it would help him to relax. The hot water felt good on his body and he closed his eyes for a few seconds to clear his thoughts; then it dawned on him. Bo's anniversary was coming up and that's why the dreams were happening so frequently.

The two of them were inseparable, so close. They did everything together and went everywhere together; they were both wild and crazy. Emanuel opened his eyes and turned off the water. Taking another deep breath, he reached for the towel and quickly dried himself off, wiping the extra moisture off his face than he glanced in the mirror. He laughed softly hearing Bo call his name. *"E man, come on."* Emanuel's eyes were red from the tears. The thoughts and images of Bo had once again overtaken him. He shouldn't be alive, he thought; he should be right in the grave next to his cousin, his boy.

Boris Giles better known as "Bo" was two years older than Emanuel; street smart and daring which led him to do foolish things. Very attractive to the women but he was no genius but he was good at what he did; he could run his ass off and received a full scholarship at Wiley College for track but only finishing his second year and dropping out after getting his beautiful girl Vanessa, who was half Portuguese and half African American, pregnant and that was the beginning of his downfall. Bo had come from a single parent home being raised by his mother who tried her best to raise him the right way but it wasn't easy. Bo had a mean streak in him which Emanuel believed came from the resentment he had toward his father for leaving his family.

Emanuel, whom his friends called E, had both parents at home who had been married for over twenty years. They were determined to keep him on the straight and narrow path; at least they tried to. They were strict and Emanuel had to abide by their rules as long as he lived under their roof. He had to attend church which he never complained about because that gave him access to meeting some pretty nice-looking girls. A lady's man; and he knew it.

Even though he was younger than Bo, E was more mature for his age and with his swagger and charm, it wasn't hard to convince anyone that he was the shit. He had the looks and the intelligence to become whatever he wanted graduating with top honors and being accepted at Harvard University. His plan was to be a physician but one night changed everything and his plans were put on hold.

By the time E graduated from high school, Bo was already running the streets. Vanessa moves to another state, taking his son away, and giving him another reason to be bitter at the world. He couldn't find a decent job and couldn't keep one so he started a hustle and was selling a little something to make ends meet. One night he and this dude named Kato were doing their last drop for the night and was jumped and robbed. Word was out that Kato had set Bo up because he knew that Bo would be held accountable for the money and the dope that they had on them. E knew that some shit was going to go down if Bo didn't have this money so he came up with a plan to help save Bo's ass. E set up a meeting with one of his boys in the hood. He made some connections and before he knew it, he along with three others including Bo, Derrick who they called Dek, and Sam were out on the corners selling dope. The guys were fearless and trustworthy and the money started coming in so fast it was ridiculous. It wasn't too long before Bo got the money back plus a whole lot more and Kato got the beating of his life.

E was the mastermind behind the transactions that took place. He found himself doing things that he would have never imagined; it came with the job. Those who didn't conform by the rules of the game got a serious beat down especially those who didn't have his money when it came time to collect. Emanuel never enjoyed it but Bo did; he got a kick out of it. When the money really started coming in, so did everything else including the women and E was making a name for himself. After sometime on the streets, he became highly respected so business was good. He now had six guys including his cousin, but they now hustled for him. His plan was to make x amount of dollars and stop. He was really smart that way; *"Always have a plan,"* he would say. While his boys did their thing, E had a legitimate job working at a hospital which allowed him to get familiar with the medical scene. He didn't want his street life to interfere with his dream yeah, he still had a dream.

Unfortunately, when word got back to E's parents about his street life, they kicked him out and wanted nothing else to do with him. So, he got his own place, fully furnished it, brought a car and put a lump sum of money in the bank every week. Life was crazy, a good crazy.

E had been working the streets for five years when Monica Watkins walked into his life and then everything started to change. He was crazy about her; from her beautiful coco brown skin, to her long flowing dark hair. It was something so sexy about her. To E's surprise, she was still a virgin and the anticipation of getting with her was nerve wrecking. He was falling in love with her fast and was willing to wait as long as she needed him to. It's amazing what love will and can make you do; he would often think.

Monica was different from any girl that he had been with and he knew that he was going to have to come correct to be with her. She helped put him back on the right track but it wasn't easy. Monica was from a middle-class family who were very religious and strict too. Her father was the principal at the middle school in Chicago and her mother worked at the church. They lived on the other side of town; I guess you could say the better side. Monica made him want to change from his evil ways, even got him to go to church a couple of times; something he had not done since he had left high school. Her parents despised him in the beginning. They thought that they knew just what he was about, especially her dad. The more he tried to impress them the more they didn't like him. I guess he was considered not good enough for their little girl so E started using his inner-charm and his intelligence to convince them and he did. But all the while E did his thing in the streets, that old familiar voice would often lurk in the back of his mind; the words of his Pastor, his mentor, the one person that he couldn't fool, the one who kept reminding him of the consequences of street life and the question of what was it going to take for him to get off the streets; Imprisonment or death. His Pastor tried to instill in him that the longer he stayed on the streets the harder it was going to be for him to get himself off the streets; he spoke from experience. E knew that the Pastor was right and his love for Monica was already confirming it.

E found out the hard way that your personal life does not get top priority when you're dealing with life on the streets. He had his head so far up in the clouds with Monica that he failed to see that putting his cousin in charge was a big mistake. He had finally won Monica's heart and nine long months later, the two of them were ready to take the relationship to the next level. E was more than ready and was heading home to put the plans in order but his thoughts were interrupted when he noticed a message on his phone and looked down to check it.

"Yo E get back as soon as you can yo, Bo's cuttin up man get here!"

"What the hell is going on with these" he said pressing down hard on the gas pedal and heading home.

E pulled into the driveway to his house and turned off the ignition. He didn't know what to expect because Bo could be crazy at times. With pistol in his belt, he got out of the car and checked his surroundings and everything seemed to be ok. It was times like this that he was glad his piece was legal. He walked in the house and up the steps to the living room. Now he knew what Dek was talking about and he couldn't believe his eyes. Bo was sitting on the sofa with drugs all over the table, gun lying on the side of him, which was most likely illegal, and that glass pipe up to his mouth. He could smell Bo as he walked closer to him and the foul odor was horrid. Bo looked up at him and didn't even try to stop what he was doing; it was like he was invisible to him. E stood in disbelief. His cousin, his road dog, his main ace had allowed himself to get strung out on this shit. E walked over to the table and knocked over everything that was on it then he grabbed Bo by the top of his shirt and started beating the hell out of him.

"Come on man you don't want to do this, E come on," Dek said running in the room after hearing the commotion. He and Sam managed to pull E off of Bo but not before Bo fell unconscious. Sam picked him up from the floor and put him on the sofa.

"How long has this shit been going on!? E hollered.

"For a while man, Sam responded.

"And no one bothered to tell me?" E asked.

"E you know how crazy Bo is and he threatened us man and you know he will do what he says he gonna do. For the past couple of weeks man, it was getting pretty bad so I had to tell you." Dek explained."

"He threatened you bullshit." You think I would have put him in charge of my shit if I knew this?" E said pacing the floor.

E managed to calm down long enough to call a meeting with the other members to see where they stood. To his surprise, Bo had missed up big time. Several detectives had already been to the house asking questions and now they were being watched. E didn't want to take the risk of getting his boys into trouble over something that his dumb ass cousin was doing so he was going to do what he had to do on his own; these were good people just trying to make some extra cash to help take care of their families.

The money and the supply that Bo had to distribute were gone. He and God knows who else, had went through $100,000 worth of dope and to top that off, monies were missing and not accounted for. E now owed the supplier a certain percentage of that and now he had to pay that off to get things back on track. It was going to take some extra time to get the money now that the police were on their tails. E was disgusted and fed up but he knew that he had to fix it so two days later, he found himself at Darren Hardy's house being padded up by one of his boys. He had never had a problem with Darren and he was hoping that it stayed that way but E was well aware that when you start fuckin up with people's money that was a whole new ball game.

CHAPTER SEVENTEEN

Darren was originally from Jamaica but had been in Chicago for about seven years. His place was hooked up. The foyer was huge with light grey walls with white crown molding and the floor was covered with grey and white marble. Black art graced the four corners of the walls and a giant chandelier hung from the ceiling that you could see from the outside window. His office was right next to the indoor swimming pool which displayed a picture of Bob Marley at the bottom. This man had been in the business for years and you could tell.

"Hey what's up?" E said while they searched him from top to bottom.

"He'll see you now" one of his boys said.

E opened the door to the study and Darren was sitting in his chair at his desk.

"Hey my man, come in, shut the door." Darren said.

One guy was standing at the door and another was seated on the sofa. Darren got up and shook E's hand.

"Hey what's up," E said.

"Nothing but the money and that's a good thing, sit."

"Ok, well I'll get right to the point; I have a situation and I want to run it across you." E said never taking his eyes off of Darren.

"Ok you two can leave now, I got this." Darren ordered giving his boys a wave of the hand to leave the room.

Darren was thinking of how E was going to handle the situation because he already had a good idea of why he was paying him a visit in the first place.

"I'm listening," Darren said.

E continued to talk and was determined to remain as cool as possible even though the looks of the man that sat across from him was very intimidating. His blue-black skin, big apple red lips and the color of eyes that E had no name for; Eyes that had the look of don't fuck me because I will kill you in a heartbeat. E couldn't help but notice the scar that ran across the side of his chin and he could only imagine what he had done to deserve it.

"So, you have my word I'm going to get your money but it's just going to take me a little longer than expected to get it." E explained.

Darren didn't say a word for a few seconds but all the while twirling a ball in his hand.

"I like you E, and I never forgot what you did for my son and because of that and only that, I'll give you the time that you need to get my money because I know that you are a man of your word." "Not only did that son of a bitch fuck things up for you, he fucked things up for me too and he's done it before." "I knew that you didn't know anything about it by the way he was acting when he came up in here talking shit." "Because he's your family, I wanted to give you the common courtesy of waiting until I talked to you first." Darren explained.

Darren went on to explain several incidents involving Bo and money deals and E was starting to fill sick to his stomach. This man could have taken him and Bo out at any time and he would have been clueless.

"I will tell you this," Darren said putting the ball down and leaning forward and looking right into E's eyes. "I also am a man of my word ok, and if the dumb mother fucker fucks me one more time, I'm gonna take him out of his misery and I hope that you don't fool around with his dumb ass and get taken out too." "Now get the hell out and get my money," he said.

E was ready to get the hell out of there so he got up to leave.

"Remember," Darren said.

E turned around to face him.

"This is not personal its business." "I have no problem with you unless you make it one" Darren said.

E nodded his head as if to say ok and got the hell out of there. Darren got up and watched E get into his car. He knew that if this had been anyone else E and his dumb ass cousin would have been found chopped up in a river somewhere; he didn't play when it came down to his money. He liked the boy and could never understand how he got mixed up in this life anyway but he was doing his thing and Darren liked the way he did it. Thanks to E, Jamal was now doing well.

After leaving Darren's, E went home and talk some sense into Bo. Bo promised to get help and he had his girl make arrangements for him to go into rehab in a week. Everything was set and Bo seemed sincere and ready to go and E was going to make sure that he kept his promise. That morning for Bo never came and E would soon see the effect of the consequences of his actions.

The reservations were made and E was determined to give Monica the best night of her life. He had been ready for months to finally get this relationship to the next level but now that it was going to happen, he was nervous as hell. He realized that he had never actually made love to a woman before and had never given it a second thought until now. Monica wasn't just another woman under his belt. What he had with her was different. All he wanted to do was please her, never once thinking about himself. This must be love he thought, and Monica definitely had his heart and Kandi noticed it too.

Kandi worked for one of the best escort services in town and she was ten years his senior. E had known her for some time and she was the first real woman that he had ever slept with. Of course, Bo had introduced the two and all the bragging made E curious as to what she could do for him. He gave her, her props; she definitely gave you your money's worth. He could talk to her about anything and she would listen. So, when E showed up at her door just wanting to talk Kandi knew something was up; Him talking as she listened.

"What I do to you E, is what you do to her." Kandi said with a playful smirk. "Just take your time and be gentle you'll know what to do." And she gently kissed him on the cheek. E was ready.

It was a Friday night and he had just picked up a bottle of champagne and a dozen of roses and was on his way to pick up Monica for what he thought would be the perfect night and then, he got the call. This was the first time that Dek had ever called him by his full name and E could tell that something was terribly wrong. Tears swelled up in his eyes and without hesitating, E turned the car around and headed back home. He was soon to find out that Darren was definitely a man of his word; in just two weeks Bo was dead.

When E got to the house, Dek, Sam and a couple of the other guys were standing outside. The look on their faces told the story.

"Where is he?" E asked when he got out of the car.

"You don't want to see him like that" Dek said.

"I said where is he?" E demanded to know.

"On 12th and Spruce', Dek answered.

E shook his head; he knew the area all too well. They all got into the car and headed to 12th street. Sweat began to form around the edges of E's head as the car pulled up slowly and then came to a stop. Dek got out the car first and E was behind him.

"Over there man," Dek pointed.

Tears began to roll down Dek's face and he knew that there was no holding E back. The area was dark; with thick bushes lined up against the fence; it had once been a dump for old used tires. E didn't see him at first but as he got closer, his ace, his best friend, his family, laid in a pool of blood; body cut in half from the waist down. It was the most gruesome thing he had ever seen. A sight that was sure to haunt him for the rest of his life. E backed away; his legs became weak. He tried and tried to hold it back but it was no use; vomit gushed out of his mouth. Flash backs of him and his cousin raced across his mind. Good times, the bad times; this is not happening, this can't be happening, he thought. E didn't really know what happened next. He remembered walking away. He walked away from the scene. He wanted to walk away from this life; the life that he knew he had no business getting mixed up in. He heard his named called in a distance' he kept walking. Cars blowing their horns at him but he kept walking. In one night, all the money, women and cars no longer mattered. It took this to make him see the light. God why didn't you take me too, E thought. Still in a daze, E didn't hear his named called. Pastor Bryant was just locking the doors to the church when he noticed E walking.

"E, my God what has happened" Pastor Bryant asked looking into a distraught face.

For the next three days E said nothing; his body paralyzed by waves of shock. Pastor Bryant took him into his home where they talked and prayed. In three weeks, E was on a plane headed to Cambridge, Ma. leaving that life behind never to look back. A couple of years later he would learn that Darren Hardy was in hell right where he belonged.

Emanuel put the towel down and gazed into the mirror again. "*You got a second chance to do things right this time,*" he thought to himself.

"I won't mess it up" Emanuel said out loud. And he hurriedly put on his clothes preparing to spend the evening with Tina.

CHAPTER EIGHTEEN

"You are a pathetic individual and a poor excuse of a man" Diane screamed.

"And I guess you're Miss perfect huh? Brock hollered. "Because you go to church now you think you're better than me huh?" "The reason I don't have anything is because of you"! "You ruined my fuckin life"! "You're no better than me and your fuckin niece," Brock said with a devilish laugh and a facial expression that Diane did not want to even acknowledge. "You were right there in the mix so don't put all the blame on me." "You knew what was going on and you liked every bit of it"! Brock said.

Diane turned to face him.

"You leave my house and you leave now and don't you ever come back"!

"Hey, I'll leave but I'll be back to get my things when you're not here." Brock said in a drunken stupor and turned and walked out the door.

Why did she allow this loser to get to her? Diane thought. Over and over again his words played in her head like a rehearsal for an upcoming play. She hated how he made her feel and she had no one to blame but herself. Maybe just maybe he will be gone for good, Diane thought and she closed her eyes in a silent prayer as she made her request known to God.

After hearing the shouting match between her parents, Brook got up off the bed and began hitting herself in the head hoping that the blows would somehow block the harsh words that had been exchanged; words that she didn't want or need to hear. It was a constant reminder of just how dysfunctional her family was.

"Can't take this shit" Brook said and she got up off the bed and went to the closet to get what seem to be the only thing that made her numb, sending her into her own little world of make believe. *"No hurt, no pain for now,"* Brook thought as the alcohol began to settle her brain; just peace. Peace that made her believe that she lived in a perfect world with a perfect family; a family that had nothing but love for each other, the kind of family that you would see on the cover of a fan at church. The mother, the father, and the children all dressed in their best with smiles of pure joy and happiness. That is what Brook longed for; A normal life with a normal family. The way it used to be but the thought of Macy brought her back to reality and Brook took the bottle and threw it at the wall.

"You all can go straight to hell" she said before balling up on the bed and falling asleep.

***

"Excuse me that's Eva right?" The stranger asked looking at the name plate that sat on the desk. Eva looked up to see one of the most gorgeous men that she had ever seen; very seldom she was lost for words but at this particular moment she was speechless.

"Yes, and can I help you?" Eva smiled.

"Well, I hope so." he said. "Is there a patient here by the name of Tina Robinson?" He asked her.

Eva checked the roster in the computer. Nothing was coming up so she double checked it again. *"The longer I can have this gorgeous man in front of me the better,"* she thought. Yes, she was married but it was absolutely nothing wrong with looking and he was something to look at.

"Sorry sir but that name is not coming up in our roster," Eva explained.

"I know that she was a patient here, could it be possible that she was sent to"

"Excuse me sir but did you say Tina Robinson?" Ronnie asked in a rather feminine voice.

"Yes" the stranger replied.

"She was a coma patient here for 10 years and was released about three years ago." "Last I heard she was doing well." Ronnie said.

"Oh, so she is alive?" The stranger asked.

"Pretty much," Ronnie answered.

The stranger responded with a nod and said thank you before walking away. There was no doubt that the woman he had seen at the mall was Tina Robinson. It had to be. This was crazy and he knew that once he relayed the information, it was going to make matters a little more complicated. He had to do what he had to do and the sooner he did it the better it would be.

"Damn," Eva said as the guy walked away.

"Pat is going to be mad that she missed that" she said laughing.

"I would like to take him home with me."

"No, I would like to take that home with me." "You know your husband would whip that ass." Ronnie said, and they laughed and gave each other a high five.

CHAPTER NINETEEN

Emanuel looked at the clock and it was getting late. He had just finished cutting up the fruit and cheese that he had brought for later on in the evening. After having dinner and seeing a movie with Tina, he had planned to bring her to his house just to chill out for a while and if anything else transpired between the two of them, he knew that it would be the making of a very special evening; at least that is what he was hoping for.

The fire was lit and Emanuel tried to make the atmosphere as cozy as possible. A white cashmere throw rug covered a small area on the floor in front of the fire place making a comfortable spot for him and Tina to sit. As they sat side by side sipping on red wine, they watched the reflection of colors coming from the flames and it gave the room a warm and romantic feeling. Tina loved the restaurant that Emanuel had chosen and complimented him on how fabulous the dinner was. She loved the intimacy that the restaurant provided and it was like they were in total seclusion with just the two of them enjoying each other. The movie was funny and quite romantic starring Richard Geer and to Emanuel's surprise, he was one of Tina's favorite actors.

"I guess I can tell you now," Tina said looking over at Emanuel.

"Tell me what" he asked wondering what it could be.

"My divorce is final."

Emanuel smiled and placed his glass on the table.

"Come here you" he said putting his arm around her and placing a kiss on her temple and then he reached for his glass to make a toast.

"To new beginnings," he said.

Tina held up her glass.

"To new beginnings" she said to him.

Emanuel leaned forward and placed a kiss on Tina's lips; A kiss that Tina didn't want to end.

"This has been a perfect evening Tina" "So I guess I can tell you now." He said.

"Tell me what?" She asked.

"Tell you that I'm in love with you but you already knew that right?" He asked smiling at her and giving her a look with his eyes that she should answer yes.

Tina laughed.

"Yes, I kind of guessed that, and I'm in love with you too" she said with the sincere conviction that showed in the most beautiful eyes that he had ever seen.

Emanuel knew in an instant that he had Tina's heart. He took their glasses and placed them on the table. Their eyes met and he leaned over and began kissing her endlessly, beginning with her forehead and going down her neck; his hands finding places, making it seem so magical to both of them. Giving and receiving a joint effort. Tina felt like nothing else mattered but being right there. Here and now, she thought. Feeling like she was losing control which felt like a good thing. Racing through her mind were questions that no longer needed answers. Every doubt and wonder no longer mattered; she could finally put them to rest.

Emanuel was ever so thorough, making sure not to miss any area that would surely give her ultimate pleasure. *"How did he know that I liked it like this?"* Tina thought with her eyes closed as she tried desperately to control her breathing but he touched all the right places at the right time sending her body in complete tumult. Emanuel began to slowly remove her clothing.

"Are we ok with this?" He whispered to her and she nodded yes.

The passion that he felt was like an explosion waiting to happen. Her body was absolutely stunning. *"Hold on boy,"* he kept telling himself, your almost there. Tina opened her eyes and could see that Emanuel wanted her so bad and she needed and wanted him too. She began to help him undress. Her hands shaking and needing him like an addict needs a fix. She couldn't seem to do it fast enough; her eyes witnessing the nakedness of a perfect body. He was truly blessed Tina thought and blessed in more ways than one. Emanuel reached over and got something off the table. He had placed a condom there just in case and thought, *good boy.* Tina closed her eyes and thought, *"Oh good I didn't have to ask,"* and she waited eagerly for his entrance; He kissed her with such passion that she could hardly contain herself and then she felt his lips connect with that most sensitive place and she moaned with undeniable pleasure for she was no longer in control. Her hands held his head tight yet gentle in position, making sure that he wouldn't move as she reached that special place. Her moans made him want her even more and he held his ground and waited for her. His kisses started up again beginning with each thigh and working his way up, tickling her with his tongue along the way. Their eyes met as he planted the most passionate kiss as he climbed between her, lifting her hips to him, entering her, sending them both to a place that was made only for the two of them. Every thrust, every kiss, was like hitting a nerve ending in their body, both exploding.

A half hour later, Emanuel and Tina laid exhausted but truly satisfied. Their expectations were above and beyond what they could have ever imagined; they blew each other's mind. Sleep soon overtook them, giving each one time to recuperate. Emanuel laid in a peaceful sleep but for Tina it was anything but…

The little girl ran across the grass; her light-brown pigtails dangling from side to side.

"Mommy, mommy, you said," she yells.

Tina runs toward the little girl who she realizes is Macy and just as she gets close enough to touch her, Macy disappears.

Tina awoke startled and confused. For a split moment she had forgotten where she was and the sudden movement awoke Emanuel.

"Babe are you ok?" Emanuel asked.

"I will be, please hold me," Tina asked him.

Emanuel sat up and pulled her to him and held her close. He could fill her body trembling.

"Do you want to talk about it?" He asked her.

"No, it was just a silly dream that's all."

"Ok I'm here if you need to talk ok?"

"Ok" she said.

Emanuel knew all too well the effects that dreams could have on one's consciousness. He knew that it wasn't just a silly dream as Tina laid in his arms apparently still shaken up from it. He kissed her and held her tight until her body relaxed and they both fell asleep once again.

CHAPTER TWENTY

Tina had finished packing and was finally ready for the move back to her house. It had been five years since her recovery and she felt that she had to prove to herself and to Diane that she was ready to make this move. Diane's attitude had already made her put it off numerous times leaving her with doubts and countless nights driving pass the house longing to go in but too afraid to. Thank God for Emanuel for his words of encouragement gave her the boost that she needed and now she was ready. With her car filled with boxes, Tina pulled up in front of her house, took a deep breath and turned the ignition off.

"I wish Emanuel was here." She said getting out of the car and walking up to the door. Tina had such a strange feeling as she opened the door and slowly walked in. Bits and pieces of memory flashed before her. Every corner and every detail of the house was like looking in a photo album. She obviously had good taste; the house was beautiful and maintained very well over the years leaving Tina with no added expenses for upgrading. Everything had been done so all she had to do was move in.

The house was huge; a two-story Colonial with lots of windows. Tina was grateful that her ex-husband had not sold the property but had rented it out and the lease had been up months ago. She smiled feeling proud that she could finally say that she had got her life back. A new love, new business, and now she was back in the house that she had obviously once loved and was falling in love with it all over again.

The staircase was beautiful and Tina put her purse down and went up the steps. Each room had its own special detail and this was exactly the kind of house that she imagined living in. Tina stopped and was once again caught off guard when her memory entertained her with an intense love making scene with Tony in the same room that she was now standing in, her bedroom. A sudden sense of guilt flooded over her and she thought it strange.

Downstairs was even more beautiful. Tina was going to have fun decorating and she couldn't wait to get started. The kitchen was amazing with granite counter tops that complimented the cherry wood cabinets and the stainless-steel appliances just made everything pop. The living room and dining room were both spacious and when Tina opened the door to the maid's quarters, an eerie sensation came over her but at the same time she was astonished at how big the room was. It would be a perfect space for her office, she was thinking. There were also doors on the other side of the room that led outside to the back yard which was huge. There was at least an acre of land that was surrounded by a fenced. Trees that had already started losing its leaves were scattered about and Tina had already begun to visualize how beautiful it probably was during the summer months. Maybe, just maybe, she would have an in-ground pool put in and arrange some outdoor furniture with a fire place and all to complete the look that she was aiming for. She was even thinking about putting some benches in the yard which she thought was a good idea especially during times when she would entertain quest.

Overall, Tina was overwhelmed with joy. Happy and satisfy that the move was not a depressing moment for her. Standing there looking at it all, she concluded that she had definitely made the right decision.

The leaves were finally changing and fall was fast approaching. Tina gazed at the different shades of color that hung from each tree. What a beautiful sight, she thought and she smiled as she and Emanuel held on to each other like letting go was a sin. Emanuel was surprised that he had got another day off so soon and he took full advantage of it by spending as much time with Tina as possible. No telling when he would have another day to spend with her especially with the holiday's approaching.

"I didn't know how I was going to feel once I got settled in the house but it's not bad, not bad at all" Tina said looking at Emanuel.

"Good I'm glad everything went well for you babe." "I just wished that I could have been there since your sister wasn't but as you know my schedule can get crazy sometimes; but I'm here with you now." Emanuel said grabbing and tickling her until they both fell down in the grass. Tina laid beneath him and their eyes met.

"I love you" she said kissing him on his lips.

"I love you too" Emanuel said to her and he wiped a leaf away from her hair.

"So, when can I get a tour of the house?

"We can go right now if you like." She said kissing him again.

"I would love to" he said, and he got up from the ground and lifted her up to him.

The house was everything that Tina had said it was; it was her all over. She was happy and her happiness was important to him so he was going to make sure that his lady stayed that way. He made it known to her that he was ready and willing to support her in any way that he could to keep that smile on her beautiful face. The rest of the day they spent in bed, ordering out from their favorite Chinese restaurant, and making love until near exhaustion.

"It can't get any better than this," Emanuel thought as he watched Tina who slept cuddled up next to him.

It wasn't long before Emanuel had also succumbed to a much-needed sleep but he was awakened shortly after, by Tina's sudden bouts of twisting and turning. Periods of moaning also captured his attention and he would hold her close to him, showering her with gentle kisses which seem to calm her. Watching her reminded him of himself. Struggling with issues that were beyond his control. He knew what it was like, he knew what it felt like. So, he wanted to remind her that he was there for her, to talk, console or just to listen. Yeah, he would remind her.

Cynthia stood outside Tina's house and rang the doorbell. She was so glad to have Tina back in her life and was excited about getting started with helping her remodel her home once again. Cynthia already knew the layout of the house and had come across some great ideas with fabrics and designs that she wanted Tina to see.

She and Tina were best friends throughout high school and while in college they still managed to keep in touch. After college, Cynthia moved across the country for a while to pursue her career in Interior Decorating and Design and was quite good at it. So, when she got the call from Tina about remodeling the house again, she made it her top priority. This would definitely keep her busy for at least a couple of months. Cynthia loved her like a sister and was so glad that Tina was able to pick up the pieces of her life and get back to living.

"Hey you, come on in here." Tina said.

"Hey," Cynthia said giving Tina a hug.

"And how's that fine Negro of yours," Cynthia said and they both laughed.

"Good and you know we have to catch up on some things, don't you?" Tina asked still feeling the effects of Emanuel from the night before.

"Yes, we do but business first." "I'm going to take these things upstairs and I still have some other things that I need to bring in for the room down here."

"Ok I will get out of your way so you can do your thing," Tina said.

While Cynthia headed upstairs, Tina made her way to the room that would soon be her office. The same eerie feeling came over her again and she walked over to the window to open the blinds. It was gloomy outside but the weatherman had predicted sunshine later on in the day.

"It looks like it's going to pour out there." Tina said and was about to leave the room when her slipper got caught on something in the floor. She pulled her foot, but the slipper would not loosen so she pulled it again. Still, it would not loosen so she took her foot out of the slipper and bent down to pull it loose. The third pull not only loosened the slipper but the whole floor panel came up with it.

"What the hell." Tina said pulling the slipper from the panel.

She was about to place it back in its place when she noticed something laying in the opening of the floor. She took the slipper and wiped the dust webs away to get a better visual, and there lay what looked like two brown books. Tina reached in the opening and picked up one of the books and to her surprise, it wasn't just a book but it appeared to be that of a diary.

"This is strange" she said examining what she held in her hand.

"Tina where are you? Cynthia hollered.

Tina jumped to the sound of Cynthia's voice.

"I'll be right there" Tina yelled back grabbing the other book out of the opening, and blowing the dust webs off of it. Tina placed the panel back in its rightful place, and left the room.

Cynthia was undecided about what color and style she wanted to use for Tina's drapes; both looked great.

"Ok I'll let Tina make the final decision on this one" Cynthia said out loud.

Tina entered the room and placed the diaries on the table. Cynthia held up two different pictures and showed them to her.

"Ok, which styles do you like best, the valance with just the blinds or this one with the drapes with the silk scarf?" Cynthia asked holding the two pictures up for Tina to see.

"Am I not paying you to do this?" She asked Cynthia playfully.

"Yes, and decide now missy" Cynthia said. Tina looked at the two pictures.

"Ok this one" Tina said pointing to the drapes with the silk scarf.

CHAPTER TWENTY-ONE

Brook's day at work had turned out to be a pretty good one. The new Adjuster was pushing up on her big time but Brook wasn't feeling him. Her main focused was on Antoine but he wasn't giving her the time of day. Why did life have to be so complicated and confusing at times? She thought. This new guy was going out of his way to get with her but no, she wanted the one who probably would wind up hurting her in the end but Brook didn't care. She wanted Antoine and she was going to do what she had to do to get him even if she lost herself in the process. As she pulled into the driveway, Brook took out her phone to call Antoine again. She had to remind herself to talk like a lady instead of a "drunken sailor" as her mother would put it but Antoine always seemed to bring that bad side out in her. For once she was going to do things his way just to prove to him that she wasn't the conniving little bitch that he thought she was. She wanted to change her ways for him. To lose him would mean that Macy had won once again even in death and she wasn't having it.

"Oh, I'm so surprised that you answered your phone" she said to Antoine. What are you doing?" She asked him.

Antoine hesitated and hit himself in the head for forgetting to screen his call.

"Nothing just sitting here thinking." He answered.

"Thinking about what" she asked.

Antoine paused again.

"Look I don't think that it's a good idea for us to be seeing each other so let's just chill ok; with everything that's happened, I don't want to do this anymore."

Brook didn't want to admit it but the signs were all there. She just didn't want to accept it; the infrequent calls and when she did get through to him, he was so distant and uninterested and the sex went from three times a week to none. Still, Brook didn't know how to take it. She knew that Antoine could never love her like he did Macy but she was ok with that. His words brought everything to light. It was one thing to act like he didn't want her but to hear him say it was definitely a wakeup call for her. Brook could feel the rage building up inside her and with no hesitation, she did what she does best, she let Antoine have it from the depth of her being.

"You know what you make me sick, you dumb prick!" Brook yelled. "I didn't hold a gun up to your head, did I?" "Now all of a sudden you on this guilt trip and you know why, because you are an asshole, the hell with you" Brook said and she threw the phone in her purse.

As the tears ran down her face, Brook took her hands and wiped them away. She wasn't in the mood to try to explain to her mother what was going on in her life so once she got in the house, she went straight to her room and closed the door behind her. She needed a quick fix; A little something to take the edge off so she opened the closet and removed the blankets that were on the floor exposing the one thing that would make her world livable. She drank right out the bottle.

There goes my damn good day, she thought.

Antoine knew that the only reason why he was able to tell Brook that he didn't want to see her anymore was because he had left town to stay with his uncle for a while. At least this would give Brook sometime to get over the situation, and over him. How can two people who obviously bring out the worse in each other have a chance of being happy? They took each other there. The mere fact of how they got together and why they got together never seemed to bother her. Brook was a very pretty girl and a very outgoing person and if she ever got her head on straight, she would probably make someone very happy but he wasn't the one. She had to stop wanting to be in control and wanting to have things her way all of the time like no one else had an opinion or a reason. Sometimes she could be as sweet as sugar and then if something was said that she didn't like, it was like a switch was hit and she would go off into Lala land. Her ways had turned him off completely. He hoped that Brook would find that someone special to share her life with at least that is what he was hoping for but Antoine knew her all too well. Right at that very moment, Brook was probably planning a "How to get back at Antoine" scheme and ready to put it in full force. So, who was he really fooling, only himself?

CHAPTER TWENTY-TWO

The warm water was soothing to Tina's body and it helped to loosen up the tension that she was feeling since her move into the house. All the running around and trying to get situated had finally caught up with her. Tina took the stopper out of the tub to let the water out. She grabbed her towel off the edge of the tub and was barely dry when she heard the phone ring and hurried to answer it. She was elated, it was Emanuel.

"Hey you," she said.

"Hey babe, listen" Emanuel said disappointedly,

"Uh oh I can hear it in your voice, what's wrong?"

"I won't be able to make it tonight; there was an emergency here and I can't get away right now".

"Aw its ok I understand"

"I will make it up to you, you know that right?"

"I sure do" Tina responded in a sexy voice.

"Ok babe, I have to go" Emanuel laughed quietly.

Tina sent kisses through the phone and Emanuel send them back to her.

It was a Friday night and Tina didn't want to be alone. She knew Cynthia was away and Diane for some reason was avoiding her but she was going to try to call her again. Tina put on her nightgown and grabbed the phone to call her sister.

Diane noticed a call coming through from Tina and was hesitant to answer it. She dreaded hearing Tina ask over and over again about coming to her house and she knew Tina could be persisted and would not let it go.

"Lord" Diane said and picked up the phone.

"Hey girl it's me, Tina said.

"Hey" Diane answered.

"Listen, Emanuel can't make it over tonight; he had an emergency at work so I was thinking, won't you come over for a while and have a sister night like keep me company" Tina asked.

Diane rolled her eyes.

"Girl that sounds nice but I have so much to do around here and that daughter of mine is no help." "A couple of the members from church are coming over tomorrow afternoon and I have to get things ready" Diane explained.

As Tina listened to the same excuses that Diane was giving her again, she noticed the diaries that she had placed on the dresser earlier that morning. That would occupy her time.

"Well, maybe another time than." "Oh, the strangest thing happened this morning." "I found two diaries."

Tina was going on and on and Diane was becoming more irritated and the static coming from the phone wasn't making it any better.

"Diaries, what did you say?" Diane asked. "Tina holds on I can barely hear you; I have another call coming in."

Diane clicked the phone over and Brook was frantic on the other line.

"Mother you have to come and get me"! "I'm at the police station"! Brook screamed.

"Brook hold on." Her mother said.

Diane clicked the phone back over.

"Tina, I have to take this call; God, I'll call you back."

Tina could hear in Diane's voice that something was wrong.

"Ok talk to you later" Tina said and Diane clicked the

phone back over to Brook.

"I hope it's not that daughter of hers again," Tina said out loud and she got up off the bed and looked out the window.

Thoughts of her own daughter invaded her mind and Tina wondered what kind of relationship they would have had. A closeness that would have brought Macy running to her with her boyfriend problems and seeking motherly advice; and hanging out at the mall together, picking out the latest fashions. Or would they have been constantly at each other's throats; distant and cold toward each other. The thought brought tears to Tina's eyes and she quickly pushed them out of her mind.

"I think I need a glass of wine." Tina said and she picked up the diaries off the dresser and headed downstairs.

"*It's nothing wrong with a little wine that settles the stomach and clears the mind.*" Tina heard a voice say.

***

"What's going on Brook?" Diane asked.

"I got pulled over and I was drinking but I'm not drunk." "Can you please come and get me from the police station; they won't let me leave alone! Brook pleaded.

"Ok, I'll be there as soon as I can." "Lord give me strength." Diane said and she got her coat and left to go to the police station. Minutes later, Diane stood face to face with her daughter and tried to make sense of it all.

"You know what; you need to do something with your life before it's too late" Diane said to her daughter.

"Oh, mother please"!

"Oh, mother please, what?" Diane asked. "You're drinking and carrying on and you don't even seem to care." "That officer was nice enough to give you another chance and that doesn't happen every day so what's going to happen the next time Brook?" "What if you're not so fortunate the next time and you kill someone or yourself?" Diane scolded her.

Brook tried to get in the car but Diane wouldn't let her.

Brook began to cry.

"Why are you drinking so much anyway?" Diane asked her.

"You're asking me why I drink so much mother; you don't know, huh." Brook asked sarcastically.

Diane stepped aside letting Brook get inside the car.

"Trying to talk to this girl when she's like this is useless, Diane said under her breath and she walked to the other side of the car.

Mommy said, "Kids will worry you to death if you let them, you have to put them in God's hands."

CHAPTER TWENTY-THREE

It had just started to rain and Tina could hear the rain drops hitting against the window. The warm temperature in the room made it cozy and Tina got comfortable on the sofa. The rain always put her in a romantic mood and she thought how perfect it would have been if Emanuel were there with her but the only romance that she was going to get was reading two old books that she had found in the floor of her soon to be office.

Tina picked up one of the diaries and started going through the pages. The handwriting seemed to be that of a child and Tina's attention was drawn to the date written across the top of the book, November 20, 2001; five days after her accident. *What a coincidence* she thought as she ran her fingers through the pages trying to find who the author was.

"Ok who the heck is Me?" Tina said out loud when she noticed the word "Me" written as the author. She turned back to the fourth page, then the third, the second; and there on the first page written in pencil was the name Macy Nicole Robinson. Tina could feel her heart beating faster; her breathing sporadic.

"Oh, dear God"! She said placing her hand near her heart.

The tears began to build up and Tina began to cry as she held the little book close to her heart. It was as if her baby girl was in her arms and she found the strength to relax herself as she began to read.

November 20, 2001

Hi diary. Jessie gave me this book. She said that it is called a diary and she told me to write down how I feel and it would make me feel better. I have so much to say. A whole lot is in my head. My mommy was hurt really bad. Me and daddy went to see her. I talked to her but she

can't hear me. I miss her so much. Aunt Diane is calling me. I will write again to you tomorrow. Macy

November 29, 2001-Thanksgiving (Thursday)

Hi diary. This is the worst Thanksgiving ever. I heard daddy and Aunt Diane talking. Mommy might not ever wake up. I don't feel thankful. God won't wake mommy up. Having dinner at Aunt Diane's. I try to tell her that mommy doesn't put nutmeg in her sweet potatoes but she hollered at me. She said that she's not my darn mother. She used the cuss word though. She's always yelling at me. I will write tomorrow. Macy

"Why would she say that?" Tina mumbled and she noticed that after this entry, Macy began using Me.

November 30, 2001-Friday

Hi diary. Daddy took me to see mommy. I talked and talked to her. I hope she can hear me. Daddy sits in the dark all the time and cries. Jessie went home early today. She was sick. I made peanut butter and jelly for me and daddy when we got home but he didn't eat it. God won't listen to me and Daddy won't talk to me either. Jessie is busy and she tells me to write. Diary I guess you're all I have. I will write again tomorrow. Me

December 4, 2001

Hi diary. Daddy took me to school today. My friends made me this great big card and everyone signed it. Mrs. Wilson gave me a big hug and she told me that I could talk to her any time. I have to eat. I will talk to you again to soon. Me

December 10, 2001

Hi diary. I am sad today. Daddy just told me that Aunt Diane might be moving in with us. He said he was going to talk to her tonight. I told him I was just fine and Jessie would be with me. He told me that Jessie is getting too old. God please don't let Aunt Diane and Uncle Brock come here. Me

December 15, 2001

Diary. My daddy is leaving me. He said he has to get away. I think he got some bad news from the doctors and he won't talk to me. He said that he would be back soon. I think he's lying because he's taking a lot of clothes. Me

December 20, 2001

Diary-Mommy I need you. I miss you sooo much. Aunt Diane moved me out of my room. She told Jessie that we didn't need her any more. I didn't even get a chance to tell Jessie good bye. I'm in her room now. Brook is in my room. Aunt Diane told me she doesn't want to look at me.

Tina took the sleeve of her nightgown and wiped her swollen eyes. Each word was ripping into her heart.

December 25, 2001

Diary-I had to stay in my room most of the day. I got in trouble. I tried to tell Aunt Diane that Uncle Brock stares at me for no reason. I didn't get to open any of my gifts. I gave my Christmas list to Daddy before he left and I know that he gave it to Aunt Diane because I seen him give it to her. She didn't know that I was watching them. I miss Mommy.

Tina had read so much until her vision became blurry and her head throbbed with pain and she closed her eyes to help relieve the pressure.

"My God" she whispered and she felt her body giving in to the exhaustion that was weighing her down; and finally, she drifted off to sleep.

CHAPTER TWENTY-FOUR

Emanuel knocked on the door and hoped that Tina wouldn't mind the early morning visit. He missed her so much and wanted so desperately to see her. The knock startled Tina and it took her a few seconds to realize that it was the next morning and that she had not gone up to bed but had fallen asleep on the sofa. She heard the knock again and wondered who it could be so early in the morning. As Tina got up, the diary fell to the floor and in an instance, everything that she had read the night before was coming back to her. She reached down to pick the book up and got the one off the end table and placed them on the shelf. To her surprise, Emanuel was standing at the door looking fine even in the early morning light.

"Just a sec." she hollered.

Tina closed her eyes and took a couple of deep breaths to clear her thoughts but her body still felt shaky and she hoped that Emanuel would not sense that something was wrong.

"Hey you" she said opening the door and pulling Emanuel to her and holding him tight; he felt her body shaking.

"You ok" he asked moving her away from him so he could look at her face.

"Huh yes, I'm ok" Tina said and she pulled him through the door and closed it.

"Sorry about the early visit but I couldn't wait I had to see you and tell you in person." "I gave some thought about our conversation that we had the other day and I'm going to take you up on your offer."

"My offer?" Tina asked.

"Yes" Emanuel smiled at her.

"What?" Tina asked with a puzzled look on her face.

"Woman you have a roommate."

Tina smiled remembering their conversation and pulled Emanuel to her.

"Are you serious? Tina asked practically jumping in his arms.

"Yes, but don't get too excited ok." Emanuel laughed. "I still have some things I have to take care of" he said picking her up and carrying her upstairs.

Emanuel playfully pushed Tina onto the bed and began taking her nightgown off; His eyes never leaving hers as he climbed onto the bed, pulling her to him. Tina began to kiss him while he pulled her on top of him; both hands grabbing at her buttocks. She needed his touch, his lips on hers.

"I missed you baby." He mumbled in between kisses and at the same time trying to remove his clothes.

"I missed you too." She said to him.

Tina closed her eyes and tried to block out everything that she had read to concentrate on the handsome man that was beneath her. Emanuel's sexy voice was turning her on and she took the initiative and putting one leg on each side of him, taking her hand, she allowed him to enter her and she quietly called his name. Emanuel placed his hands firmly on her hips while pushing himself inside her creating a perfect rhythm going faster and faster while they lost themselves in each other. He had never seen her like this; the more aggressive one; but he liked it, he liked it a lot. She was giving him all that she had, holding nothing back.

Suddenly, Tina was caught between anger and ecstasy as her mind drifted to a passage written in the diary and without warning, the word bitch uttered from her lips as she reached her sexual peak; Emanuel in unison with her, groaned loudly with full satisfaction. Feeling embarrassed, Tina wondered if Emanuel had heard her for, she was loud but then again, so was he.

With their breathing slowly becoming normal again, Emanuel held Tina close to him as their bodies recovered. He kissed her with his last ounce of strength and his thoughts were of how special it was to actually make love to someone that he was in love with; it was beyond feeling satisfied. As he watched Tina sleep, his curiosity took over his thoughts. Never in the heat of passion was he ever called a Bitch. He thought it strange; this was the first. *"What the hell,"* he thought. If she could deliver like that, she was welcome to call him whatever she wanted.

Tina folded the clothes and placed them in the basket to take upstairs. A pair of Emanuel's socks had got in her wash and she grinned. The man sure could rock her world and thoughts of their lovemaking from the day before made her grin again. She was still feeling a little embarrassed about that word that slipped out but he never mentioned it so maybe he did not hear her. She still had not mentioned the diaries to him and felt compelled to keep it that way for the time being. While still in deep thought, the sound of the phone brought her back to the present and she quickly began to tense up realizing that the one on the other end was her sister. *"Relax she told herself"*; she didn't want Diane to think that anything was wrong even though she knew that she could never look at her sister the same way again. If she could just find the time to finish the diaries, she truly believed that there was a whole lot more that would reveal itself.

"Yes" Tina answered.

"Hey Ting what's going on?" Diane asked.

"Nothing much just getting some laundry done, what's up?" Tina asked. The mere sound of Diane's voice was making her blood boil.

"Sorry girl for not getting back to you; so, the soap opera of my life continues." "That trifling husband of mine was picked up last night; I mean ex-husband." Diane explained.

"Oh, the divorce is final?" Tina asked.

"Yes, it is and thank you Jesus" Diane said with much enthusiasm.

"So, you're free at last uh?" Tina asked.

"Yes indeed." "Well, my little get together was nice; girl we think we have problems until you hear someone else's; I tell you." She told Tina.

"Yeah, you never know what goes on behind closed doors," Tina said sarcastically.

Diane's mind was once again invaded by an incident that she had with Macy and she closed her eyes tight in hopes of blocking it out. "*God please,*" she said to herself."

"Your right about that" Diane managed to say and the guilt took its rightful place.

"So, when are you coming over Diane?" Tina asked once again.

"Soon, well uh I'm on my way to the market; do you need to get anything?" Diane asked hastily.

"No, I'm ok for now thanks."

"Ok I will talk to you later than." Diane said hanging up so quickly and not even giving Tina enough time to say good-bye.

Still shaken up Diane hung the phone up. She knew that God had forgiven her for all her wrongs but maybe the problem was not being able to forgive herself. She just couldn't shake it off. Tina hung the phone up and with her hands on her hips she sensed that something was terribly wrong with this picture. There was a reason why Diane was always making excuses not to come over to her house and whatever the reason, Tina was determined to find out what it was.

"Trust your intuition," Tina heard a voice say. *"If something feels wrong it probably is."* "Yes, we will see" Tina said.

CHAPTER TWENTY-FIVE

"Yes, my holiday was fantastic and this is my week to get caught up." Tina laughed. "Yes, I will have the contracts written up and ready to sign in about a week; yes, that's fine, great thanks".

Tina hung up the phone and breathed a breath of fresh air; she was finally caught up with the work that she had left on her desk before the holiday. The 4th of July had come and gone and it had left her busier than ever but she didn't want to complain; business was great. Tina barely had time for herself so to help with the work load, she hired an assistant and the way the business was blooming she would probably have to hire yet another person. Regina was great. She was referred by a temp agency and Tina was reluctant to hire her at first but Regina reassured her that having an infant son would not interfere with her job performance and it didn't. She was always so professional and her computer skills were a plus. Tina hoped that the next person that she brought along would be just as good.

Tina had not talked to Diane in almost a month and it could remain that way as far as she was concern. Her attitude toward her sister was changing and it was not for the better. She had completed the first diary and was about to start the second one and the more she read, the angrier she was becoming. An ugliness was building up inside of her, changing her and she couldn't talk about it not even with Emanuel and they basically talked about everything. He must have noticed a change in her too because he was always asking her if she was ok. He was always talking about how important communication was in a relationship. No matter how hectic his schedule was he always checked home to make sure that she was ok. He was so sensitive to her needs and she loved him for that. *Maybe she just needed some time to herself*, she thought.

Regina had two more letters to complete before taking her lunch break. As she glanced at her boss, she could tell that something was bothering her but Regina couldn't figure out what it was. Sometimes she looked so angry and distant but she never had an attitude toward her. She was great to work with and the woman didn't play. She really had to stay on top of things to keep up with her; she was good at what she did. Regina smiled as she looked at her son's picture. She missed him so much and couldn't wait to get home.

"Regina" Tina called.

"Yes Ms. Robinson," Regina answered walking to her boss's desk.

"I've just decided to take a couple of days off so can you cancel any appointments that I have this week and reschedule around the middle of the month and I won't be taking any more calls today either."

"Yes mama" Regina said walking away.

"Oh, by the way" Tina added. Regina turned around to face her.

"That means you have the next three days off too with pay."

"Yes mama"!

Tina turned the computer off and headed upstairs to pack a light bag for the next couple of days. Glancing at her watch, she realized that it was the perfect time to call Emanuel; she knew that he would not be answering his phone. As she dialed his number, she crossed her fingers hoping that he wouldn't answer and sure enough, his voice message came on and she was relieved. Now she wouldn't have to answer any questions that he might have had regarding her brief trip.

"Yes" Tina whispered and she listened to the message and waited for the beep.

"Hey Emanuel, listen I know this is sudden, but something has come up and I have to go away for a couple of days to take care of some business, and don't worry everything is fine ok." "I will see you in a couple of days love you."

Tina put the phone down and began to pack and not too long after, she was on the highway heading for the Radisson. It was at the end of September but it was a hot afternoon. The humidity was causing Tina to sweat and the silk blouse that she had on stuck to her skin leaving a very unpleasant feeling. She should have changed into something a little more comfortable but it was a little too late. She pushed the buttons putting the windows up in the car and hoped that the air conditioner was now ready to kick in.

The forty-five-minute ride was not bad at all until Tina ran into traffic causing a complete stand still. As the traffic began to move slowly, it was evident that an accident had occurred resulting in the closing of one of the lanes. Tina waited anxiously and after a half hour, the traffic began to move freely again.

Chapter Twenty-Six

Diane walked passed Brook's room and was taken back by the smelled of alcohol. Brook was stretched out on the bed listening to the radio.

"Have you been drinking again?"

Brook didn't answer her mother or even acknowledged that she had come into the room.

"You need to come to church with me sometime; get your life together girl" Diane said to her and she picked up clothes off the floor.

"Everything is always church this and church that; where was church when Macy was here huh?" Brook asked her mother in a rather cold tone.

Her words caught Diane off guard leaving her shocked and speechless.

"What do you mean?" "I was good to that girl, so don't you talk smart to me."

"You know Mother there's a special place waiting just for you." "I know about everything that went on in that house and yet you have the audacity to ask why I drink"! Brook shouted.

Diane turned around so Brook would not see the shock and the hurt on her face. She had never given it a thought of any possibility that Brook knew about what had gone on. She thought it was something her and Brock would carry to their graves.

"But guess what mother?" Brook said sitting up on the bed.

"What doesn't come out in the wash will surely come out in the rinse." "Isn't that what your grandmother use to say huh?" "Did you know that

Macy kept a diary?"

Diane couldn't argue with her or even try to defend herself; Brook's words were cutting her like a knife. Diane thought that she heard Tina say something about a diary months ago but it had to be just a coincidence, Diane thought. Then her mind drifted way back to a place that she didn't want to go; recalling several instances when she had seen Macy writing but had never questioned her about it. As she thought back, Macy was always writing.

"I know where she kept them; "Did you know that mother?" Brook asked knowing that her mother didn't have a clue.

Diane walked over to Brook and grabbed her off the bed so hard that Brook thought she would fall to the floor.

"Now you listen to me, how dare you talk to me like this and if anything like that exists, you need to tell me about it before it gets into the wrong hands"!

"What was done was done.

Diane let go of her.

"I have turned my life around and I have asked God almighty to forgive me." "I can't change the past but I can try to change things for the better especially for Tina."

Diane began to pace the floor.

"You will never know what it was like growing up in this family with your grandparents." "I could never live up to their expectations especially when I got pregnant with you." She said turning toward Brook. "I never regretted having you, never. "When I got pregnant with you it was like I was a disease to them even after your father married me; that still wasn't good enough for them." "Tina was always praised for everything that she did and I was always overlooked; Tina had everything and I had nothing."

"The way they catered to her made me hate her"! Diane paused and turned her back to Brook. "I allowed my hatred for her to control me; I wanted to destroy everything she had even if it met taking it out on her daughter and now it haunts me e-v-e-r-y s-i-n-g-l-e day." Diane professed, crying uncontrollably. "And the really sad part about it is, Tina loved me, and did for me and she didn't even know that I hated her"!

Diane said turning to Brook.

"So, if you know anything about some diary you need to tell me now"!

Brook reached out for her mother and the two of them held on to each other.

"Baby I am so, so sorry please forgive me" Diane whispered in her ear.

Mommy said, "Life can be hard but it's what you choose to make it."

Chapter Twenty-Seven

Tina opened the door to the hotel and sat her bags down. Her stomach growled and she realized that she had not eaten anything since breakfast. Immediately she picked up the menu that was sitting on the table and opt to order from room service. After placing her order, Tina walked over to her bag and pulled out the diaries and placed them on the table along with a pair of pajamas, socks and her shower gel. She took off her clothes and grabbed the shower gel and headed for the bathroom to take a quick shower.

The cool shower was just what she needed. She lathered up twice and then she took the shampoo that they provided and lathered her hair up once and she let the water run down her face; oh, it felt so good. After rinsing off, she quickly turned the shower off and dried herself putting on some deodorant and her favorite body lotion, White Diamond. She loved the scent and Emanuel did too. He loved how soft it made her body feel. She was missing him already.

The room was still a little chilly from the air conditioner and Tina grabbed her pajamas and socks and put them on. Glancing at her phone, she noticed a missed call from Diane but she had not left a message. *Good,* she thought. She really wasn't in the mood to talk to her anyway.

"Who is it? Tina asked when she heard a knock at the door.

"Room service Ma'am," the man responded.

Tina opened the door, to get her food, gave the waiter a five-dollar tip and closed the door behind her.

"Hum, smells good." She said lifting the lid off the tray to expose cream of chicken breast, mash potatoes and string bean casserole. She immediately began eating while putting her things away.

With the last bite of chicken, Tina anxiously cleared the table and prepared to get comfortable. A glass of wine would have been nice and she was sorry for not bringing a bottle with her. The view from the balcony was amazing. Lights shone everywhere and the sky was filled with tiny lights of its own. The humidity had dropped and you could feel a slight breeze making it a perfect evening.

So, while Tina was preparing a quiet evening of reading, Diane on the other hand, was determined to put an end to the craziness. Neither she nor Brook was aware that Tina had already left; they were on their way over to her house.

"What are you going to say to her?" Brook asked her mother.

"Well, she has been begging me to come over there for months so now she can stop begging." "While I have her in one room, you go and see if you can find the diary and I will try to keep her occupied." "Let me call her now and let her know that we're coming."

Diane felt the nervousness creeping in her spirit and she hoped that Tina didn't pick up on it. She had not talked to her in a while and Tina had not returned her calls and was probably pissed at her for not coming over there so she was hoping that the visit would be welcomed.

"That's strange." Diane said handing the phone to Brook.

"What?" Brook asked noticing the puzzled look on her mother's face.

"She's going to be away for a couple of days so let's hope that she remembered where I told her to keep her key.

Diane and Brook stood at Tina's front door. The house was dark giving indication that no one was presently in the house and sure enough, the key was in the place where she had told Tina to put it.

"Thank God she remembered now let's pray that the alarm system hasn't been installed yet." Diane said, letting out a sign of relief when she realized it wasn't.

Brook entered first and went into what was now Tina's office and Diane followed her.

"It's over here" Brook said pointing to the floor as she remembered it.

Brook kneeled down and ran her hand across the floor looking for a slight difference in shape.

"It's not here anymore," "She must have had someone come and fix it"!

"Are you sure it was there?"

Brook turned to her mother.

"Yes, I'm sure."

"Why didn't you just take it when you had the chance? Diane asked becoming impatient.

"No one knew it was here Mother; "Macy didn't even know that I knew." "I followed her in here one day when she was high and I saw her pull the wood out of the floor." "You couldn't see it if you didn't know it was there,"

"Well, let's hope that no one has found it," Diane said looking at Brook.

"Can we go now?" Brook said being more than ready to leave.

Diane followed behind her and locked the door and placed the key back in its space.

The ride home was quiet. Both women had thoughts and concerns of their own. Diane didn't know what Macy could have written in the diary; she could only imagine. For a brief second, Diane had put herself in Macy's place and if Macy had written down her life story Diane was sure to be a part of it; the dark part. So, for now she was going to try not to think or worry about something that may not even exist anymore. Hopefully the diary was buried underneath the floor with all of the secrets with it.

Brook on the other hand had already read more than enough and what she did read had convinced her to never want to read any more of it. She had just assumed that her family was like any other family but that was so far from the truth. The diaries had changed her life.

Mommy said, "What doesn't come out in the wash will sure enough come out in the rinse."

Mommy, I hope this isn't one of those times. Diane thought to herself.

CHAPTER TWENTY-EIGHT

Tina pulled back the bedspread and propped the pillows up so that she could get comfortable on the bed. She reached for the diary that was on the night stand and she began to read. Every word and every paragraph was like a roller coaster ride. The more she read the more it took hold of her emotions; crying one minute and then laughing the next. A warm sensation came over Tina and she could feel a sense of panic come over her. She wasn't prepared for what came next. A mother's nightmare coming to life; Macy describing a sexual experience, rape.

June 15, 2003

Diary- Please God send someone to help me. I hurt so bad. I tried to get away from the monster but he was too strong. I hurt all over. I tried to scream but he put his hand over my mouth. Blood was on me. The monster told me not to tell or he would kill me and mommy. He told me not to look at him. I tried to pray but I can't. The next day I told Aunt Diane because I had blood on my sheets. She told me that I was stupid and that every girl goes through this. She said that I started my period.

"Monster?" Tina said trying to distinguish if what she was reading was fact or fiction. It was like her brain was fast forwarding so she had to take a deep breath and try to relax while she re-read the paragraph again.

June 20, 2003

Diary-The monster is back. He came in my room real late. Aunt

Diane and Brook wasn't home. The monster came in my room with no clothes on. He told me not to look at him again. He had something gross on his leg. This real big thing. I was so scared I couldn't move. He hurt me over and over again.

Tina realized that even though Macy never mentioned Brock, she somehow knew that she was talking about him. She closed her eyes and bits and pieces of a conversation that she had with Diane started going off in her head; Diane talking about Brock and using explicit details explaining their first sexual experience. Tina held her head with her hands, rocking back and forth and trying to concentrate. Everything was coming together in slow motion. She's remembering.

"Oh God"! Tina whispered. She remembered.

"So how was last night big sis; was it good or was it G-R-E-A-T-?" Tina asked.

"It was all that and a bag of lays potato chips." "Girl he got the body and he knows how to work it, work it."

Diane moved her body in motion.

Tina's remembering.

"One thing though," Diane laughed.

"Oh Lord here we go." Tina said.

"Well, he took his clothes off and we were about to get in the shower and I happened to looked down to see what I was going to be working with and he had this big, bumpy thing I don't know what you would call it in his groin area." "It scared me at first and I guess he seen me looking so he told me that it was a birthmark but he made me forget all about that shit."

Tina began to cry and suddenly she felt a churning in her stomach and just as she made it to the bathroom, everything that she had eaten was now coming up with a vengeance. It felt like everything was closing in on her and she backed up into the wall desperately trying to get herself together. Ghosts were invading her mind and everything was coming back to her; like a movie being rewind. The puzzle pieces of her mind were now coming together. Arguments, accusations, affairs; her best friend warning her of her sisters jealous but Tina just couldn't believe it, didn't what to believe it; hearing her mother constantly putting Diane down and telling her that "she would never be like her sister." Seeing someone bending down looking under her car the night of the accident; Tina sees it all; her beautiful baby girl.

"Oh God, no, no, no" she screamed.

Distraught and shocked, Tina fell to the floor. Her pajamas now spoiled from her own vomit. A face displayed with tears and a heart filled with unconceivable hurt; a spirit broken. How would she ever recover from this? She kept thinking.

"Damn you all" she yelled out holding her head like it was all too much to take in.

"*Just keep praying girl,*" *Mommy said.*

"No!" Tina yelled crying out to the voice that now had a face, Mommy.

While Tina was falling apart, Emanuel was just finishing up his rounds and was going back to his office to check his messages. Tina had called and he was anxious to talk to her being that she had called around the time when he was making his rounds.

"Hey Doctor" Mrs. Moss spoke.

"How are you Mrs. Moss?" "Working late aren't you?" He asked.

"Yes, but I'll be leaving out of here soon" she assured him.

"Well, you have a good night and be safe," he said to her.

"Ok now."

Emanuel sat down at his desk and checked his message from Tina.

"Out of town for a couple of days, what's up with you woman." Emanuel said out loud while deleting the message.

He got up from his desk feeling some kind of way and headed for the cafeteria. Lately he was feeling like Tina was keeping things from him and her message had just confirmed it.

CHAPTER TWENTY-NINE

Tina stood on the balcony with her arms folded around her. She held her face to the sun letting it dry the tears that were now streaming down her face. She was so hurt and angry until she could not think straight. She wasn't even aware of the time that had gone by nor did she care. It really didn't matter. Her body was physically exhausted. Her mind was equally. She closed her eyes and thought. *"Emanuel is not here to rescue me this time so I can't lose it, not here and not like this. If I do, they win."*

"They will pay for this Macy; they will." Tiny said and she meant every word of it.

It was hard to accept the harsh reality of the chain of events that led to her daughter's suicide. Abandoned by her own father and abused by her family; the people that she should have been able to trust. Beaten, raped, and impregnated; feeling like she had no choice but to drown out her abuse with drugs.

"Oh, they will pay dearly," she whispered.

Tina knew that she would never feel the same toward her family again. She was determined to repay every bad deed that they had done to her daughter but to do that she had to get herself together. It had been twenty-four hours since she slept or had eaten. She had to rest her body and mind and she had to force herself to eat even though she had no appetite. Tina went back into the room and ordered room service again and then she slept, sleeping well into the next afternoon. The sleep had done her body good so she got up and took a quick shower, got her bags and walked out the hotel a different person; a person on a mission.

The radio was playing full blast and Tina hoped that it would help drown out the many thoughts that were running through her mind. The tears had ceased. There were no more and without giving it a second thought, she stayed on the highway and headed toward Everlasting Haven. An hour later, she was pulling up in the church parking lot praying that she would see a white Lincoln.

"There it is" she said out loud.

Tina parked her car as close to the church entrance as possible and prayed that she didn't run into anyone that she knew. She could hear the sound of the choir as she approached the door and she hurriedly went inside and headed straight to the Pastor's office. Tina knocked at the door and was so relieved when she heard his voice.

"Come in" Pastor Peterson said when he heard the knock at the door.

"Hey PP" Tina said.

"Tina, oh my goodness what a surprise" he said getting up from his desk. "My child what brings you here at this time?" And he reached out to hug her.

"Aren't you glad to see me?" Tina asked him.

"Yes, I'm always glad to see you my dear; come, sit" he said directing her to a place on the sofa.

"I can see that something is troubling you my dear; I'm here to listen all night if I have to." Pastor Peterson said taking her hand.

"It's not going to take all night that's for sure but something, she paused, something has hurt my heart, I mean really hurt my heart and I can't go into details right now but I will say that its regarding Macy."

Tina could feel the tears beginning to build up again and her emotions were running on overload.

"I didn't want to ask you this before because I was so afraid of the answers that I might get but I'm ok now." "Pastor Peterson, tell me about my daughter, anything please!"

Pastor Peterson removed his glasses and began to speak.

"Let's have prayer and then we will talk."

As he prayed, Tina's thoughts were not where they should have been. All she could think about was her plot to take vengeance out on the people who had hurt her daughter. Vengeance will be mine for a little while that is, she thought to herself.

"Amen," she said after Pastor Peterson had finished the prayer.

"I hope that what I'm about to say will bring some peace and comfort to you." He told her. "My dear, I didn't see too much of Macy when she was on the streets but when she had got herself together the second time, Macy would come to see me just about every Sunday for the last three months of her life." "During that time, she was three years clean and you would have never been able to tell all that she had been through by looking at her." "Macy was a beautiful young lady; just like her mother might I add."

Tina looked at him and smiled.

"She was happy and very excited about her new job and she seemed to be so at peace with herself and I do believe it was because she was at the point in her life when she could finally find it in her heart to forgive herself." "She was so hard on herself." He continued.

Tina got up from the sofa and began to pace the floor.

"After service, when I wasn't too busy, we would sit and talk for an hour or two and sometimes she would even stay for dinner." "She seemed so happy and I thought that everything was going well for her." "I guess that's why her death troubled me so." "I kept asking myself if there were any signs that maybe I didn't see and I get absolutely nothing." "I could usually tell when something was really bothering her but she seemed fine." "Something drastic had to happen within a week's time that I saw her. "I don't know what it was." "When I heard of her accident I was dumbfounded; "I found out the morning of the memorial service because I had been away." "I got a call from I believe it was Sister Mary's niece and she was the one who told me about Macy." "I turned around and went right back out the door." "I was told that Macy was cremated and I found out weeks later who actually officiated the service." "By the time I got there it was over; it only took maybe a half hour; I just didn't understand it." "It seemed like no one knew anything." "Tony didn't stay long enough to even say hello." "I tried to get in touch with him later but the contact information I had for him was not updated so I had no way of getting in touch with him."

"Was my sister at the service?" Tina asked.

"I don't recall, like I said everything was pretty much over when I got there." "Sit my dear" he told her.

Tina sat next to him and he took her hand again. She listened even though it felt like something was ripping her heart out.

"I know this is not easy for you Tina." "Sometimes things happen to us or to the ones we love and sometimes we don't understand why but we just have to trust God and let his will be done" Pastor Peterson told her.

"Did Macy ever mention anything to you about being abused?" Tina asked.

"Abused? No, she didn't" Pastor Peterson responded. "I will say that I do believe that her drug abuse stemmed from something deep within and it's something that she would not talk about." "It's a lot that she never told me but I found out well, to tell you the truth, from mere gossip and that was because her cousin made sure that whatever Macy did, she was sure to tell it."

"Cousin?" Tina asked.

"Your niece was friends with a couple of the young girls here at the church." "This one time in particular, I had to speak with Brook regarding some of the things that she was saying about Macy." "She told me, I guess in so many words, that I needed to accept the truth" "You could tell just by her tone of voice that she had this thing against Macy." "She talked with so much dislike when referring to her; but no matter how disturbing the news was, when I confronted Macy about it, she would always tell me the truth and we would talk about it." "Some of the stuff was the truth and most wasn't according to Macy and I believed her." "She even shared with me that she knew it was her cousin that was saying things about her and the only thing that Macy ever said was when it comes to her cousin, the ones who hurt are the ones who hurt the most."

"The ones who hurt are the ones who hurt the most" Tina repeated. *My God,* she thought and closed her eyes when she realized that they were the words her grandmother would say.

"Thank you, PP," Tina said giving Pastor Peterson a hug.

"Your very welcome my dear."

"So, how is your doctor friend?" Pastor Peterson asked.

"He's good"; he's been very busy lately but we always try to make time for each other."

"Do you love him?" He asked her.

"Very much," Tina said and she managed to smile.

Pastor Peterson nodded in agreement.

"Remember my dear; always take God into your relationship."

"I sure will."

"Husband how long?" Rebecca said not realizing that her husband wasn't alone.

Tina and Pastor Peterson looked up at the same time.

Ting is that you?" She asked.

"It's me" Tina said giving her a fake smile.

"How are you daughter?"

"I'm ok"

Rebecca sat down next to her and shot a quick glance at her husband as to say what is going on.

"I have an idea, Pastor Peterson said. "Why don't we grab a bite to eat at the diner on Cherry, my treat?"

"Alright now, that sounds good to me" Rebecca agreed.

"Sounds good." Tina added.

"Good, I'm done here anyway so than let's get going."

Pastor Peterson grabbed his jacket, Rebecca turned off the lights and they headed out to the diner.

CHAPTER THIRTY

Tina pulled in the drive way and Emanuel pulled in right behind her. The timing was anything but perfect. Tina thought that maybe she would have had time to freshen up and get herself together but that wasn't the case.

Tina got out of the car to meet Emanuel and the look on his face was priceless. She realized just how much she loved him and when she looked into his eyes, she didn't know rather she wanted to laugh or cry. She only hoped that he did not sense the pain that she now carried in her spirit. She had become so ashamed of her family and as bad as it was, she had to stay in control of the situation. Only God knows how she would do that.

"Don't you ever just leave like that again woman" Emanuel said to her, giving her slaps on her behind as if to punish her.

"I won't" she said and she covered his face with kisses.

"You promise?" He asked in between kisses.

"Yes, I promise" Tina said and she planted the kiss that sealed the deal.

Emanuel took her by the hand and Tina opened the door. Neither said another word. Emanuel walked toward the steps but Tina pulled him back. As he stood there and watched, she started to remove her clothes and he helped her, gently pulling her on nipple with his lips while his hands cupped her buttocks and she moaned with pleasure. She helped him remove his clothes and he was ready for her and she was ready for him and the two became enthralled in each other.

Tina sat at her desk the next morning with the sole purpose of getting some work done but her mind was somewhere else. She grabbed the remote and switched the channel to the movie Halloween; they had been advertising it for the past week and how fitting, she thought. Tina wondered if she had the guts to do what Michael Meyers did and she grinned at the thought but she didn't want to kill anyone. She wanted to hurt them, seek ways to destroy them, make them suffer.

Tina glanced out of the window at the houses decorated for the upcoming holiday and a glimpse of memory of how Tony had taken Macy out for Halloween reminded her of a little of what use to be. She had gotten her memory back for the most part but she was going to keep it between her and the man upstairs and besides, by keeping it to herself no one would be able to trace anything back to her for the things that she was planning to do.

"She tried to talk to you but you were so wrapped up with your own little life, ignoring all the signs." "How could you have been so blind to your daughter's needs?" "But you know what, you weren't blind, you just didn't want to deal with it" Tina said out loud. "Oh, but I know how to break you really good." "Let's see how happy you and your little wife will be after I get finish with you." Tina promised out loud.

After their divorce was final, Tony had finally married the woman that he was living with. From what Tina understood, his precious wife knew nothing about her or Macy.

"How could you deny your own daughter you sorry bastard?" Tina mumbled.

Tina knew exactly what she wanted to do to Tony but she was going to need some help pulling it off. Way back when they were married, she had hired this guy to find out if Tony was having an affair. Tina remembered the guy would do just about anything if the price was right and she was willing to make the price right. The only problem was that she couldn't remember his name but she knew who would. She just had to be careful not to make it obvious that she had gotten her memory back. Maybe if she played her cards right, she could pull it off.

"Hey you" Tina said.

"Hey what's going on girl?" Cynthia said happy to hear from her.

"Nothing much; just trying to get some paper work done." Tina said.

"I hear you; nothing much on my end either." Cynthia admitted.

"Ting, we have to have a girl's night out soon, I mean real soon."

"I hear you, and we will girl" Tina promised.

"Ok…question" "Do you know of any private detectives who are really good like scandalous?

Tina had her fingers crossed.

"Why girl, what are you up to?" Cynthia asked laughing.

"Oh no not for me; a colleague is going through some things and she wants to hire someone who is good." Tina lied.

"Well, the only one I can think of is your cousin Mack, Mack Turner and his crew."

"My Cousin?" Tina asked playing it off while moving her lips to silently say bingo.

"Well not really a cousin but he was raised by some distant relative of yours." "Hum, it's funny that you asked about him." "I saw Mack the other day going toward Cool Luke's on 36 and Mott, he works there."

"Oh ok" and Tina wrote the address down.

"Rough area now; I was dropping off my assistant who lives a couple of blocks from there." Cynthia mentioned.

"Ok girl thanks; I will definitely call you soon so we can plan our night out." Tina assured her.

"You better I'll talk to you later girl."

"Bye Cyn" and Tina hung up the phone.

In three days, Tina was getting out of her car and walking toward the entrance at Cool Luke's. Paying close attention to her surroundings, she knew exactly what Cynthia was talking about when she said rough area; that was an understatement. She felt like someone would come up behind her at any minute with a machete. Men were hanging around the entrance and she held tight to her purse.

"Hey sweet thing," one man hollered and Tina smiled but kept walking.

The place was dark and Tina wasn't a hundred percent sure if she would recognize Mack even though she remembered images of him. Tina glanced around the room until she found the bar and began to walk toward it.

"Hi have you seen Mack?" She asked the bartender.

"Over there" he said pointing toward the pool table.

Tina glanced over at the pool table but there were five guys standing there.

"So, which one is Mack?" Tina asked.

"The one with the blue shirt on," the bartender answered.

"Thanks, can I have a rum and coke please?"

"Baby you can have anything you want." The bartender said with a wicked smile.

Tina got her drink, and when she seen Mack walk away from the table, she hurriedly walked toward him.

"Mack" Tina called out.

Mack turned around when he heard his name.

"Hey how are you?" Tina asked.

Mack backed away with a puzzled look on his face.

"Ting is that you?" He asked her.

"Yes, it's me in the flesh."

Mack's face lit up with a smile that spread across his entire face. He was not bad to look at neither. He was quite tall, clean shaved with a baldy that shined like a new coin.

"Damn girl," Mack said giving her a hug. What the hell are you doing in here? He asked smiling.

"Mack, I need your help," she said looking up at him.

"Ok let's grab a table."

Mack got the impression that she didn't want to be seen so he led her to a booth located in the back of the room.

"Do you want another drink?" He asked her.

"No, I'm good thank you."

The place was filled with smoke and the music was jumping to the beat of Marvin Gaye's "Got to Give It Up." Tina was so glad that the lights were dim giving way to a slim chance that someone might be able to recognize her.

"Mack please don't question anything that I'm about to tell you." "I need you to take care of some business for me and I guarantee you, the price will be right." Tina explained.

"Ok let's hear it" Mack told her.

It took Tina a little over an hour to tell Mack in details what she needed him to do and how she wanted him to do it.

"Can I still trust you?" Tina asked.

"Always but you do remember how I roll right?" Mack asked giving her a stern look.

Tina nodded yes.

"Ok so once I start, there's no turning back under no circumstances." Mack warned her.

"I won't want you to; Tina told him. "I will meet with you in two days at our spot at the park." "Do you remember where?" Tina asked.

"You remember that?" He laughed.

"Yes, I do" Tina assured him.

Tina was amazed at how things were starting to pop up in her head out of nowhere. She had no idea about the park until she actually said it. Tina concluded her meeting and was about to leave when Mack volunteered to walk her to her car. She was glad about that and she let out a sign of relief.

"It's good seeing you again Ting" Mack said.

"Good seeing you too" Tina said while getting in her car.

Mack took out a key that opened up a side panel in his car. He removed a phone which he only used for his special business deals and he placed a call to his boy.

"Hey man what's going on?" Mack asked.

"Nothing much you tell me" Duces said.

"Two things I need to talk to you about my man." "Tina Robinson is alive and looking good as ever." Mack explained.

"I know I bumped into her months ago and the shit blew my mind"

"Damn, how awkward was that?" Mack asked.

"Very"

"Ok I have several jobs for you; a little heavy and some pretty good money too if you're interested." Mack explained.

"How much?" He asked.

"Ten thousand, are you interested?" Mack asked him.

"Yes."

"Good, this is good people that we're dealing with so I need you to be up on it." "I need you to be on call and ready to go and I will call you with the details in a couple of days." Mack explained.

"Ok" he said.

"Alright later," Mack said hanging up and placing the phone back in its spot.

Chapter Thirty-One

Emanuel walked into the jewelry store a proud man. For weeks he kept putting it off but now he knew that he was ready for a serious commitment and he knew Tina was ready too. She was his heart: his soul mate and he could finally say that he was done looking. He had found her.

"Hi can I help you sir?" The sales lady asked as she admired the handsome man that had just entered the store.

"Yes, I hope you can." "I'm going to propose to my lady and I need to look at some rings."

"Do you have anything in mind?" She asked him.

"Something exquisite, your very best," he said.

"Ok right this way sir." "Oh, by the way, my name is Cathy and your name is?"

"Emanuel please to meet you" he said shaking her hand.

"Have a seat Emanuel and I'll show you what we have."

The saleslady pulled out a classic five-carat prong set round diamond.

"This is nice, real nice," Emanuel said looking the ring over.

"And this one is one of my favorites, seven-carat platinum diamond." She spoke.

"Sweet, I like this one even better," Emanuel said shaking his head in approval.

Several hours had passed by and Emanuel had finally picked out what he thought was the perfect ring for Tina. He wanted to give his woman nothing but the best because Tina was one of those women who would appreciate whatever he gave her even if it came from a crackerjack box as long as she knew that it came from his heart. That's just how she was and he loved her for that.

"I've made my decision, and I'm going with this one" Emanuel said holding up the seven-carat platinum diamond ring.

"Lucky her" Cathy said.

"No lucky me" Emanuel said.

After taking a shower together Emanuel and Tina laid beside each other. Emanuel had expected another passionate lovemaking session but he sensed that Tina had a lot on her mind and didn't seem like herself. He felt guilty because he knew that his schedule prevented him from seeing her as much as he would like to but when they did get together, they went out of their way to make the most out the time that they had. He loved her with all his heart and he promised himself that he would put all of his energy into making their relationship work but he needed her to be open with him. Their time together was limited right now and he wanted all of her not just her body but her mind too.

"Babe, is there something wrong?" Emanuel asked again.

"No just tired that's all." Tina said looking up at him.

"Are you cheating on me?" He asked jokingly. Tina looked up at him and grinned.

"Are you serious?" She asked him turning his face to meet hers.

Emanuel laughed and did not answer.

"No, I'm not cheating on you silly." "I love you, only you; you got that?" She asked him.

"I guess I do but you're the one who went on a little trip and didn't tell me where you were going and you still haven't told me."

Tina began to laugh. "Are you jealous?" she asked him.

"A little" he said laughing too.

"Baby it wasn't that kind of a trip and I will tell you when the time is right ok, and it has absolutely nothing to do with another man, trust me." She explained.

"All jokes aside Babe you know that I trust you, it's just that you always seem to have things on your mind and I just need to know that you're ok." He said looking at her in a caring way.

"Yes, something is on my mind but I'm ok and like I said I will talk to you about it when the time is right and the time is not right now." Tina assured him rubbing her fingers down the side of his face.

"You know we're acting like two old married fobies." Tina said laughing.

"Oh no, don't you use that married word not for a long time coming." Emanuel said purposely choosing words that would make his proposal to her come as a total surprise.

"Ok Ms. Lady come here" Emanuel said pulling her closer to him.

Tina laid in Emanuel's arms feeling a bit baffled. "*I didn't know he felt like that,*" she thought as Emanuel fell fast asleep while she laid there still pondering on that married thing.

***

Tina got out of her car and headed to the spot where she was supposed to meet Mack. She was still feeling a bit tired from earlier in the morning. She and Emanuel had fallen asleep last night without making love but they made up for it by having a full body workout before he left for work and it left her grinning to herself.

It was a pretty nice November afternoon. The sun was shining bright and you could feel snow in the air. Tina dressed in a purple and black jogging suit, and even though she was a bit tired, she began to jog around the park so that it wouldn't be too hard to explain why she was there if she just happened to bump into someone that she knew. When Tina got to the spot, Mack was just coming around the corner.

"Hey how you doing" he said giving Tina a hug.

"I'm good" and she handed him an envelope.

"Everything you will need is in here so call me at the number that I gave you when it's done ok." Tina said.

"Ok" He assured her.

They said their good-byes and Tina started jogging back to her car. Short and sweet she thought and that's how she liked it.

Mack walked back to his car taking the long way and pulled out his business phone.

"Yo what's up," Mack asked.

"Hey you tell me" Duces replied.

"Listen carefully here's the details and he give him specific instructions on what he is supposed to do. Mack trusted him with his life and always had.

"I will meet you at the spot in 10 minutes with the plane ticket" Mack instructed.

"Ok I'm leaving now, later." Duces said.

Duces waited about 20 minutes and then he seen her come out of the motel. He walked toward her not exchanging a word, handing her a white envelope with $5,000 dollars in it. He kept walking never looking back, got in his rental car and headed back to the airport.

CHAPTER THIRTY-TWO

Monday mornings were always hectic for Diane. No matter how much she planned the night before, she always found herself late for work and this morning was no exception. Thank goodness her boss wasn't around because she had to go pass him to get to her office. She had barely taken her coat off when Sonia suspiciously walked in her office.

"Have you heard the latest?" Sonia whispered.

"No, I just got here." What's going on?" Diane asked.

"Girl get settled and meet me in the ladies' room" she said and walked away.

Diane sat down at her desk and turned on the computer. Two people had been fired within three months and she wondered by Sonia's comment, who had been next. Diane checked her calendar and could feel that it was going to be one of those days and she let out a deep breath and went to meet Sonia in the lady's room.

"Girl another one bites the dust." Sonia said as Diane came in the door.

"Who?" Diane asked.

"Henry Capano," Sonia explained.

"Get out of here" Diane whispered.

"They tell me it's some kind of investigation going on and it looks like they're going after the big boys." Sonia said.

"Well girl I guess we will see how it all turns out." "It's a shame people losing their jobs hard as times are, girl keep me posted." Diane told her.

"I sure will, talk to you later."

Diane and Sonia walked out of the ladies' room both going their separate ways and both curious as to what was going to happen next.

***

Tina sat at her desk and tried to get as much paper work done as possible. The less paperwork the better but she was finding it harder and harder to stay focused on what she needed to do. She had deadlines to meet, certified letters to prepare for Regina to type up, and a couple of appointments that she could not cancel. What usually took her a week to do, was now taking her double the time to complete and not sleeping well was only making matters worse. Thank God for Regina or the pressure would really be on, Tina thought. She closed her eyes and took some deep breaths and the anxiety eased when she thought of the invitation that Emanuel had sent to her. It was incredible and personalized with his special touch. Tina knew that whatever he had up his sleeve it would be unforgettable.

Out of the corner of her eye she saw it. The light on her phone was blinking and beeping at the same time. She knew that it could mean only one thing and she reached for the phone.

"Hey," Tina said.

"Case closed." The voice on the other line said and the call was disconnected.

"Nasty" Tina said turning off the computer and heading for the kitchen in hopes of having a private celebration of her own.

Tina took the bottle of Barolos from the cabinet, a treat that she had for such an occasion as this. Why did this have to happen in her family, she kept asking herself? Why couldn't she have come out of the coma and come back to a loving family, a normal family. This was like living a nightmare over and over again and then she thought of Brock.

"You will never hurt another baby again" she said out loud taking one last swallow of her wine before throwing the empty glass against the kitchen cabinet.

"*Mommy said, "Do unto others as they do unto you."*

"You damn right Tina grinned. "You damn right."

CHAPTER THIRTY-THREE

Tony had just walked in the door drained from another day at the office. His practice was doing pretty good and the money was coming in and that kept everyone happy, especially his wife. Sheila was great with the kid and good at maintaining the upkeep of the house so he didn't mine her being a stay-at-home mom and wife. She held the fort down in every area and that's why he couldn't understand how he allowed himself to get caught up in the same situation that almost destroyed his first marriage.

He had been on edge for weeks since his little one-night stand with some chick that he met at the lounge. The whole thing puzzled him and he still didn't understand how something that started out so innocent could have ended the way that it did. He had stopped there after work just to grab a beer. A very attractive lady sat next to him and they got into what he thought was an innocent conversation. Before he knew anything he was leaving and checking into a motel. What scared Tony the most is that he couldn't even remember what the woman looked like or if he had used protection. He never made it a habit of carrying condoms around with him especially since him and Sheila never used them. For the past week he had to make up excuses to avoid having sex with her until he got himself checked out. She was everything he wanted and needed in a woman and he just couldn't understand how he let it happened again.

"Sweetness I'm home, where are you, hello" Tony hollered.

There was no aroma coming from the kitchen indicating that dinner was either ready or it would be soon. The house was dark and if it wasn't for Sheila's car in the driveway, Tony would have thought that no one was home. He sat his brief case down and headed upstairs. The glow from the night light illuminated the master bedroom giving it just enough light for Tony to see his wife sitting on the floor; her back up against the wall.

"Why are you sitting in the dark are you crazy or something" he asked her.

He hit the light switch exposing a face smeared with tears and eyes that were red and swollen. As he kneeled down beside her, that's when he saw them; sexually explicit pictures of him and a woman. Before he could get a word out, Sheila slapped him so hard in the face that he lost his balance and fell backward. Tony sat there in shock not knowing what to say.

"How could you do this to me Tony, how could you?" She kept asking him over and over again. "I've been too good to you; I don't deserve this."

Tony stood up and sat on the side of the bed.

"Baby I'm so sorry." He said to her.

"Sorry?" "You're sorry?" "Yes, you are." "You are a sorry ass bastard!"

What else could he possibly say to her? He couldn't even lie with the evidence right there in front of him. Sheila continued to yell and Tony reached down and picked the pictures up from the floor. He couldn't believe what he saw. Someone was all up in his shit. The pictures were taken from every angle, every position leaving nothing left for the imagination. Tony couldn't think of anyone who would do such a thing.

"Yeah, you take a good look at your nasty self." "You need to get your things and leave." "I can't even look at you right now."

"Get out!" Sheila screamed.

Tony got up and threw the pictures on the bed. He was hurting because he knew that he had hurt his woman and she didn't deserve it. She was a good woman and a good mother but there was no use in trying to say anything else. His best bet was to get some of his things and leave. He had to give Sheila some time to calm down and he did just that. He got his things and left.

Mommy said, "*First time you do something wrong, it's a mistake; second time is a choice.*"

"*Here we go again*" Tony thought, *"Damn!"*

CHAPTER THIRTY-FOUR

Emanuel had ran an extra two miles to loosen up the tension that he was feeling. Even though there was no doubt in his mind that Tina would say yes to his proposal, he still felt edgy. He was elated when his request to have the week of Thanksgiving off was official. It gave him plenty of time to plan the most romantic weekend ever starting with sending Tina an invitation requesting her presence to dinner. The week would start off with days filled with fun and excitement and of course, plenty of love making which would all lead up to his proposing to her, and ending with a visit to his parents. Everything had to be perfect and Emanuel wouldn't expect anything less. This was also Tina's sixth anniversary since her accident and that made it even more special. He made reservations for dinner at a cozy spot called, Au Pied de Cochon, one of Tina's favorite restaurants which was not far from the hotel where they were going to stay.

The roses, candles and champagne were on order at the hotel and Emanuel had just left with Mr. Wallace to finalize the arrangements for the main event. Now the time was upon him and he was laying out his tux and was about to get a fresh cut and shave so that he could look good for his woman.

Emanuel had the limo driver pull up at Tina's house at exactly six o'clock. The brother didn't play. His time was definitely his money.

"Wow right on time." Tina said looking at the clock.

Tina looked in the mirror one more time making sure everything was flawless and then she went and opened the door expecting to see Emanuel but to her surprise, she was greeted by a limo driver dressed in a tuxedo and all.

"Hi" Tina said smiling as she looked around for Emanuel.

"Good evening Ms. Robinson, I would like to escort you to the car."
The driver said.

"Good evening, let me grab my coat." Tina said still looking around for
Emanuel.

Tina hurriedly went and got her coat off the sofa and made sure the door
was lock. The driver gave his arm to her as he escorted her to the limo. The
suspense was killing her and just as they approached the door, Emanuel
exited from the limo and greeted her. Wow, Tina was thinking, the man was
looking ever so fine. A black Brioni tuxedo graced his body and he looked
at her with such passion that it took her breath away. There Tina stood
complementing him with a brown mink coat draped across her shoulders
giving way to a red evening gown that Tina had matched perfectly with red
stilettos that were fit for a queen. Her hair hung loose with just a little curl
and her make-up was flawless.

"You are absolutely stunning." He told her.

"You like" she asked him.

"No, I love" he told her.

Tina smiled at the man standing in front of her. The evening was just
getting started and already Emanuel was making her feel oh so special. He
took her by the hand and gently kissed it and helped her into the limo. Once
in the limo, Tina noticed that all around the inside was draped with red
roses. Emanuel gently leaned over to kiss her and Tina said nothing else for
fear of crying right there in front of him.

The stunning couple arrived at Au Pied de Cochon right on schedule.
The place was beautifully decorated as usual during this time of year. *How
did he know that this is my favorite spot?* Tina thought and Emanuel must
have read her mind because he leaned over to her and gently whispered
"Cynthia." After sharing a delicious meal, Emanuel picked up his glass to
make a toast.

"To the finest woman I know who I just happen to love very much" Emanuel said and Tina picked up her glass and they tapped their glasses together.

Leaning closer to him, Tina passionately placed a kiss on Emanuel's lips.

"Are you ready?" Emanuel asked.

"Yes" Tina said but the truth was she could have sat there all night just with him.

Emanuel waved to get the Maître Di's attention.

"I'll take the check now please." He said.

The opera "Carmen" was amazing. Neither had ever been and it was highly recommended by one of Emanuel's colleagues. Two hours later, the limo was pulling up at the Hyatt Regency Hotel. Emanuel got out first and he held out his hand and Tina took hold of his as she made her way from the limo into the hotel.

"Emanuel this is so beautiful" Tina said once inside.

Tina marveled at the detailed structure of the building that she had heard so much about but the closest that she had ever got to it was looking at pictures; to be there in person was simply breathtaking. As her and Emanuel entered the hotel hand in hand, they were barely able to take their eyes off each other. The stunning couple was also getting the attention of those around them. People stared and smiled picking up on their vibe as they made their way to the elevator. Tina was truly happy and it was showing.

Mommy said, "A good man is hard to find so when you find him, you better keep him."

CHAPTER THIRTY-FIVE

Emanuel had just taken his eyes off of Tina for a second and then she stopped him in his tracks. He had often wondered what would happen if their paths had ever crossed again and now, he knew. It was as if time had stopped and he stood motionless not having a clue as to what to say or do next.

"Emanuel Cartwright?" She asked him.

Emanuel did not say a word. She really had not changed at all; maybe a few pounds here and there; the same hair color, same mouth, nose and lips. You could tell that she had taken care of herself over the years.

"Monica Watkins?" Emanuel whispered.

They stared at each other for what seemed like an eternity. Either could find the words to say. Memories were rewinding; going back into time. Thinking about what would have or could have been. "*Not here and not now,*" Emanuel thought.

Tina glanced at the woman and then back to Emanuel. "*What the hell is this?*" She said to herself.

Tina could tell by the expression on their faces that something was going on or something had gone on between the two. To what extent was the question?

"Tina this is Monica, Monica this is Tina." Emanuel said not taking his eyes off of Monica.

Neither of the two ladies said a word for different reasons. Not even a how do you do.

"Babe" Emanuel managed to say. "I need to speak with Monica for a minute." "Let me get you a seat here in the lobby ok?" "Monica, I'll be right back."

The radiant glow that had shone on Tina's face seconds before was now replaced with a face of someone that had just sucked on something bitter. Emanuel found her a seat and he assured her that he would explain everything as soon as he got back.

Tina's mind filled with all sorts of things. As she thought back at the times when she and Emanuel shared stories of past loves; her high school sweetheart and a brief relationship during her first year of college before meeting Tony.

Emanuel on the other hand, had briefly mentioned someone that he had really cared for but he never went into great details about her. Now Tina wondered if this woman who had stood before her was part of his past, present or was she going to be his future.

Emanuel was not prepared for this; of all nights, not this one. He knew that he had less than a half hour to sort this mess out or the whole evening would literally go up in smoke. Thank God Monica was still standing in the same spot when he came back to meet her.

"How are you?" he asked her.

"I'm well" Monica responded.

"I guess I owe you an explanation, no wait a minute let me correct that, I owe you an explanation and apology." Emanuel admitted.

"You do, don't you?" Monica asked.

"Yes, I do but there is one problem."

"And what might that be?" She asked.

"The timing is not good for me so is it possible that we can meet tomorrow, just tell me where and when and I will be there." He said.

"Well, I can meet you here in the lobby tomorrow morning around nine is that good?" She asked him.

"Yes, that's fine so I will see you than."

"Ok" Monica nodded and started to walk away.

"Monica" Emanuel called out.

Monica turned around to face him.

"I'm sorry." Emanuel said and he turned and walked away.

Monica watched Emanuel as he turned the corner.

Thank God I'm happily married, she thought and hurriedly went to join her husband and their friends.

***

Tina got up from her seat and began to walk. She wondered if she looked as stupid as she felt. Her intention was to go in the ladies' room and cry her heart out but she decided to go straight to the limo and demand that the driver take her home. Things between her and Emanuel were good yeah maybe too good.

Mommy said, "Some things can be too good to be true, and it usually is."

"The damn truth," Tina thought.

CHAPTER THIRTY-SIX

Emanuel had no idea as to what was going through Tina's mind but he knew that he had to hurry and get her to the room before the evening would be ruined. When he turned the corner, his heart fell when he noticed that Tina wasn't sitting where he had left her. He loosened up his collar and started looking in every direction. *"Maybe she's in the ladies' room,"* he thought, and he started walking in that direction; he had no time to waste.

"Sir" Emanuel heard someone say.

Emanuel turned around to see the limo driver standing behind him.

"Your lady friend is waiting for you in the limo."

Emanuel walked as fast as he could to the main entrance and tried to remain cool as possible. He approached the limo and opened the door and found Tina sitting there mad as hell. If looks could kill, he would have dropped dead right there on the spot.

"Tina, I want you to listen to me, ok."

"You son of a bitch leave me sitting there while you go talk to that heifer." "No wonder he didn't want to hear the married word; he's probably screwing her, standing up there giving each other the gooey eye and shit. Forget you I don't need you or this shit." Tina wanted to say but it was only in her thoughts.

"Now Tina, I love you baby with all my heart but you have two choices; either you can sit here and cuss me the hell out and then I can take you home or you can let me finish what I started, but I'll tell you one thing, I will not let you walk away from me just because of what you may think you know."

"So, can you please come with me now and I will explain everything to you later ok?"

With words of persuasion, Emanuel took Tina's hand into his and gave it a gentle caress and with no more time to waste he practically pulled her out of the limo back in the hotel and into the elevator. When the elevator stopped at its designated spot, the attendant gave Emanuel the signal indicating that everything was ready and set to go so he took the key and swiped it to open the door to the room. Emanuel was nervous as hell but he managed to give Tina a smile before stepping aside and allowing her to enter the room first.

As Tina entered, her eyes had to adjust to the dimmest in the room and what seemed to be hundreds of long-stem red roses and candles lit everywhere. Rose pedals covered the floor in a path that apparently had a resting place which Tina could see leading to the balcony. Emanuel was hoping that she got the hint and followed the path; and she did. His heart began to race with the anticipation of not knowing how Tina was going to respond.

Tina turned around and looked at Emanuel not knowing how to feel or what to say. There next to the balcony door, was a little table set up with a beautiful table centerpiece made with roses and more candles with little crystals spread across the top of the table. A bottle of Champagne sat in an ice bucket with two champagne glasses on each side along with a tray of chocolate covered strawberries, which were Tina's favorite. Tears began to run down her face and she was totally confused of being caught between the feeling of not liking him minutes before but loving the hell out of him for what he was doing now.

Emanuel's phone started to vibrate letting him know that the main event was just about to take place so he led Tina out on the balcony and gently placed his arm around her waist and pulling her close to him.

"Baby look up" he told her.

Tina looked up to a star filled sky and there in sparkling letters were the words, Will You Marry Me? Tina stared at the sky and placed her hand near her heart. It was so much happening that she didn't even have time to catch her breath. It was like being on a natural high, then coming down and then being lifted back up again higher than what she was before. It felt weird to her.

"Tina."

Emanuel stood there waiting for her answer.

"This is so beautiful Emanuel and I want to say yes but I have three questions that I need to ask you."

"Go ahead." Emanuel said.

"What is she to you, do you love her and did you sleep" Tina was so emotional that she turned away from him before asking the last question.

"I can't deal with this." She said.

"Look at me" Emanuel said turning her around to face him and getting so close to her that she could fill his breath.

He lifted her chin up and Tina was too afraid to look at him for fear of what she might see in his eyes. She began to rub her hand up and down his chest. She didn't know what else to do.

"Take a deep breath and relax." Emanuel told her.

Tina closed her eyes and took several deep breaths and her body began to relax.

"Look at me" Emanuel said again.

Tina looked straight up into his eyes.

"She was someone in my past that was very special to me; I did love her and no I never slept with her." Emanuel explained.

Tina could see the truth in his eyes and she allowed Emanuel to kiss the tears from her face.

"Yes" she told him.

Emanuel went in his pocket to retrieve the little red box and he slowly took the ring out and got down on one knee and placed it on Tina's third finger left hand. Tina covered her mouth in amazement.

"Oh, this is beautiful"! She said as she cried.

"So, did I do a good job?"

"You did a wonderful job"!

"Perfect" he said.

Emanuel picked her up and they kissed again; their tongues exchanging places.

"She's in trouble now I'm going to tear this ass up," he thought.

Mommy said, "Makeup sex is the best sex in the world that is when you're married" and Tina smiled at the thought.

***

Monica sat and listened intensely to Emanuel speak. *"Oh, the look on this man's face,"* she thought. Emanuel was fine when she first meant him and now, he was looking even better with age. She displayed the face of a woman scorned and let him go on and on about the night in question. She would have never thought that after all these years he would still be so sensitive about the matter. She even thought that she seen tears in his eyes. The laughter was building up and Monica didn't know how much longer she could keep it inside.

Emanuel sat there pouring his heart out; he couldn't help but notice the look on Monica's face. A face that looked as if she would, at any minute, rise up and beat the hell out of him. God, he didn't want any drama from this woman, not in this place or any other place. Then Monica did the unthinkable and it shocked the hell out of him.

"You should see your face." She said to Emanuel bursting with laughter.

"*This damn woman is crazy,*" Emanuel thought as he sat there staring at her in disbelief.

Monica managed to calm down and she became a little more sympathetic to the matter. She didn't want to come across as some crazy person but from the look on Emanuel's face it was already too late.

"Emanuel" Monica said taking his hand. "You did hurt me but I got over it." "I found out the whole story from your friend Derrick." "Yes, this could have made me a very bitter young woman but I knew that it was best for me to let you go under the circumstances." "I have a wonderful husband that I met in law school and we are both attorneys in the Chicago area; he's a born again Christian and we're happily married with two children, so life's been good for me."

Emanuel noticed the glow on Monica's face when she talked about her family and he knew that she was ok. He put his head down and started to grin.

"Ok I've been punked, wow" he said. After all these years, I thought that you would have hated me."

"No Emanuel, I never hated you, I am so glad that you beat the odds and did well for yourself in spite of and I am happy about that."

They talked for another hour sharing stories and talking about their hopes and dreams and even exchanging numbers.

"Your fiancée is very lucky to have you, and on that note, Dr. Cartwright, I have to get going" Monica said getting up from her seat and Emanuel did the same.

"Give me a hug woman," he said as he reached out to embrace her for old time's sake.

You take care of yourself." She said to him.

"You do the same." He said and gently kissed her on her forehead.

Monica gave him that smile that used to melt his heart away and then they said their good-byes.

Emanuel always felt better after talking to Tina. She seemed to give him the boost that he needed to deal with the chaos's of life. He was relieved that she sat and listened without an attitude when he shared his story about Monica. Tina had even agreed that they should meet and talk to bring closure to both of their lives. So, the weekend getaway had went considerably well in spite of what could have happened. They were definitely in a good place and his heart was happy about that.

CHAPTER THIRTY-SEVEN

Sheila had just finished packing when she heard a car pull up in the driveway. As she rushed over to the window, she was surprised to see Tony getting out of the car. He must have sensed something was wrong because he was home way too early from work. As she watched her husband exit the car, she wondered how this could have happened to her marriage when she had done above and beyond all that she could do to make her husband happy. She thought that she was doing a good job at it but, evidently, that wasn't the case.

Sheila was tired of feeling miserable and the thought of him sleeping with some bimbo was physically making her sick. She no longer slept in the same room with him and no way would she allow him to touch her; it just wasn't working out so why was she still there, she kept asking herself. Tony had begged and begged her to give him another chance and he had promised her from his heart that he would never cheat on her again but she just didn't trust him anymore and that was a major problem for her. What do you do when you have done your best and you still fail at it? That's how she felt; it was so frustrating to her. There was no doubt that she still loved him but love without trust wasn't going to work. Sheila took her suitcases downstairs just as Tony was coming in the door.

"What are you doing?" he asked her.

"I'm leaving Tony." Sheila said to him.

"Sheila come on please don't do this, not now please." He begged her.

Tony had felt it coming but he thought that he could convince her to stay and work things out with him. He could see the hurt in her eyes every time he looked at her and it was nothing that he could do to convince her that he would never hurt her again.

"Can we please talk about this baby please?" He asked her.

"Ok let's talk." "You know I put everything I had into this marriage." "I trusted you and I went out of my way to please you." "You crossed the line and betrayed that trust and I just can't forgive you but I will thank you for thinking enough about me to use protection and I thank God for that." She said to him.

Tony was quiet for a few seconds and silently thanked God too. Evidently, he had missed something.

"I'm so sorry that I hurt you, I love you Sheila just stay with me; we can work through this ok all I need is another chance, please I know that you still love me, don't you?" He asked her.

"I do, and I would be lying if I stood here and told you that I didn't but another chance, really?" "It looks like you didn't love me or respect me enough so why should I give you another chance?"

Tony reached out and tried to pull her to him.

"Don't; please don't touch me!" She hollered at him and Tony backed away from her. It was as if his touch hurt her and that broke his heart.

"What about our son Sheila?" "He needs both of us he deserves that." "You're not going to stop me from seeing him are you?" Tony asked.

"No, I would never do that Tony." "In spite of what you did to me, I know that you love your son and you are a good father to him but you should have thought about our son when you were out there with your head in places where it should not have been," she said and then she walked outside to her car and he followed.

"Goodbye Tony." She said to him.

Tony went back into the house and pulled himself a drink. Everything that Sheila had said was the truth. He knew that he had messed up but one thing that he wasn't going to do any more and that was beg. He needed a vacation; go somewhere to clear his head, to give him time to think things over. He picked up the phone to call his secretary to put things in order. Maybe in time Sheila would have a change of heart but in the meantime, he was going to focus on raising Tyler and being a good father to him. That was something that he had failed to do with Macy and he would regret that for the rest of his life.

CHAPTER THIRTY-EIGHT

Brock took his key and locked the door behind him. Even though it was cold outside he decided to walk the short distance to the corner store. He felt good; better than he had felt in years and he looked mighty damn good too he thought to himself.

One day he took a long look in the mirror and decided that he wasn't going to let that bitch of an ex-wife win the battle. He stopped drinking, lost the beer belly and cleaned himself up. He got a job as a truck driver and even though it wasn't what he wanted to do, the pay and the benefits were good. The job allowed him, for the first time in his life, to get his own place which was much better than sleeping at the shelter. The one-bedroom apartment suited him just fine and he had brought some used furniture that he found at the thrift store down town. He loved every minute of his freedom because he didn't have to listen to nobody bitchin all the time and he could do what he wanted to do when he wanted to do it but the one thing that didn't change in Brock's life was his lust for young girls. The want, the need, the control; it was in him; in his heart, his spirit.

Brock put his cigarette out before entering the store. A young group of girls were just coming out and he held the door open for them just to get a lustful peek of their asses. He always had a thing for young girls even before his college days. Whenever he was on the road, he treated himself to the youngest prostitutes that were available. The younger the better he thought. Just thinking about it really turned him on. Brock had done some things that should have landed him in jail for a long time but no one ever found out. He thought that he was invincible.

"Let me have a pack of those Salam's my man." He told the cashier.

Brock then paid for his order, picked up his cigarettes and headed out the door. The wind had picked up so he fastened up his jacket and decided to take a short cut through the woods that was next to an old abandoned garage. Sometimes people used the trail in the woods to get to the other side. Brock stopped for a few seconds to light up a cigarette and hearing a noise behind him, he turned around but no one was there. He never liked taking this way home but the cold night air and the wind was kicking his ass. He had just entered the woods when he heard the sound of scuffing feet again but before he could turn around, someone grabbed him from behind. A hand with a cloth covered his nose and Brock's cigarette fell to the ground. He tried to fight but the lightheadedness had already started to take effect and he felt himself fall to the ground landing on his back. Brock felt the tight grip on his jacket and that's when he felt the first blow right in the face.

"Don't kill me please" Brock hollered.

"No, I'm not gonna kill you"; I want you to live through this motherfucker." The man said to Brock.

Brock took another blow to the face and he struggled to get a good look at his assailant's face just in case he spared his life but the face was covered with a black mask. The third blow to the face knocked Brock out and he laid on the ground motionless.

Hearing voices from a distance, Duces removed the mask from his face and placed it in his pocket. He turned Brock over and removed anything that could identify him from his pockets. He then lifted him up and dragged him over toward the old vacant garage. His job was half way done and he had to hurry up and make it happen.

Tina pulled herself a cup of coffee and sat down at the kitchen table. She and Emanuel had stayed up a little too late just enjoying each other's company and she was feeling it. She loved that about their relationship. They never grew tired of each other. She was still feeling a natural high and couldn't stop thinking about the events that had taken place. Meeting Monica at the hotel, the engagement, meeting Emanuel's parents and now they were both dealing with his new position at the hospital. If she thought that Emanuel's schedule was hectic at the nursing home, the hospital's schedule was putting extra demand on his time but Tina wasn't complaining. This was Emanuel's dream and even though they would be spending even more time apart, it would leave her with more time to concentrate on her path of revenge. The phone in her office began to ring and Tina got up to answer it.

"Hey" Tina answered.

"Case closed" the voice said and then hung up.

Mommy said, "Sooner or later your mess will catch up with ya."

"Yes," Tina said laughing with joy.

CHAPTER THIRTY-NINE

The first day at the hospital was crazy and Emanuel didn't even have time to break for lunch. From the looks of it he probably wouldn't get a chance to have a normal meal for dinner neither. He witnessed so many sick people from all walks of life but nothing would prepare him for what happened next.

"Oh no, what"! One of the nurses said on the phone.

"Doctor Cartwright, we have a black male between the age of fifty to fifty-five with a partial severed penis." "The medics are on their way now".

Emanuel had just finished discharging a patient and still had the chart in his hand. He along with several others stood there in disbelief. He knew that there were some crazy people in the world but this had to top the list. Emanuel could see the approaching lights from the ambulance and he braced himself for the worse. When the paramedics wheeled the man in, Emanuel noticed that not only had the man sustained a nasty injury, he had also taken a beating. Someone definitely did not like this man, and he placed his gloves on to examine him.

After removing the gauze that was placed on the man's private area, Emanuel was kind of glad that the unidentified man was still unconscious. The flesh hung as if it was about to fall off and there was a substantial amount of blood lost. "*Oh God what mad man or woman did this,*" he was thinking. Surgery was crucial.

Hours had passed when Emanuel had finally entered the hospital room of the unidentified man just as the nurse was replacing the bag of antibiotics. The guy was black and blue and still unconscious from surgery. The police report indicated that he was found near an old vacant garage and there were no leads as to who could have done it. The man was well dressed and well-groomed ruling out the possibility of him being a homeless person and the lack of identification made it difficult in finding out who he was, therefore contacting his family was impossible.

"Who did you piss off," Emanuel whispered looking at the man who laid before him.

Emanuel would have to be the one to tell this man that he would never have the same quality of life that he was accustom to. The surgeon did what he could, but the damage was too severe. Emanuel noted his patient's chart and right after he left the room, the man began to mumble.

"What's going on, what's going on?" He moaned.

The pain was unbearable. He couldn't move, could barely talk. He felt weak. Something didn't feel right; he couldn't explain it. He dreamed. The blows, the kicks and then he was unconscious again and remaining that way for the next two weeks.

CHAPTER FORTY

Tina sat down at her desk and began to plan her sister's sweet revenge. "You hurt me the most sister, now I am going to hurt you." Tina said out loud as if Diane was in the room.

Tina remembered an incident that involved her precious sister at a previous place of employment. Diane almost went to jail for embezzlement but walk away a free woman thank God for one of Tina's friends who returned a favor by taking Diane's case. Diane claimed that she didn't do it but Tina knew that she did and she also knew that Brock was the mastermind behind it all. It was never supposed to be resurfaced but Tina knew anything was possible.

Deep in thought, Tina jumped when she heard the phone ring and reached to answer it.

"Hey you what's up?" Tina asked Emanuel.

"Sorry I didn't get a chance to call you last night but just checking on you babe."

"Oh, don't worry about me Emanuel, I'm fine." Tina said.

"Good, uh things are a little hectic here and you will never guess what happened to this guy that was brought in." Emanuel said.

"What happened?" "I hope nothing out of a horror movie." Tina said with some concern.

Tina listened, while she slowly sipped on a cup of tea that she had just made.

"This guy was brought in beaten up and his penis was almost severed."

Emanuel explained.

Tina began to choke spilling the tea all over herself.

"Shoot, what did you say?" She asked him.

"You heard right; the guy had severe trauma to his penis" he confirmed.

"Are you serious? Tina asked in shock.

"Yes, unfortunately and we almost lost him." "They had to send him to us because the county hospital wasn't equipped to take him."

"Baby are you ok?" Emanuel asked when he heard Tina coughing again.

"Yeah, I spilled this tea all over the place; just have to clean it up."

"Well, I'll let you go then and I will call you when I'm on my way home." Emanuel said.

"Ok and good luck with that patient, love you" she said to him.

"Thanks, and I love you back."

Tina's heart began to race and she got up to wipe the tea that she had spilled; her mind was trying to process what Emanuel had just told her. Was this guy Brock that he was talking about. The guy was beaten and the last time she had talked to Diane, Brock had moved downtown and that's where the county hospital was. Everything was adding up; everything except that nasty injury. Maybe she was totally wrong about everything but either way time would surely tell.

***

"What's going on, what's going on?" He mumbles again.

"Sir, can you tell me your name?" The nurse asked.

The man slowly moved his head in the direction of the voice. He felt hot but his body shivered. He ached all over. He was starting to remember. He wanted to answer but he couldn't. He could hear himself mumble something. The pain had eased. As a matter of fact, he couldn't feel anything.

"Brock Casey," he mumbled.

"Mr. Casey, can you give me a contact number for a relative, next of kin?"

Brock managed to give her the information that was requested before falling unconscious again. He dreamed about being back in his hometown, with images of his momma and her sweet face. He loved her so much but he had hurt her so many times. He didn't want to leave her but they both knew that he had to. Wanda Logan wasn't his first but he couldn't tell her that. He couldn't tell her that his dirty habits started even before he realized that they were dirty. He couldn't tell anyone. What happened to Brenda he often wondered. She had to experience his wanton advances on more than one occasion but no one knew but it wasn't his fault; it was passed on to him. His eyes opened again. No one was in the room now. He could hear Brenda screaming as he tried to hold her down. *"Be quiet!" He told her.* He could hear his momma say, *"Son you have to go; you will have a better life with your aunt."* Maybe he could start with a clean slate. Diane was supposed to save him.

"Save me," Brock mumbled and he fell unconscious again.

***

Emanuel was able to contact Brock's daughter, Brook. It was such a sensitive matter so Emanuel suggested that Brook contact Diane or Tina but Brook practically cursed him out for making the suggestion so he left it alone and wondered what that was all about.

Brock laid in his bed looking out the window. He felt such hopelessness. This had to be the lowest point of his life. Feeling deeply depressed, his body still ached from the beating that he had taken and he wished that he had not survived it. They were letting him go home in a couple of days and he wondered how he was supposed to go on with his life; a life that had limitations that he just couldn't accept. He knew that one day karma would come back at him but he had no idea that this would be the way that it would go down. The therapist tried to get him to open up but he wouldn't. He was afraid to talk; afraid that if he did, the truth would be known; his secrets.

Brock didn't want to think anymore; it hurt too much to do so. He felt that a life without his manhood was no life at all and it couldn't have happened at a worse time. He was finally living his life the way that he wanted to. He had got himself together only for this to happen. He felt like such a fool. A fool for thinking that he could actually be somebody. Be better than his dad or granddaddy. It was tearing him apart. Karma was definitely a bitch.

"I can't live like this; damn it I can't." He mumbled and wept.

CHAPTER FORTY-ONE

Diane arrived at work late again but this time she wasn't trying to break her neck to get there. She was still fuming from the mess that was going on at the office and the attitude she had was evident. It was some sneaky mess going on and HR was being so secretive about everything. People were brought in for interviews but no one seemed to know for what and it seemed like every other week someone was either getting laid off or fired.

"Oh no," Diane thought. She had been there too long to put up with this kind of foolishness. With two promotions under her belt, she felt in no way threatened by what was going on around her and as far as she was concerned her position there was secured.

"They better be glad I know the Lord" she said picking up the phone.

"Yes Mr. Barns" Diane said.

"Diane, hold all of my calls until farther notice."

"Ok" she said and she hung up the phone.

Mr. Edward Barns, a puny, medium height, white man had been head manager at the company for over twenty years. He was never happy when it came to firing people especially those who had contributed a lot for the company's sake but he had a job to do.

"Ok let's get this over with on Friday maybe around four." "I have all of the documentation here." Mr. Barns said.

"Ok sir." Patrick responded and shook his head in agreement.

Diane was so into her work that she failed to notice that she had worked well into her lunch.

"Good Lord" she said looking up at the clock and noticing the time. "Oh no, there will be no more of that not from me anyway" and she got up to get her pocketbook and left for lunch.

Once Diane got in the car, she pulled out her "to do list" from her bag so that she could run some errands while on her lunch break. She hated stopping anywhere after work. She liked to go straight home, have a light dinner, put on her pajamas and chill for the evening with a good book or entertained by a good movie.

"Ok, dry cleaner's bill, phone bill and electric bill" Diane was saying as a reminder of what bills she needed to pay.

It took her longer than usual to run her errands which left her with no time to stop and get a salad. She was desperately trying to cut back on fast food but today she found herself heading right to the drive through at Popeye's. After placing her order, she pulled up just in time to see this fine-looking black brother walking towards the entrance. They made eye contact and Diane returned a smile for a smile and it didn't take long for her mind to start wondering.

Since her divorce, Diane had not been in the company of any man other than her church members and she couldn't even remember the last time that she had been in the arms of one either. Her head was so jacked up from her ex that she couldn't imagine getting involved with anyone. She had to get herself together before she tried to share her life with anyone else and that seemed like a long time coming.

Diane got her order and was stuffing French fries in her mouth and didn't see the guy walking up to her car.

"Excuse me" he said to her.

Diane turned toward him and was totally embarrassed by the amount of food that she had just stuffed in her mouth. Of course, the guy was grinning from ear to ear.

"How are you doing my name is Steve, what's your name?"

"Oh Sorry, it's Diane." She said trying to chew the food up as fast as she could.

"Hi Diane question, are you married or seeing anyone?

"No to both and what about you." Diane asked still trying to chew the remaining fries that were in her mouth.

"No, I'm not married and I'm not seeing anyone. Do you think that I can get your number?"

That question started a conversation and Diane found herself feeling like a young teenager and realizing that she was going to be a little late getting back to work.

***

It had just started to rain and Tina was meeting up with Mack again. He had informed her earlier in the day that their meeting place would be at a different location due to the weather. It didn't matter to Tina as long as it was short and sweet and that it was. She put on her sneakers and got the envelope off the table and headed out to meet him. His directions were on point and Tina had no trouble finding Mack's car so by the time she pulled up, he was already out of his car. She rolled down her window and handed him the envelope and as fast as he got out of his car, he was just as fast getting back in. Boom…it was done.

CHAPTER FORTY-TWO

It was mid-afternoon and Brook was just leaving the hospital. Her dad looked ok, considering his injuries, but mentally he was a basket case and she couldn't help but feel sorry for him. When Brook was young, she remembered the good times when she loved her dad but as she got older and became aware of his dirty little secrets, she kept her distance from him. She began to live in her own little world pretending that her dad was this perfect person and everything was normal in her household. Brook knew all too well the bad habits that her dad had inherited and she closed her eyes but couldn't erase the thought that maybe he had pissed someone off by doing something inappropriate to their daughter. Brook knew that was what brought him to Atlanta in the first place.

Way back when, her dad had got into some trouble in his hometown, Mississippi. He had just started high school when his mother found out that he had sexually molested a female student and whisked him off to live with her sister in Atlanta to keep him from going to jail. From what Brook understood, her dad's family was full of freaks; everybody fooled around with each other. Her dad was just a little boy when his dad left his mom for another woman who was his own cousin. There were other stories even surrounding her dad being sexual abused by his dad's father. Brook heard these stories played over and over again as her parents would scream at each other and her mom would throw it up to her dad thus where he came from. Some things should never be heard in the ears of a child.

Brook blamed her parents as the main reason why her relationships with men never seemed to work. She demanded affection from them and when she didn't get what she wanted, she made their lives miserable as hell until they ended up hating her. Wiping the tears from her face, Brook tried to look at the bright side of things but there wasn't any. Even though Emanuel reassures her that her dad would be ok the injury that he had sustained was devastating to him and there would definitely be some major adjustments in his life. Emanuel had even set up an appointment for him to see a therapist to help him deal with his state of depression. Brook pushed the thoughts from her mind and picked up the phone to dial her mother's number and as usual she didn't answer the phone.

"Why does she even have a phone" Brook said out loud and she dialed the number again.

Diane was just pulling in the parking lot at her job when she heard her phone ring again and she reached down in her bag to retrieve it. Diane didn't like carrying big bags because it was so hard to find anything in them.

"Hello" Diane said.

"Mother where are you?" Brook asked.

"At work why?"

"I just left the hospital; Dad's been in there for the past couple of weeks."

"What's wrong with him?" She asked while going through her things.

"He was beaten pretty bad mother and uh his thing was almost cut of."

"What did you say"! Diane yelled.

"Yes, mother his private part was almost severed." "I just spoke with Emanuel and he said that dad will be ok physically but mentally he's not coping well at all."

"Emanuel?" Diane asked.

"Yes mother, he's dad's doctor." "He's made arrangements for him to see a therapist to help him deal with his depression." "When I went in to see him, he couldn't even look at me; he said that he wishes that they had let him die."

"Oh my God, how did it happen?" Diane asked.

"A group of kids found him lying on a side street near a vacant garage; the police questioned them but they don't have any leads as to who did it."

"This is just too much." "I will talk to you when I get home, ok baby."

"Ok" Brook said in a low whisper.

There was no question as to how Diane felt about her ex-husband. She disliked him immensely but still she didn't want to see him or anyone else for that matter, sustain that type of injury. She knew that there were some messed up people in the world, but Diane felt in her heart that no matter how evil some people were, they just didn't inflict that type of injury on someone without just cause. Brock had done something to someone and this was their way of paying him back. He was only getting back the pain and misery that he had caused in so many other people's lives.

Mommy said, "You reap what you sow."

"Lord have mercy." Diane said. She sure knew about that.

CHAPTER FORTY-THREE

The more Diane looked at the clock the longer the day seemed to be. The whole week had been like that and today was Friday and she couldn't wait to get home. There was a time that she hated to leave anything lingering in her bin and would have stayed late just to have a fresh start on Monday but not anymore; it would have to wait.

"Yes" Diane said answering the phone.

"Diane, I need to see you in my office." Mr. Barns said.

"Ok I'll be right there."

Diane put the phone down, grabbed a pen and some paper and went next door to Mr. Barn's office. When she approached the door, Diane thought it was strange that the door was shut. Even in his meetings, Mr. Barns always kept his door open or ajar but never completely shut. Diane knocked lightly on the door.

"Come in." Mr. Barns said.

Diane opened the door and came face to face with not only her boss, but Patrick Dunlap, President of Human Resource. She felt a churning in her stomach and she knew that this had nothing to do with taking notes or anything of the sort. Patrick couldn't even look at her.

"Diane take a seat please." Mr. Barnes said and he began to explain the reason for their meeting.

Diane could not believe what she was hearing. "*This cannot be happening to me she thought.*"

"Diane, the company has been doing some back ground investigations on some of our employees, just a random background search." "In this search we came across some incriminating evidence that will affect your position here." "In 1995, we found that you were involved in a lawsuit filed by Martin and Marx, your prior employer, for the mismanaging of funds." "There was a discrepancy on your application that you filled out here when you first applied for the position." "When asked if you were ever involved in any lawsuits or criminal cases you responded no on your application but we found information that proves otherwise." "On a personal note, I want you to know that you have always been a model employee, you have an excellent work history and have been one of the main contributors to this company for the past 10 years; but, because of false information that you placed on your application, it is with great empathy that I have to terminate your position here with TRZ."

Diane thought that this incident was buried away in her past; something that she was told would never resurface again. She couldn't argue with her boss because the fact of the matter was, he was right and she was wrong, so what was the point. Mr. Barn's voice became a distant echo and without saying a word, Diane got up slowly and left the room.

"What am I going to do?" Diane whispered as she shut the door behind her.

Most of the employees had already left the office so Diane quickly got a bag from her drawer and put her things in it. Papers and notes tacked to her cubicle she pulled off and trashed. Everything in her drawer she cleared out placing all company property on her desk including the company's manuals and the company's key. Twenty years she had put into this company and this is what it all came down to. Diane put on her coat and prayed that she wouldn't run into anyone as she was trying to leave the building. She could no longer hold the tears in; they ran rapidly.

Diane got on the elevator and made her way to the main entrance. *"Coast is clear,"* she thought and she walked as fast as she could out the door and to her car. The evening was cold and windy and she didn't even bother to close her coat. She wanted the cold air to numb her making her less aware of what had just happened. Two co-workers from the second floor had just come out and Diane quickly turned on her car which caused them to look in her direction. They waved and said "have a good weekend," and Diane thanked God that they were walking in the opposite direction because in that instance, she lost control of her emotions. Diane wept barely able to make it out of the parking lot. It was the longest ride home and when Diane got there, she found herself pacing the floor and wondering what she would do next. Not too many people knew about the charges that had been brought up against her because it wasn't something that she talked about or shared with anyone. Only two people knew and that was Tina and Brock. After all of these years how could Brock benefit from telling and Tina could barely remember her own name let alone remembering something that had happened years ago. So, Diane wondered who else it could have been. Caught up in her thoughts, Diane didn't see Brook when she came in the room.

"Mother what happened?" Brook asked.

Diane looked at her daughter and wondered how she was going to explain this.

While Diane was at home struggling with the realty of losing her job, Tina and her friends were enjoying a girl's night out. It was going on seven o'clock and Tina was meeting some of her close friends for drinks and dancing. She couldn't remember the last time that she actually had been able to go out just to have some fun; she sure did deserve it. When Tina pulled up to the club, she was lucky enough to get a parking spot in the front and from what she could hear, The Havana was jumping; Tina walked inside where Cynthia was waiting for her and they hugged and hurriedly walked to their table where the rest of the ladies were waiting. Drinks were served and everyone was rocking to the beat of "Jam Tonight" by Freddy Jackson.

"Ok ladies I have something to show you." Tina said loudly looking around the table.

"Show us what?" Tammy said.

Tina pulled out her left hand that exposed a diamond as big as her finger.

"Oh shit"! "Ok is this what I think it is"! Cynthia asked almost jumping out of her seat.

"Yes, it is"!

"Girl, start from the beginning; how did he propose?" Payton asked.

"We were having wild sex and he just whipped the ring out and put in on my finger." Tina laughed as she moved her body in a very sexual kind of way. Everyone at the table burst out laughing.

"I'm lying, let me stop." Tina said still laughing.

Tina began telling them about the proposal from the time the limo picked her up to meeting Emanuel's parents and everything that happened in between.

"Damn that is crazy; he took that shit right out of a romance novel." Brenda said and they all laughed again.

"Ok girl we are so happy for you, congratulations." Cynthia said and they all raised their glasses to her.

"Ok there goes my jam ladies let's get our groove on." Tina said when the DJ played "The Electric Slide" and they all got up from the table and partied and danced the whole night away.

It was pass three o'clock in the morning when Tina got home from the club. Feeling a little buzz, she wanted nothing more than to go straight to bed but the chirping sound from her office stopped her and when she went to check her message the person on the other end said, "Case closed." Tina hung up the phone and left the room smiling.

"I hope you're crawled up under a rock somewhere." Tina said in a delightful kind of way.

"Are you comin with me, come let me take you on a party ride and I'll teach you, teach you, teach you I'll teach you the electric slide." Tina sang and giggled as she went upstairs to bed.

CHAPTER FORTY-FOUR

Emanuel was finishing up with his paperwork. It had been a crazy day. From a combination of broken bones, gunshot wounds, burns you name it, he treated. He had been so busy that he didn't have time to check in on Tina to see if she had enjoyed her night out with the girls. He also wanted to tell her that the unidentified man that had been brought in just happened to be her ex-brother-in-law.

The sun was just peeping its face out, when Emanuel left the hospital. He was tired and glad that he no longer had that long drive to take to get to his condo. He was relieved that he was able to sell it as fast as he did for the price that he wanted; it had worked out well for him. Now he was on his way home to Tina.

Emanuel tipped toed up the steps to avoid waking Tina up. He quietly undressed and slowing got into bed, moving as close as he could to her. He loved the smell of her body, her hair and the softness of her skin. As tired as he was, he knew that if she awoke, it would be on and sleep would have to wait for its rightful place but Tina didn't wake up and Emanuel fell fast asleep with her body close to his.

Tina stretched out in the bed and was awaken by the smell of his scent. The scent of the one that held her heart and she slowly turned over to confirm it. Tina marveled at the man who laid next to her and she leaned close to him and planted a kiss gently on his lips. Emanuel's eyes opened and the smile that Tina knew all too well greeted her with full effects.

"Good morning gorgeous." He said to her.

"Good morning, would you like to take a bubble bath with me?" Tina asked.

"If you go and get it warm in there first, deal?"

"Listen to you, it's a deal" she said laughing. And she got up and headed to the bathroom. Emanuel laid there with his eyes closed wishing that every morning could be like this.

"Oh Baby, have you talked to your sister or your niece?" Emanuel asked.

"No, I haven't why?" Tina yelled from the bathroom.

"Do you remember the patient that I was telling you about?" Emanuel asked her.

Tina stopped what she was doing and she thought of Brock.

"Oh God" she whispered and she came out of the bathroom.

"Who?" She asked playing it off.

"So, I assume that you don't know uh?" Emanuel asked sitting up in the bed.

"Know what?" Tina asked.

"Well, sorry to be the bearer of bad news but that patient that had the injury to his penis was your ex-brother-in-law."

Tina's adrenaline level hit the roof and her heart began to race.

"My ex- brother-in law, you're kidding right?" Tina asked.

"No, I'm not kidding, it was Brock Casey." Emanuel confirmed.

Tina didn't know what to say.

"I talked to your niece and I felt pretty bad having to explain everything to her but, she insisted that I not call her mother or you, so I left it at that" Emanuel said.

"So how is he?" Tina asked waiting patiently for him to answer.

"With the injury that he sustained, he will never have the same quality of life ever."

"So, does that mean that he can never have sex again?" Tina asked him.

"You are correct." "The surgeon did his best but the injury was just too severe." "I'm sure your sister knows by now but please don't mention what I have told you, ok?" Emanuel said.

"Ok baby I won't." "I'll have to give Diane a call later and see what's going on with her." Tina said in a sympathetic tone of voice but inside she was jumping for joy.

"Now on a happier subject, how was the girl's night out, did you get any phone numbers?" Emanuel asked jokingly.

"We had a lot of fun and no, I didn't get any numbers smart ass" and Tina leaned over the bed and kissed him.

"Let me get that bubble bath going."

"Ok you do that and hurry up please, he's waiting for you." Emanuel said looking down at himself and grinning.

Emanuel was smiling the whole time on his drive back to the hospital. Tina sure did rock his world. He loved her and he wanted to be loved by her. Tina gave him that iff that he needed. As Emanuel approached the hospital parking lot, his mind went into work mode and he saved his little private space in his memory for Tina to keep him company for the ride home.

Emanuel barely had time to get his gloves on. Blood was everywhere and he had to find out exactly where it was coming from.

"Ok let's get an IV hooked up over here now and a monitor"!

"What happened here?" Emanuel shouted.

The paramedics was informing him that it was a domestic situation and that the woman had been stabbed three times; once in the upper right arm and twice in the right side.

"Do we have a name?"

"No doctor, we're working on it." The nurse responded.

Everything was happening so fast and then the moment that every doctor dread; the sound when a heart stops beating. Emanuel glanced up at the monitor and in seconds he reached for the defibrillator.

"Clear please"! Emanuel shouted as he made contact with the woman's chest; nothing happened. "Again, clear." He shouted.

He was not ready to lose a patient; not today if he could help it. Then suddenly the monitor picked up a heartbeat and the woman's condition stabilized for the moment and as Emanuel let out a sign of relief that's when he noticed it. Emanuel turned the patients face toward him.

"My God I know this…I know her!" Emanuel said frantically, trying to stay focus.

"Ok let's prep her for surgery," he ordered and everyone moved swiftly around to get the job done.

Emanuel had never had a close call like this one especially with someone that he knew and that made it ten times worse. He removed his gloves and thanked God that Patty didn't die on him.

"Damn it" he mumbled. And he watched as they wheeled her to the operating room.

Later in the day Emanuel was informed that Patty had managed to place a 911 call from her home before passing out from her injuries and the police were now searching for her husband as a person of interest. Within hours he was arrested and charged with attempted murder.

CHAPTER FORTY-FIVE

Tina sat in her office trying to come to terms with her feelings. She hated Brock for what he had done to her daughter and she was glad that he would never get the opportunity to hurt another child again but somebody had done her a favor. Someone had done what she was thinking, what she wanted, but didn't have the nerve to ask someone to do it. A good ass whipping would have been sufficed, but someone thought otherwise; someone knew what Brock was capable of. Tina didn't know whether to keep quiet or approach Mack about it. As far as she was concerned, Brock deserved everything that he got that night. All of them were getting what they deserved and she was enjoying every second of it but the more Tina allowed herself to go after them, the less human she felt and she didn't like the feeling. She kept making excuses like she had a right to do what she was doing but she hoped that one morning she wouldn't look in the mirror and find a total stranger looking back at her.

Tina got up to get one of the diaries from off the shelf. She kept them out of sight so that no one would notice them. It was her Brother Robert's turn to feel her sweet vengeance and she sat down on the sofa and turned to the page with the yellow sticky that referenced where Macy had written about him.

November 2, 2010

Dear diary-Don't feel too good today. I didn't take my meds. I don't like the way it makes me feel. Just didn't feel up to it. Still upset over Uncle Robert's remarks. He hates me so and the bad part about it is I don't know why. Nothing makes sense anymore. I know he has money and I didn't ask for a whole lot just enough to carry me over. He cussed at me and treated me like I was dirt. But what hurt the most was the comment he made after I left. I stood near the door after he practically

threw me out. He told this guy you can do what you want with her. I can't deal with this anymore. - Me.

Tina wiped the tears from her face.

"Baby I am so sorry; he will regret this for the rest of his life." Tina said angrily.

She knew how Robert loved his money but little did he know that his money was going to be missing real soon. She had planned on hurting him exactly where it would hurt the most and that was in his pockets.

Robert hated her and blamed her for ruining his chances on a business deal when she refused to co-sign on a loan for him. Yes, she could have helped him but it was a large amount of money and she didn't think that it was a wise decision at the time and months later, her decision proved to be the right one and he never spoke to her again.

"And that's ok you don't have to like me but after I get done with you, you will definitely need me before I will need you, you can bet on that." She said.

An hour had passed after meeting with Mack and Tina headed to the grocery store to pick up a few things. Emanuel would be home for the entire weekend and she wanted to make sure she had everything she needed. Her mind was still pondering on the conversation with Mack and the puzzled look on his face after she had mentioned the gruesome injury that Brock had sustained. Mack didn't have a clue as to what she was talking about and he assured her that everything would be taken care of and not to worry. Tina had always been under the impression that Mack was the one who was doing the jobs but that wasn't the case; she had no idea who worked for him and she didn't want to know. She just didn't want anything traced back to her.

Tina paid for her things and got in her car to go home. She needed to call Diane and when she got in front of her house, she pulled her phone out and called her. She had not talked to her sister in a while and she didn't miss her either. As long as she kept Diane thinking that she was upset with her for not coming over her house was a good thing. She couldn't have her suspecting that it was anything else.

"Hello," Diane said distraughtly.

"Hey girl I haven't heard from you in a while." "What's going on?" You sound like you're sick are you ok?" Tina asked sarcastically.

"No, I'm not ok."

"What's wrong?" Tina asked with a smirk on her face and preparing to hear a long-drawn-out story about her getting fired.

"Let's see, now where do I begin." "I lost my job and I have filled out a dozen job applications and no one is calling me back, then again, who's going to hire a person with a record." Diane started to cry. "Oh, and by the way, my ex-husband killed himself the other night because he couldn't cope with life anymore." "You know, I despised the man but I didn't want to see this happen to him." Diane said in between sobs. "Brook and I are on our way to the funeral home so I will call you later ok." Diane managed to say before hanging up the phone.

Tina was stunned. Death was too good for him.

Mack sat in his car still in deep thought over the conversation that he had with Tina. Duces knew the rules and if anything was to go wrong, he knew to contact him as soon as possible but he had not heard from him. It was very few people that Mack trusted and he trusted Duces with his life. Duces could handle himself in a very professional manner but he also could be very cocky at times but something just wasn't adding up. They had done some scandalous shit which came with the job but this was supposed to be a serious beat down and to inflict this type of injury on someone was personal shit. Duces had never changed the game and Mack had to find out what was going on. He had a reputation to live up to and he didn't what to get caught up in some unnecessary shit.

Mack had been working this hustle for years. While locked up in the pen on a grand theft charge, he learned the ropes from some guy that use to be a private investigator that was also serving time for slicing the hell out of his wife. The guy had done some wild shit and Mack listened and learned all that he could and when he served his time, he went into business for himself. Duces was the first guy that Mack hooked up with when he was released from prison. He was a pretty boy, smart, loyal and a trickster at heart. Duces had some tricks of his own, tricks that Mack had never heard of before. His dad, whom they called Dek, had been a gangster back in the day and he had taught him very well. He and Duces were partners in crime but Mack could honestly say that they were friends too. Duces shared little about his life but it was on those rare occasions that he would open up about his family. This puzzle was complicated and Mack couldn't figure out where to put the pieces. He had to catch up with Duces. Still in thought, his phone rings and it's his boy.

After questioning him about the incident with Brock, Mack had no choice but to take the ride to Duces' place to see what was going on. He had insisted that it would be better for him to see it than to try to explain as to why things went down the way that they did and when Mack arrived, he got the shock of his life. Duces assured him that he was handling it so he had no choice but to trust him.

CHAPTER FORTY-SIX

Emanuel was still hype after leaving the medical conference where he had met up with some of his old buddies. They were all doing rather well and they made a pact to get together real soon. The traffic was moving rather slow and Emanuel picked up his phone to call Tina and hoped that she wasn't too busy to talk. It would sure help to pass the time away and maybe he would even mention setting a date for their wedding which he had been trying to do for weeks.

"Hey," Tina answered trying to sound a bit preoccupied.

"Hey Baby what's going on, what's wrong?" Emanuel asked hearing it in her voice.

"I have some bad news Emanuel." And she paused for a few seconds. "Brock killed himself."

"What? When?"

"Yes, the other night." "I talked to my sister a couple of hours ago and huh, that's what she said."

"That's too bad; I am sorry to hear that." "You know he was seeing a therapist at the hospital to help him deal with the depression and I had recommended that he continue with his sessions after his discharge but unfortunately we have no control over the situation if they don't choose to go." Emanuel explained.

"So, I guess what I wanted to talk to you about is not appropriate at the moment uh?"

"What?" Tina asked.

"Setting a date for our wedding," Emanuel mentioned.

"Yes, we will talk later when things settle down deal?"

"Sure babe I understand." "Look I'm going to stop at the hospital for a minute and I will see you later ok, love you?"

"Ok." She said to him.

Tina wasn't the type to pretend but felt it necessary to show some emotions for the man that she hated. She surely couldn't reveal her true colors. Not to Emanuel; not to anyone.

Emanuel could sense that Tina was obviously upset over Brock's death. She didn't ask about how his day went and she didn't even say I love you back. Emanuel was a man that picked up on things like that and he wanted to do something special for his lady. From a woman's perspective, it's nothing like a box of chocolate covered strawberries. That would surely cheer her up and he planned on doing just that.

"Hey Ms. Patty," Emanuel said in a low whisper.

Patricia smiled when she heard his voice and opened her eyes to see Emanuel standing next to her with a beautiful bouquet of flowers in his hand.

"Hi Emanuel, oh thanks," Patricia said when she saw the flowers. "You can sit them right over there where I can see them." She said tiredly and pointing to the table.

"I was on my way home and I thought I would stop by and see you for a minute." "How are you feeling?" He asked her while placing the flowers on the table.

"Sore, real sore and so tired" she responded. "It was my fault Emanuel." She said in a low voice and Emanuel took hold of her hand.

"No one deserves to go through this Pat regardless of whose fault it was." He told her.

"You know I use to think that his jealousy was cute at first, but each time we fought he hit harder and harder and I would laugh at him." "I really thought that I could beat his ass." Patricia said trying to laugh. "And I was until he…" Patricia stopped talking. The memory was just too overwhelming and Patricia squeezed his hand.

"Look I want you to concentrate on getting better ok?" Emanuel said.

"Ok" Patricia said softly.

"I'm off this weekend but I will check on you first thing Monday morning ok."

"Ok please do."

Then Emanuel got close to her planting a kiss on her forehead and removing a tear that was now running down her face.

"You rest and that's an order." Emanuel said to her.

"I will and thanks for dropping by, I really appreciate it."

"You're very welcome." He said ready to leave the room.

"Oh Emanuel" Patricia called to him and he turned around.

"I heard that congratulations are in order." She said to him and managed to smile.

"Thanks Pat" And he smiled back at her.

Patricia laid in silence as Emanuel left the room. She felt like crap and it took so much out of her just to speak. She had never imagined that her husband would have done such a thing. He always talked shit about what he would do to her if he ever caught her cheating on him so she thought that she was playing it safe. Evidently, he took it to heart when she came home late which started an argument that escalated into a fight. She had never seen him that angry and before she knew anything she was fighting for her life. She knew that she was wrong and the guilt swelled up in her for being responsible for pushing her husband to that point. As the tears ran down her face, Patricia made a promise that she would never take another man for granted because the next time she may not live to tell it.

Emanuel was glad that he had stopped in to see Patricia. It had been touch and go there for a while but now he was able to finally hold a conversation with her, God was good. Her wounds were healing very well but mentally she had to be going through it. Emanuel could never understand how a man could beat up on a woman plus go as far as to perpetrate those kinds of injuries especially to the mother of his children. He was taught that women were precious gifts to be loved and treasured. He could recall plenty of times when females would make him pretty angry but never to the point where he would raise up his hand against them but then again, he had never been cheated on either. He wondered if it were him that walked in Don's shoes, how he would have handled it and to what extent would he have gone. It was definitely something to think about and he hoped that he would never cross that line and find out.

Emanuel had just left River's Candy Store with a big box of chocolate covered strawberries. This was sure to put a smile on his lady's face; anything for his lady.

CHAPTER FORTY-SEVEN

Tina got up earlier than usual to type up a letter that she was sending to Mr. Ford. She proof read it a hundred times making sure that everything was in perfect order. Along with the letter, she was sending a check for a very generous amount that would surely make her brother Robert a very unhappy man.

"Ok done" Tina said and she placed the letter with the check in an envelope, sealed it and placed it in her purse and then she heard the phone beep.

"Case closed," the voice said when she answered. Tina smiled.

"Money, money, money, money," Tina sang as she went upstairs to shower but not before eating two of the chocolate covered strawberries that Emanuel had brought her. He was so thoughtful, and she loved him for it.

***

"What the hell are you talking about? Over drafted by how much?" "You have to be kidding me." "Well, there must be some kind of mistake." "You damn Skippy!." Robert said slamming the phone down.

Robert sat down in his chair than got up again and walked to the window. He loved the view. He could see miles and miles away and he had to admit that he had made some very difficult decisions while looking out that window. Something seemed to speak to him, direct him. Completely frustrated, he turned around and picked up his phone again.

"Leah," he said,

"Yes sir?" she answered.

"Get my accountant on the phone now." He yelled.

"Yes sir."

Robert waited anxiously for his phone to ring and in seconds, he was on the line with his accountant.

"Gary this is Rob ok, you need to tell me what the hell is going on." "I just got off the phone with Bank International and they told me that there was an overdraft amount of three hundred and fifty thousand dollars on my business account and the balance in my personal account can't be right." He explained.

"Ok Mr. Lewis let me pull up your account information."

Robert thought that he would explode at any minute. It seemed like everything was going from bad to worse.

"Mr. Lewis, it is showing that your account is in the rears." "Apparently, there has been an excessive number of activities on both accounts especially in the last two months." Gary tried to explain.

"How the hell is that possible?" Robert asked him. "I keep track of everything so you tell me how did this happen?" Robert demanded to know.

"Mr. Lewis, your signature is on the checks sir and it looks like you approved all of the transactions yourself."

Robert began to sweat profusely and loosened his tie to help give him the relief that he was looking for.

"You listen very carefully; I want a copy of everything that was approved and signed; I want copies of everything that has left this building for the last six months I mean everything"! "Fax it to me, everything"! Robert said.

"Yes, sir I will have that information for you as soon as possible." Gary assured him.

Robert slammed the phone down again in disbelief. His mind roamed around trying to figure out what the hell was going on. There was a large amount of money missing, and his workers still had to be paid. He had to think of something or he would run the risk of losing everything. He didn't trust anyone when it came to his money.

He had built his construction company up from scratch by borrowing money from a mutual friend who had connections with the mob. When he got his business up and running, he was able to repay every dime that he owed but not without paying a heavy price. He became indebted to certain people. The long hours he spent in the office, sacrificing everything and practically selling his soul to keep it going got him high on his own self-gratification and he praised himself for becoming a very successful business man. Now he realized that his whole future was at stake. If this information leaked out, he knew that he would lose the Ford account which was his biggest account; it could ruin him. The thought of losing it all weighed heavily on his mind.

Robert sat back down in his chair and started to rub his temple to relieve the headache he felt coming on; than his thoughts went to Norma who he had been seeing for some time. He knew that she loved him and wanted a committed relationship but he was incapable of loving anyone except himself. When he grew tired of one woman and became bored, he dropped them like a hot cake and got another, but Norma was an exception. He did not love or trust her or any other woman for that fact, but she was young and she kept the fire burning in him. He had been seeing her long enough to become comfortable with her and leaving his personal information lying around when she was in the house; like his check book, bank statements and even his credit cards. She had access to all of it and she definitely had the motive.

After having a heated argument, Norma got pissed off at him when he refused to purchase some jewelry that she had on hold at Tiffany's. She left and he had not heard from her. Robert slammed his fist down on his desk. He couldn't believe that he had been so stupid.

"This shit can't be happening"! He said as he got up and looked out the window again.

No voices, no answers; he heard nothing.

Mommy said, "You put your trust in things, it will disappoint you every time."

CHAPTER FORTY-EIGHT

Tina took a little extra time getting ready for Brock's funeral. She wanted to look fabulous. As far as she knew, all of her siblings were going to be there and she wanted to rub it in their faces the fact that not only did she look good, but that she was doing good. Her business was blooming to the point that she was thinking about buying new office space to accommodate all the new clients that were coming in.

"Ok and that's going to do it." Tina said standing in the mirror putting on her little black hat. She was ready.

She had to admit that the black suit that she had picked out really rocked. She found it at a boutique in the city and it complemented her shape in every way. What would Hollywood say? She looked like money. Tina had always had a fine taste for fashion and for this day she wanted to flaunt it. She couldn't wait to see the faces of her siblings. She wanted to see the hurt, pain and the misery.

Tina got her sunglasses off the seat and put them on. "I'm so glad Emanuel had to work" she said looking in the mirror for a final check. "Ok let's do this," she said and she got out of her Mercedes and headed for the entrance to the funeral home.

Robert stood in the foyer trying to decide if he was going to stay for the entire service. Brock was not one of his favorite people but he had his reasons for being there. Just as he looked up, he saw his baby sister walking right toward him. No getting out of this, he thought.

"Perfect" Tina thought to herself when she seen Robert standing alone.

With her head held high and chest out, Tina strutted across the hallway toward Robert. When she got close enough to him, she could see that his financial woes were taking its toll. Robert was known for his fine expensive suits and his muscular swagger but today he didn't look so good. He looked haggard and it was evident that he had lost weight. Tina had purposely gotten the word out that she had contributed a large amount of funds to the Ford account and she could tell by the look on his face that he was aware of it. As Tina approached him, she took off her sunglasses and was so tempted to ask him about his business affair but she didn't want him to connect her with anything that was going on in his life.

"Hello brother." Tina said.

"Tina" he responded.

"Good to see you but sorry it had to be under these circumstances." She said slowly gazing at him from the top of his head to the bottom of his shoes.

Robert noticed the look that she gave him and without any other words exchanged, he walked away. Good job, she thought as she went to the back of the room to take a seat.

Mommy said, "Vengeance is mine saith the Lord," but in Tina's mind vengeance was hers and it was almost repaid.

***

Robert sat in his car outside Wayne's Funeral Home. The funeral had been over and done with but he stayed behind dwelling on the fact that he was going through the biggest scandal of his life. He had no choice but to pull out of the Ford contract and that was devastating to him and his business. The bank and the authorities were investigating the situation and Robert was informed that it would take some time before they would actually find out what happened. The signatures on the copied checks looked like his and it looked like he had authorized the business transactions but he knew that it wasn't him and he had no way of proving it. To add to his misfortune, Norma had got a hold of two of his credit cards and ran them up to the limit making over five thousand dollars worth of merchandise purchases. Yes, he had to admit that he had been screwed all the way around.

Robert put his head back against the seat. He didn't want to admit it but his baby sister looked like she was riding high on her horse these days to say the least, and he wondered if she had any inkling as to how bad things were going for him. He wasn't a hundred percent sure if she knew about his mishap and he was furious when he found out about the large amount of money that she had contributed to the Ford account and it made him feel sick every time he thought about it. He knew that Tina was financial secured even before her accident but he had no idea that she was rolling the way that she was right now. In a coma for ten years, and able to get right back up on her feet, and doing better than what she was before, damn he thought; life still had been very kind to her in spite of. Mommy would have said that she was blessed and highly favored.

For once in his life the guilt was creeping up on him. Robert knew about Tina's will even before her accident and the amount of money that she was entrusting to each of her siblings but of course, she had to die before they could receive it. That's when he started scheming to make it happen; the accident that didn't kill her but unfortunately, left her lingering on for ten whole years. Robert shook his head in disappointment. For a split second he even allowed himself to think of asking Tina for a loan but he knew that his pride would never let him do it.

Mommy said, *"You have to treat people the way you want to be treated cause you never know who you might need"*.

CHAPTER FORTY-NINE

Tina kicked off her shoes, threw her hat onto the sofa and made her way upstairs. She was furious at Mack and she let him know it.

"How dare he question my actions, son of a bitch!" she said out loud."

After the burial, everyone had gathered at Diane's for the repast but Mack had called her for an emergency meeting so she had to cut her time short at Diane's but not before she made her presence known in a most airy kind of way. While meeting with Mack, she was sorely disturbed when he questioned her about what she wanted him to do. It was his way of making sure if she really wanted to go ahead with the plans because it involved children and their lives would forever be changed.

"You're sitting here questioning me?" "I'm a grown ass woman and I have my reasons, trust me so I don't give a good damn who gets hurt." "Your job is to do what the hell I paid you to do not to question me," is what she told him.

"Calm down ok, I will do it I just wanted to make sure it's what you really wanted to do that's all." Mack tried to reason with her.

Tina grabbed the towel and dried herself off. The oil soak sure did help her to relax. To think that over an hour ago she was acting like a mad woman and Mack probably thought the same too. Damn she thought, looking in the mirror, what was happening to her. She was so short tempered these days and angry all the time. Keeping everything bottled up inside was finally taking its toll so it didn't take much for her to lash out at someone and Mack just happened to be that someone.

When she arrived at Diane's, she wanted to puke in their presence. She had to act one way around this person and another way around that person and hoped that nothing slipped out in between that would indicate that she had gotten her memory back. She had to smile when she wanted to cry, hug them when she wanted to hit them and it didn't end there. She also had to be extra careful around Emanuel too. He was very attentive and probably had already picked up on some of the things that she was doing. Could she really keep this up, she asked herself? It was exhausting for her.

After eating dinner and having another session of their love making, Tina tossed and turned and couldn't get to sleep for her brother Thomas weighed heavy on her mind. She had been close to him but he had allowed lies to come between them, and the more she tried to convince him of the truth, the more he didn't want to hear it. It really hurt her heart. His own niece was in trouble and in desperate need of his love and his help and he did nothing about it so she was also holding him accountable for what had happened to Macy.

Tina got up slowly from the bed trying not to wake Emanuel and went downstairs to once again retrieve the diaries. She sat down at her desk and turned the lamp on squinting to adjust her eyes to the dim light that barely gave her the ability to see. Slowly she opened the diary and turned to the page where Macy talked of her Uncle Thomas.

Hi Diary

I'm scared. My period has not come on yet. I went to the store to get one of those tests and I saw Uncle Thomas. When I turned around, he was right there. I know he saw what I had brought. He looked at me like he wanted to say something, but he said nothing. I remember what momma said, it doesn't hurt to speak. So, I spoke to him. I guess he hates me because he hates momma and momma didn't even do nothing. I tried to defend her one day when he was arguing with Aunt Diane. He told me to mine my business and I mined my business.

-Me

It touched Tina's heart to read the way Macy would refer to the things that she had taught her. Something that had been handed down from grandmother to granddaughter and mother to daughter; Words of wisdom I guess you could say from her grandmother whom she and her siblings called Mommy. It was her voice that Tina heard whenever she was about to fall off the straight and narrow path; and lately she was hearing a lot from her.

Tina's eyes began to water. The thought of her baby going through something like this by herself was heart breaking. The tears began flowing freely staining the pages of the diary.

"Your niece buys a pregnancy test and you say nothing; absolutely nothing." "At a time in her life when she needed somebody, anybody to listen and just care a little bit"! Tina said as she rocked back and forth, hitting herself in the head. She felt the anger building up inside as every word written by Macy seemed to possess her.

"Get it together," Tina heard her Mommy say and she rocked back and forth even more frantically.

Something was happening to her that she couldn't explain. Ever since the run in with Mack, the anger that she felt wasn't directed at Tony, Diane, Robert, or Thomas but it was directed at herself. It was torturing her. Was she too having second thoughts about what she was doing? She questioned herself.

"No, this is what I want," she said out loud. "I'm really losing it."

Why couldn't she either totally love her siblings or totally hate them. Every time she heard the words "case closed" she felt like her mission was accomplished but she was never at peace with it. It was like fighting a battle that tugged at her heart, her soul and she was not satisfied. She had never been so confused in her life. Tina closed the diary up and wiped the tears from her face.

"It's done." "Your heart will break just like mine and I will handle this one." "Sorry my brother but why should I care about your damn kids." Tina said in a whisper.

Noticing the light on in the hallway, Tina hurried and turned the lamp off that was on her desk and headed out of her office but in her delicate mental state, she failed to see Emanuel and ran right into him.

Mommy said, "The main thing that you try to cover up in the dark, always finds its way out in the light."

CHAPTER FIFTY

It was pretty calm at the hospital compared to some days and Emanuel had just come from visiting Patricia. She was doing well and he and another doctor agreed that maybe she would be going home for the holiday. Her body was healing well but Emanuel was growing concerned for her mental state. She couldn't hold a conversation without crying. Recovering from physical abuse was no joke and he recommend that she see a therapist and he was going to make sure that she followed up with it.

Emanuel realized that Patricia wasn't the only one that needed to see a therapist. He couldn't erase the image of what he had witnessed a couple of nights ago; a side to Tina that he had never seen before; angry and bitter but towards whom he didn't know. He managed to grasped bits and pieces of her words as he watched her at her desk, almost in the dark, rocking back and forth as she spilled out words about a niece who was fifteen years old and pregnant. As far as Emanuel knew, Tina only had one niece and that was Brook but she was well over the age of fifteen. It was upsetting and painful for him to watch her pour out her emotions in such a way. What was even more disturbing was when he realized that Tina was questioning her own sanity and at this point, so was he. This confirmed his curiosity all along that something was bothering her but every time he questioned her about it, she would tell him that she was ok. She wasn't ok and he was not going to let it go.

Emanuel felt guilty for not being there for Tina in the way that she obviously needed him to be. The long hours at the hospital and even staying overnight when feeling too tired to make the drive home, was also contributing to the problem. Tina had to know that she could come to him with anything. He was never too busy to talk with her or listen to whatever was on her mind. He wanted to be her rock; the one that would lift her up and shower her with his love, reassuring her that together they could do anything but it was obvious that Tina did not trust him enough to tell him what was going on. Why couldn't she talk to him? She had to have a reason but Emanuel couldn't think of one good reason why and that scared him. He loved her and wanted to reach out to her in any way that he could to help. He had a plan and he knew just what he needed to do if she let him. She had to let him in.

Mack watched Tina as she walked away. It was something different about her but he couldn't put a finger on it. *"What the hell,"* he thought. If this is what she wanted to do than he had no choice but to let her do it. This was her decision. He was going to do his part and the rest was up to her.

Tina put her sunglasses on and started the car up. Everything was set and ready to go. She knew that she had to be extra cautious in how she handled this and her supposed memory loss would prove to be a vital part in keeping anyone from suspecting her. Just like with Diane's situation, very few people knew that her two twin nephews were not really her nephews. Gossip that just happen to be true; passed on from a friend to a friend that had no business having access to confidential information. Even though it was by accident that Tina found out, she had given her word and swore in secrecy that she would never reveal that she knew anything about those two boys; the kids that her brother loved and had taken care of all their lives, the only dad that they knew. Memory loss, Tina chuckled. She remembered everything but at times she wished that she didn't.

***

Destiny laid in bed not sure of what to do about her current situation. Every time she turned around it was some type of drama in her life. Two weeks had passed since she received the letter in the mail and it was no use in putting it off, she had to do something. Lori insisted that she told no one about her boys except Thomas' sister Tina. How could Lori do this to her, how could she betray her. God knows it wasn't easy keeping it a secret.

Looking back over her life, nothing ever seemed to be easy. Living at home was like living in a hell house so as soon as the opportunity came, she moved from under her parent's roof and moved in with Thomas. Little did she know that she was already pregnant when she made the move.

What she and Thomas shared was precious for the moment but she knew that the love that they had for each other was not the kind of love that would maintain a relationship; they were not in love with each other. Thomas was much older than her. He had a good job, was a good provider and was doing well for himself. So, when she got pregnant, he was more excited about it than what she was and when they found out that she was having twins, he was tickled pink. Finding herself in a delicate way, Destiny was afraid and panicked and since Thomas had already assumed that the babies were his, he became her scapegoat; he was all that she had. She cared for him deeply but she didn't have the heart to tell him the truth. He even wanted to do right by her and marry her but she wouldn't because she knew that starting a marriage based on deceit was a recipe for disaster. So, in nine months and just turning twenty-three, she made Thomas the proud daddy of twin boys, Michael and Malone. He loved those boys.

Destiny prayed and prayed that this day would never come and she had to convince Tina to keep her mouth shut for the sake of her kids who were innocent in the matter. Maybe, just maybe when she revealed who their real father was, she would have pity on them. She hoped and prayed for that.

CHAPTER FIFTY-ONE

The wine was on ice and Emanuel was putting the finishing touches on the casserole that he had prepared for dinner. Of course, he wanted everything set up and ready when Tina got back home from the hair dresser. Emanuel had not told her that he had the day off and he was hoping that she didn't have anything else planned on her agenda for the day. He was hoping that when he sat down to talk to her, she would open up to him and let him know as to what was going on in her world; a part of her world that he obviously didn't know anything about.

"Girl this looks good" Tina said looking in the hand mirror at her hair.

"Well thanks for letting me experiment on you" Larissa laughed.

When Tina had fully recovered from her accident, Cynthia had given her a gift card to Shear Miracles to get her hair done and Tina was overly satisfied with the results. She loved the pampering that they provided and the salon wasn't too far from where she lived. She was enjoying the spare time that she had to indulge herself in the pleasures of her life after hiring two more workers to help Regina. Her business had increased immensely and everything was working out very well so with nothing else planned for the day, Tina got in her car and headed home to prepare something for dinner. The song on the radio, reminded her of Emanuel making her body miss him and it yearned for his touch.

"Stop it, don't go there" Tina said out loud and laughing as the song played on the radio taking her mind back to Emanuel and their last love session.

It was incredible. The man just had it going on, and on and on. He was the type of man that aimed to please his woman by any means necessary. Once he studied her body, he mastered how to please it. He knew what to touch, when to touch and how to touch. All the while, saying all the right things at the right moment and planting kisses in places that took her to another world. He knew when to hold back giving just the right amount of teasing but not leaving you frustrated and then giving you his all with a vengeance; a sweet vengeance.

Tina pulled in the driveway and pushed the button to open the garage and to her surprise Emanuel's car was there. Just the thought of a wall separating her from him, she couldn't seem to get out of the car fast enough.

"Hey you, where are you?" Tina yelled to Emanuel as she entered the house.

Tina knew that he was up to something because she could smell the aroma coming from the kitchen. Emanuel came around the corner and Tina dropped everything that she had and ran to be in his arms. They kissed and their bodies could tell that it had been a long time. In their minds were the same thoughts. Dinner would just have to wait.

Emanuel and Tina laid in total silence. Caressing and kissing is what was left for them to do, for their bodies were truly exhausted from the after effects of their love making. No words were spoken; they didn't have to speak. Emanuel only hoped that the rest of the evening would be as perfect as this.

"I'm hungry" Tina said looking up at him. Both realized that they had been so caught up with each other and had not eaten.

"Ok," give me a couple of minutes to warm everything up, ok?" Emanuel said getting up off the bed but not before giving her a gentle slap on the behind.

"Ok go do your thing" she said laughing and Emanuel slipped his pants on and headed downstairs.

As Emanuel passed Tina's office, he was once again annoyed by the chirping sound that came from within. He had forgotten to ask Tina about it; it always seemed to slip his mind. He opened the door and walked over to the desk and realized that the chirping sound was coming from the phone. A red light blinked on the side and Emanuel thought it was strange and reached over the desk and picked it up.

"Case closed" the voice said not even giving Emanuel time to speak.

"Excuse me" Emanuel said.

And before Emanuel could say another word, he heard a click.

"Strange shit" he said hanging up the phone and he went into the kitchen to get dinner ready.

Tina stretched out on the bed; her body feeling refreshed and renewed but her stomach was growling; she wanted food.

"Ok let's see if I can speed up the process." She said getting out of the bed and slipping on some pajamas to go downstairs.

Emanuel was just taking the wine out of the refrigerator when Tina came into the kitchen. He looked up at her and instantly he remembered as if his life had come to a pause. An unpleasant feeling came over him and he knew where he had heard those words, "Case closed." Back in the day, his boys used that term to let each other know when a job had been done; anything from an ass whipping, to something far worse than imagined. Something funky was going on with Tina and he was going to get to the bottom of it tonight. That face, that sweet face. What in the hell was she up to? He thought.

"I'll take that" Tina said reaching for the bottle of wine and looking into Emanuel's eyes.

She had seen this look on Emanuel's face before; a rather strange stare, like he was questioning something. Tina remembered the night that she had come out of her office and ran into him. The same look that he had on his face that night, was the same look that he was giving her now.

"Is something wrong?" Tina asked him.

"No" Emanuel said and walked around her to get to the table.

Tina got the vibe that something was going on; first the look that Emanuel was giving her and now the strange tone in his voice. She didn't know how to take it. As they sat down to eat, every question that she asked him, he responded with a one-word answer. The atmosphere had turned to something that was anything but pleasurable. After dinner, Tina had just loaded the dish washer and was glazing out the window. She wondered why all of a sudden Emanuel was giving her the silent treatment. The evening had been filled with such love and warmth but the atmosphere had turned cold leaving her with such an empty feeling inside. From the first time that she laid eyes on him, Emanuel had never made her feel like this. He meant the world to her and she could not imagine the thought of not having him in her life. That was something that she couldn't even conceive. The sound of his voice made her jump and she turned around and gave him a fake smile.

"We need to talk Tina." He suggested.

"Ok" Tina said looking up at him.

She put the dish cloth down and followed him into the living room. Emanuel sat on the sofa and Tina sat down next to him.

"I need to know what's going on with you Tina." Emanuel said to her. "Right after your trip I noticed a change in you but I couldn't figure it out so I didn't say anything." "Your attitude towards me hasn't changed but I just felt like something wasn't right."

Tina put her head down to avoid looking at him.

"Then a couple of days ago everything that I was thinking was confirmed when I see you in your office that night; it was as if you were a completely different person." "The crying and then what I heard you say." Emanuel explained with a frown on his face.

Tina knew exactly the night in question, and had wondered if he had heard her. *How crazy I must have looked*, she thought and she got up off the sofa. Emanuel followed her with his eyes.

"And then tonight when I came downstairs, I heard this chirping sound again." "I had heard it before so this time I went into your office and that's when I realized that the sound was coming from your phone and yes, I answered it." He admitted.

Tina turned around to face him. Her breathing pattern increased and she began to panic.

"Before I could say anything the person said case closed." "I know what that means Tina; now I need to know what the hell is going on and I need to know now." Emanuel said in a tone that she had never heard him use before.

Tina stood in front of him in total disbelief. What was she supposed to say to him; that her family was responsible for her daughter's death and now she was taking revenge out on them by paying someone else to do her dirty work? And there's Brock whom maybe would still be alive if it wasn't for her. He would probably send her straight to a nut house and throw away the key. *No*, Tina thought, she wasn't going to tell him not now or ever. She sat down next to him again and turned toward him so that they were face to face.

"Emanuel nothing's wrong ok." Tina said reaching out to caress his face but Emanuel pulled away.

"No Tina it's not ok"! "So, you're going to sit here and tell me that nothing is wrong and you want me to believe that and trust what you're telling me is the damn truth?" "Trust you after hearing that message?" "Please don't sit here and say nothing's wrong; just say you don't want to tell me ok"! Emanuel said.

"Ok your right but it's not something that's up for discussion ok, Tina admitted and she began to cry. Emanuel nodded his head in disappointment.

"Ok Tina ok" Emanuel said. "You know I love you but I can't sit around and pretend that everything is fine with you when I know that it's not"; "Something serious is going on here and I can't deal with the fact that my woman can't open up to me about something that's obviously hurting her." "I'm sorry but I can't deal with this kind of shit." Emanuel said and he got up from the sofa.

"This kind of shit got my cousin killed."

"So, what are you saying?" Tina asked him.

Emanuel turned to face her.

"I can't be in a relationship with you let alone marry you if you can't talk to me Tina"! "Do you get that"! "I'm at the hospital sometimes 24-7 and I need to know that my woman is ok and it's obvious that you're not." "And the bad part about it is you won't even give me the benefit of the doubt and trust me with whatever the hell you're dealing with"! Emanuel explained.

Tina had never heard him use this tone of voice. She wanted to grab him and tell him everything from the beginning to the end; every detail, the bad and the ugly. She wanted to kiss him and tell him that she loved him and that she didn't want to lose him but she couldn't. Tina knew in her heart that she could never tell him the things that she was keeping from him. With tears streaming down her face, she slowly took off her ring and gave it to him.

"Well, I guess this damn case is fuckin closed huh?!" Emanuel asked.

Feeling his heart scattering into a thousand pieces, Emanuel took the ring and walked out the room.

CHAPTER FIFTY-TWO

The doorbell rang and Leslie got up to see who was at the door. Her little visits of seeing Thomas had become more and more frequent and she could now say that they were finally at a good place again.

They had been separated for years and Leslie thought that maybe this time they could actually make their marriage work. She still loved him and wanted desperately to work their marriage out but she didn't want him to know just how desperate she was. After numerous failed relationships and even filing for divorce at one time, Leslie realized that none of the other guys that she had dated had come close to what she once shared with Thomas. Thomas had been so good to her and she had almost lost her mind when she found out about his infidelity. She never listened to him or let him explain his side of the story because she was so hurt; a hurt that she never wanted him to forget. They had tried quite a few times to work it out but her bitterness kept coming in between them and the fact that she couldn't have a baby with him only made matters worse.

There was a time that she wanted so much to fall out of love with him and she did try to; five guys later and a std to prove it but no matter how bad she treated him, Thomas never gave up on her. One night when she was feeling vulnerable and having her own little pity party, she let him come over and they sat down and had a pretty deceit conversation. There in her living room, she let him finally tell his side of the story and the funny thing about it was she believed every word of it. No, it didn't excuse him from his cheating but, she understood; so much for listening to a kid's story. All the wasted years trying to prove a point; that she could do what he did, and was it worth it? No not at all. So, it had been over a month since she had shared her true feelings with him to let him know that she did indeed want their marriage to work. Not only did she tell him but she showed him by making love to him like she had never done before. It was incredible and it felt like they were on their honeymoon for the first time. She loved him and those two boys and they had already discussed trying to convince Destiny on letting Michael and Malone come to Atlanta to live with them; to be a complete family.

"Hi is this Thomas Lewis' residence?" The UPS guy asked.

"Yes, it is." Leslie responded and signed for the envelope.

"Thank you, Ma'am." He said and walked away.

Leslie closed the door and was looking over the envelope to see who the sender was.

"Humm that's strange" she said.

"What's strange?" Thomas asked walking up to her and planting a kiss on her cheek.

"This is addressed to you but it doesn't say who it's from".

"Let's see." Thomas said opening up the envelope.

Enclosed was information regarding his sons, Michael and Malone, birthdates, addresses', social security numbers, birthplace, blood-types and written at the bottom of the paper were the names Destiny and Edward Spencer. Thomas flipped the envelope over to verify what Leslie had said; there was no other name on the envelope besides his.

"This is confidential information and isn't it strange he said to Leslie."

"Yes, it is strange" Leslie said back to him.

"I'll give Destiny a call later to see if she knows what this is all about." And he put the paper back in the envelope and sat it on the table.

***

Destiny kept looking at the address written on the paper.

"I know this is the correct address" she whispered to herself.

Her eyes were affixed on her surroundings; every house that they passed was like a mini mansion. Trees surrounded the area on both sides and the landscaping was absolutely breathtaking. Suddenly the cab stopped.

"This is it." The driver said.

Destiny looked down once again at the address and sure enough it was correct.

"Damn," she said looking around.

She had no idea that Tina was living like this. Destiny remembered the first time that she had met Tina. Tina had invited her and Thomas out to dinner to celebrate Thomas' promotion. She had that sophisticated rich look and was quite bougie but nice with it. That was years ago but now Destiny didn't know what type of personality she was going up against. Lori swore that Tina was the only other person that knew about her son's father so Destiny prayed that the rumor of Tina losing her memory was true.

Destiny paid the cab fare and closed the door. A grey Mercedes was settled in the garage so assuming that someone was home, Destiny walked up to the door and rang the doorbell.

"Come on please answer the door." Destiny whispered after waiting for almost ten minutes. Her nerves were a wreck and she stepped down off the step to see if there was any indication that someone was coming and then she seen someone peeping through the blinds.

CHAPTER FIFTY-THREE

Brook glanced at the speedometer and was well aware that she was driving over the speed limit. She was determined to catch up with the car ahead of her even if she had to cause an accident to do it. With no precaution at all, Brook got as close to the back of the car and hit it forcibly sending the car ahead of her almost off the shoulder of the highway. She knew that she was out of control but she didn't care anymore. Her mind was made up and Antoine was going to pay one way or the other.

Antoine gained control of the car once again and managed to get to the next exit with Brook right behind him. He had come to the conclusion that she was insane and by the way that she was driving, he could tell that she didn't care whether she killed herself or anybody else as long as she got to him. He was naive in thinking that it was safe for him to return home; Brook had lost her mind. She had spotted him at the ice cream parlor with his new girlfriend and all hell had broken loose. He managed to get his girl in the car and hastily pulled off but not before hearing Brook's choice of words that would have made even a sailor tremble.

"You know what?" Antoine said to his girl.

"What?" Veronica said still shaken up by Brook's unbelievable rage.

I'm sick of this shit, I'm not running anymore"!

Antoine slowed down and pulled into the first gas station that he came to. Brook pulled up behind him so close that he thought that she was going to rear end him again. Antoine jumped out of the car but Brook was up on him first; she went berserk on him. He tried to shield himself from her fierce blows but one caught him right dead in the head. As little as she was, Brook fought like a man and was strong as a bull. I guess that was the crazy in her Antoine thought and he fell back against his car. Antoine was always taught to never hit a woman but he was at his breaking point. He had enough of her manipulating ways, forcing him to do whatever she wanted him to do but no more. He had allowed her to destroy the relationship with the only girl that he had ever loved but no more. He knew that if he didn't take control of the situation right now, Brook would have him running for the rest of his life; embarrassing him whenever she felt the need to and that was only half of the horror. The real horror was not being able to get the look of Macy's face out of his mind and the hurt that he had caused her; that beautiful face of an angel. Antoine could no longer hold back the anger. With the image of Macy still in his head, he took one hand and grabbed Brook around her neck pushing her into the side of the building. The grip disabled her from moving and with his other hand, already balled up in a fist, was ready to hit if she dared to make an attempt to lash out.

"Look you crazy bitch, leave me alone before I break your neck do you hear me?" Antoine whispered through gritting teeth.

Tension had built up inside of him and with his hand still around her neck, he pulled her to him and then pushed her with such force that she lost her balance and fell to the ground.

Brook could see the hatred in Antoine's eyes. Every vein that lay beneath his skin seemed to protrude. His facial expression changed to something that Brook had never seen before; not with him or any other man that allowed her to manipulate them. Antoine was no longer the sweet boy that she could boss around like a little puppy dog. He was dead serious and Brook believed his every word.

Antoine backed away but never took his eyes off of her and by the time Brook got up off the ground, he was in his car headed for the highway.

Brook didn't know which one shocked her the most; the words that had come out of Antoine's mouth or the force behind his push. She didn't know that he had it in him.

"I guess this is the end of that." She said wiping her clothes off.

"Why did this keep happening?" She asked herself.

In the beginning she was motivated by selfish intentions but those intentions left her falling in love with Antoine. She tried to convince herself that maybe in time he would grow to love her back but now he to, hated her. Brook thought that Antoine would give her the fairytale relationship that she longed for but once again she would have to put up another brick wall to hide the hurt that now occupied another place in her heart.

"Oh well," she thought, *"Fuck him too, next."*

CHAPTER FIFTY-FOUR

The snow was coming down harder when Tina got on the highway and the visibility was getting pretty bad. It had been five months since her break up with Emanuel and Cynthia had taken her to the Poconos for a weekend getaway and had freely given her shoulder to cry on. It was getting unbearable for Tina to stay at the house weekend after weekend alone, so when Cynthia suggested the little trip, Tina jumped on it with no hesitation.

The first couple of weeks after the breakup were the worst. Depression had set in and Tina found herself crying all the time. No matter what she tried to do, her mind lingered on Emanuel; she missed hearing his voice and smelling his scent. Not only was he in her head but her body was missing him to. She needed his touch; his body close to hers. How was she supposed to get over this man? She kept asking herself.

The break up brought back memories of her high school sweet heart Billy Walton. He had broken her heart when it got back to her that he was grinding on the wall at a party with some girl. She thought that she would never get over it but then one day she finally listened to her grandmother's advice and took control of the situation and Billy Walton became a distant stranger. *It's funny,* Tina thought, when you're young, you think older people are like aliens from Mars who speak an unfamiliar language but as she got older, she realized that her grandmother was right and her advice was always on time. But unlike Billy, the love she had for Emanuel wasn't puppy love it was real genuine love; the kind of love that runs deep down inside and Tina found herself drowning in her own self-pity. Why couldn't he just go with the flow of things? She was fine. If he loved her so much, how could he just walk away from her but then again, looking at things from his perspective Tina knew that he had a point, even a right to feel the way that he felt. Still, she wanted him back but she knew that she could never tell him how dysfunctional her family was or her little secrets. Would he even want to be with her if he knew half of the stuff that she had done?

Then there's Destiny. The look on that poor girls face when she had paid her a visit the day after Emanuel and her had broken up. Tina couldn't believe how close she came to almost blowing it all because of Emanuel's ass. She had to sit through an hour of Destiny's begging and pleading for her silence as she revealed the truth about her repeated rape by her own father. My God, it was enough to make you sick. She tried to convince Destiny that she was as dumb as a door knob as to what she was talking about, all the while hurting for her and trying to conceal her own hurt all at the same time.

"Oh well" Tina mumbled; the paper had already been sent out by the time Destiny had paid her a visit. It was a bad situation and her heart went out to Destiny but the fact still remained, her brother was partly to blame for her daughter's death and there was no getting around that.

"Tell the truth or someone else will" Tina mumbled as her grandmother would say so as far as she was concerned, her brother deserved to know the truth. Now the only thing that she could do was wait and see how everything played out.

Tina pulled up in the driveway and she could feel the loneliness settling in once again. Would she ever be able to get over this breakup, she sat in her car and wondered.

***

"Ok it's a boy." Emanuel said smiling as he lifted the baby boy up so that he could be introduced to his mother. Emanuel was relieved that everything had went well for the two of them. He had been paged a little past midnight when Samantha Stevens was brought in. Her doctor was on his way but her delivery had become difficult when the umbilical cord became wrapped around the neck of the newborn. Emanuel had worked frantically to free the cord and finally little Christian, all eight pounds of him, was out of danger.

Emanuel was so happy and as he left the delivery room he thought of Tina. Five months without her was torture. He wished that he could call her but he had made a promise to himself that he was not going to try to contact her no matter how much he missed her. He loved her but hated the fact that she would not open up to him. It was so frustrating. He tried everything to get her out of his mind; hanging out at the hospital even more so and grabbing a beer with some of his colleagues after a shift ended. Anything was better than staying at home and home these days was a small apartment that he was now renting from a friend.

One night he went to the club with the boys; something that he had not did for some time. When the ladies found out that he was single, and a doctor, they were on him like rabbits in heat. The ladies showed no shame and they let Emanuel know up front that they were more than willing to take him home for the night. One in particular was Gwendolyn Knight. Gwen was fine as a bottle of wine and was a practicing attorney in the New Jersey area. She was born and raised in Barbados and had a sexy accent. Emanuel had to agree that the conversation between them was mutually enjoyable and the offer that she made him was one that he could not refuse and it led him straight to her bed.

The sexual healing gave him what his body needed and he had to admit that Gwen definitely had skills. The woman had no shame at all and when she told him that she had not had sex in a while he believed her for her actions spoke louder than her words. The sex was only a temporary solution for his loneliness and what had transpired between him and Gwen was indeed a mistake on his part. It gave him the relief that he needed physically, but emotionally he felt even worse.

While Gwen lay sleeping, Emanuel put on his clothes feeling guilty as hell. This was a first for him. He could not remember a time when he felt guilty after having sex while in or out of a relationship. Maybe it was because he knew that Tina had definitely made a permanent mark in his life and on his heart.

Emanuel turned around and stared at Gwen. She had made it perfectly clear that she would not feel bad in the morning and he slowly walked over to her and sat on the side of the bed waking her.

"I had a nice time Emanuel," she said still half asleep. Please call me sometimes ok" Gwen said moving and stretching her body in a sexy way.

Emanuel leaned over and planted a kiss on her forehead.

"I will" he said to her.

CHAPTER FIFTY-FIVE

Destiny picked up the pair of sweats off the floor and sat down on the edge of the bed. *What a mess to deal with right around the holiday,* she thought. After receiving the second letter warning her that her boy's true identities would be revealed and the call from Thomas asking about a paper that he had received in the mail, Destiny knew that she had to tell him the truth and she needed to do it right away. Dealing with the truth was harder than what she had ever imagined and when she told Thomas about Michael and Malone, she would never forget the look on his face. It had torn her to pieces to tell him but in spite of the devastating news, he still loved Michael and Malone as his own.

Their plan was to protect the boys as best as they could by not revealing the true identity of their father so they told them half of the truth. The story was that their real father had been killed in a car accident. The news had hit the twins hard; each handling it in their own way. Michael was holding everything in and not showing any emotion at all while Malone rebelled in every way that he could think of; even resorting to using and selling drugs. Destiny just couldn't understand why Tina would want to destroy the lives of two innocent children and why did she act like she didn't recognize her. She could convince her brother of having clean hands but she would never be able to convince her. The look on her face when she opened the door that day told it all. Destiny got up and laid the sweats neatly on the bed. It was getting late and it was almost time to meet Thomas at the court house.

Thomas had arrived a half hour early which had given him plenty of time to try and relax. It wasn't easy acknowledging the fact that your son could spend time in jail. *Yes, his son*, he thought. He had accepted the truth and as far as he was concern, Michael and Malone were his sons even though they didn't have the same blood running through their veins; but the love that he had for them ran just as deep. Destiny had mentioned that she thought Tina had something to do with it but after talking with Diane, who kept him up to date on things, Tina didn't know her left from her right and besides Thomas knew that Tina would never ever do such a thing; she has a heart.

If only Destiny had been up front with him from the very beginning this wouldn't be happening but he understood how difficult it must have been for her. *"Damn, that's just the way life goes sometimes,"* he thought and through the door came Destiny with a worried look that a mother displays when her child is in trouble.

"Hi Thomas" Destiny said and Thomas gave her a hug and she hugged him back. She sure was grateful that he had left that wife of his at home. It was one less thing that she didn't need to stress over.

"Thomas what if...." Destiny began to say but Thomas cut her off.

"We're going to think positive, ok?" He said thinking about Mommy and what she would say.

"Ok." She said still feeling jittery.

"Come on let's go in" Thomas said taking a deep breath and placing his arm around Destiny's waist as they headed to the court room. He too was thinking what she was about to ask. Think positive, he thought.

After three hours had passed, the courtroom doors opened. Destiny's face was covered with tears as she held onto Thomas to keep from falling. This was something that no parent wants their kids to go through especially over one stupid mistake. This one mistake had cost their son two years of his life and to see him handcuffed and taken out of the courtroom like that had broken their heart. They could do nothing to help him but pray and thank God that he didn't get a longer sentence.

It seemed like it took forever just to walk to the car. Thomas opened the door and helped Destiny in and as he walked to the other side of the car, he hoped that she didn't feel him because he was shaking like a leaf. If he didn't hurry up and get her home, he was sure to break down right in front of her.

"Malone's going to be alright ok." He said to her breaking the silence. He took her hand into his and with all his might he tried to convince himself of it too.

"He's strong and determined, he'll be alright." Thomas said again.

"Our son is going to prison for two years Thomas." "A lot can happen to a young boy in two years." She said and she began to cry.

Thomas couldn't respond to that. He squeezed her hand and said nothing else.

Destiny was angry and she wanted to cry out. She wanted to scream to Thomas that his sister had done this. A young boy's life was about to change and it was all because of her. No, she couldn't put all of the blame on Tina because Malone should have known better but he was lashing out because he was hurting and the stupid ass Judge couldn't see that so as far as she was concerned, Tina and the judge could go straight to hell.

CHAPTER FIFTY-SIX

Monday had finally arrived and Diane found herself up earlier than usual getting ready for her second job interview. Shell's Inc. had called her back again and after much prayer, she had never felt such enthusiasm that gave her the go out and tackle the world attitude. She had been down for so long and she knew that there was nowhere to go but up.

"No more feeling sorry for myself, think positive." She whispered. "That's what Mommy would say."

Still admiring herself in the mirror, Diane had to give herself props where props were due. The trips to the gym had the weight coming off like melting butter; she felt her sexy again. Things were finally coming around and she was going to take everything that was coming her way. I guess you could say that Steve had a little something to do with this new attitude. He was good for her at this particular time in her life. He was her fixer upper and he took her mind off of all the stuff that was surrounding her. They were taking it very slow, nothing serious as of yet but who knows what he would or could bring to her table.

Diane picked up her keys off the table and said a quick prayer for her nephew. Malone wasn't a bad kid, a little too smart with his mouth but not bad. Hopefully the money that Tina had contributed towards Malone's legal expenses was enough for Thomas to hire a good attorney. Diane took another look in the mirror and then she headed out for her interview. Within two hours, Diane was on her way to see Tina and to tell her the news about Malone.

Tina sat at her desk and glanced up to see Diane pulling in the parking lot. She was so tired of pretending to like her, and the rest of them, and she hoped that it wasn't starting to show, at least not yet. Sometimes she would say things and as soon as it came out of her mouth, she knew that it was a mistake so most of the time, she would blame her outburst on her breakup with Emanuel or a medical condition that had resulted from her accident. She was really having trouble controlling herself. Whatever, Tina thought. She hated her sister and wished that she could tell her and then tell her why.

"Hey" Diane said as she came in the door.

"What's going on?" Tina asked pretending to work.

"Well Malone got two years."

"That's what happens when you're out there selling drugs." Tina said still pretending to work.

"*There she goes again.*" Diane thought.

"Tina, where is your compassion?" "That boy went off because he found out that Thomas is not his father you know that." "You know how close those boys are to him."

"He knew right from wrong and he choose to do wrong, Diane." "Now he has to deal with the consequences of his actions like we all do." She said looking directly at Diane. "I have a lot of work here."

"Ok and you have a nice day Tina." Diane told her and then she walked out the door. Diane couldn't believe Tina's nonchalant attitude. She had been saying some pretty nasty things lately but today was the worse. Diane was glad that she had not mentioned not getting the job which would have probably given Tina another reason to insult her. Diane wasn't in the mood to hear it. She knew Tina was dealing with a lot. The breakup between her and Emanuel and Lord knows what effects being in a coma had done to her. Diane wanted to talk to her on more than one occasion but she dreaded getting her head chopped off in the process. Tina was becoming more and more like a person that she once knew; herself.

As soon as the door closed, Tina laid back in her chair and threw the pen on the desk. She was elated to know that Thomas had to be one unhappy camper right now but her nephew going to prison was not her idea. Their stupid mother should have kept her mouth shut but no, I guess her conscience had got in the way. Tina got up to pour herself a drink. She had hit all of them where it hurt the most and as far as she was concerned, her mission had been accomplished but wasn't this supposed to make her happy? Wasn't it supposed to fill a void in her life and for a moment it did; but now she found herself just as unhappy as they probably were. *"Come on girl, get yourself together she told herself."* This is supposed to be a reason to celebrate and Tina poured herself another drink to calm her thoughts. The drink wasn't helping but she knew what would. Shopping always made her feel better so she decided to treat herself to something real special after all, it was almost Christmas. Tina put the glass down and got ready to go to the mall and that familiar voice once again crept into her head.

Mommy said, "You won't find happiness while bringing misery to others"

Tina picked up the glass and threw it and reminded herself to get some more because she didn't have that many left.

It was a cold night and Tina thought that maybe she would pick up a few Christmas gifts while she was at the mall. As she approached the entrance, she could see that it wasn't going to be easy getting a parking space. The mall was packed with parked cars and Tina found herself riding around for fifteen minutes before finding a spot. Once inside, it was crowded as expected and every store seemed to have their own gimmicks in trying to sell their products. Tina's sudden craving for ice cream must have been contagious because she found herself waiting in a long line admiring parents with their little one's dress in their best to meet Santa Claus. She smiled at the little faces as they lit up with wonder and amazement.

"Ma'am may I help you?" The guy behind the counter asked and Tina politely gave him her order and seconds later she was holding a double dip of eggnog ice cream and saying thank you and Merry Christmas. Then Tina's eyes caught a glimpse of what was straight before her. Her mind was telling her to move but her legs were having no part of it. Her eyes were affixed on the couple that was straight in front of her. That beautiful smile that she had fallen in love with was now entertaining someone new. Walking arm in arm with a woman, an attractive woman at that, Tina froze. It was no way she could avoid him from seeing her; Emanuel was too close but looking in the opposite direction.

Emanuel laughed as Patty shared another one of her corny jokes. When they were together, they acted more like teenagers. That's what he liked about her the most; He could just chill with her. They were so opened with each other and they could talk about anything. He thought that he had that with Tina. If only she would have opened up to him and shared what was going on with her maybe he could have helped her deal with it. It was one thing that Emanuel could honestly say about Ms. Patty; he sure was glad that she had stood him up that night or they would have been singing to a different tune. She still looked good and she was laughing more and crying less but there were still times when Emanuel would see a blank stare and he knew that once again she was pondering on the night that she almost lost her life.

Emanuel gazed forward and the smile that covered his face left the second his eyes met hers. He was as surprised to see her as she was to see him. Tina quickly glanced at the woman and then her eyes met Emanuel's again.

"*Who is this heifer?*" Her eyes asked, and Emanuel must have read them.

"Tina how are you, oh this is Patricia from Silver Care." Emanuel explained pointing his finger toward Pat. Tina didn't say a word.

"*Who the hell is Patricia?*" Tina thought. She was not prepared for this.

Hi it's nice to meet you." Pat said and Tina managed a smile.

"Hi" Tina said looking at Pat and then there was seconds of silence. *"How awkward is this?"* Tina thought.

"Well nice seeing you Emanuel and Merry Christmas" Tina said looking at him and with nothing else to say she walked away.

Emanuel watched her walk away and not knowing what to say, he said nothing.

"Well," Patty said looking at Emanuel. "I don't know how she really feels about you but the look on her face makes it plan and clear, she just seen the man that she loves with another woman, that's not good." "It's obvious that you still have feelings for her too." "You still love her don't you?" Patty asked him.

"Yeah, I do." Emanuel said.

"Then you need to fix it." "She's a beautiful woman Emanuel."

"Yeah" Emanuel said as he watched Tina disappear into the crowd.

Tina walked as fast as she could to get the hell out of the mall. Her heart was beating a thousand beats and the tears that she could no longer hold back began to flow down her face. She knew eventually that one day she would run into Emanuel but she thought in a naive kind of way, that when she did, he would have been alone. That would have given her a little more control of the situation and there was no doubt in her mind that the situation would have turned out differently. She just wasn't prepared to see him with another woman so soon. Emanuel was a handsome man and she should have known that sooner or later some woman was going to grab him up.

"God this is hard," she thought as she made her way out of the mall and dumping her ice cream into the first trash bin that she came to. Five months and he's out shopping and laughing with some bitch while she was at home crying her heart out; Spending nights alone wondering what he was doing, wanting to just hear his voice; Wanting to wake up in the morning yearning for his touch and wanting to feel him next to her. Another piece of her heart

felt like it had just broken.

"Damn you Emanuel" she said.

Tina snuggled under her coat and walked back to her car wondering how she would pick up the pieces from this mess.

"Mommy said, "It would be days like this"

"Damn you, Emanuel," she said again.

CHAPTER FIFTY-SEVEN

The ride home was quiet and Pat noticed that Emanuel seemed to be deep in thought and she would guess that Tina was the center of his attention. Funny how things turn out, she thought. At one time she desired this man so bad and, on several occasions, she was going to tell him and then show him but for some reason it was never the right moment. Emanuel was a woman's dream; handsome, intelligent, and just the way he carried himself let you know that he knew how to treat a woman. It was something about his look that was hard but gentle which made him even more attractive; and his body. Lord help me! Pat thought.

Going through the ordeal with her husband seemed to change her perspective on things especially when it came to men. Pat's desire wasn't there anymore not for Emanuel or any other man. She needed time to heal mentally and love was sure to come again but in no way was she ready for it now. Being there for Emanuel as a friend was enough for her and from the look on his face, she could definitely see that his heart belonged to someone else.

Emanuel pulled up to Pat's house and he gently kissed her on the cheek and they said their good-nights. Patty turned and waved good-bye and he watched her go into the house. As Emanuel pulled off, he reached down to get his phone and dialed Tina's number but got no answer. His sudden urge to hear her voice was over powered by his own promise to himself that he would not try to contact her. He could tell by the look on her face that she assumed Pat was his woman. He knew that the assumption of the female mind could be dangerous and he wanted to set the record straight. Why should it even matter he thought but he already knew the answer; he loved her. Emanuel dialed Tina's number again but still got no answer so with a strong rush of adrenaline and against his better judgment, he made a u turn and decided to go and pay her a visit.

It seemed like hours had passed and still there was no sign of Tina. Emanuel started the car up letting it reach a comfortable temperature and then he turned it off again. He glanced around occasionally and wondered if he looked like a fool because he was definitely feeling like one. Maybe the cold was freezing his brain and taking away his good common sense, he thought. He started the car up and glanced around the area once more hoping that maybe Tina would pull up but she didn't so without hesitation, he pulled off cold and disappointed.

Tina drove down the highway with every emotion and thought taking control of her. She wanted to go anywhere except home so she kept driving. She called Cynthia and got her voice message. She called Robin, she even called Diane but no one was picking up. She wanted to talk to somebody, anybody that would help get the voices out of her head. *"I'm not crazy"* she kept telling herself. The tears were now blocking her vision and Tina could barely see the vacancy sign that shone outside the motel as she pulled up in the parking lot. She was physically and emotionally drained and thought it was best to stay the night there. Once Tina got inside, she showed her license and kindly gave the woman her debit card. She could only imagine what was going through the mind of the woman behind the counter for Tina's eyes were red and swollen from crying. The woman asked was everything ok and Tina nodded yes.

The night was long and Tina tossed and turned as she struggled to find a place of peace. Staying awake left her with visions that haunted her; visions of Emanuel and that damn smile. The giggles shared between him and his new love; the bitch who hung on his arm. He was supposed to be her happy ever after; what happened. With sleep came the nightmares of her daughter. An image with no face yet she knew it was Macy. By her hair, her smell, by the way she moved in the wind. She didn't know which one was worse. It seemed as if all the pain in the world was cast upon her. Then there were the diaries. Every word was like a curse that possessed her mind. Her heart overflowed with hate. She could hear Macy's voice explaining what she had wrote; her heart tugging in two different directions and finally, her mind and body could take no more and Tina fell into sleep. There she talked to the one person that would make sense of it all; hearing his voice, him listening without judging. A peaceful calm, she liked it.

As the sun peaked its way through the sides of the curtains, Tina looked around and tried to gather her thoughts. She was instantly reminded of the night of hell and was grateful that she had survived it. She got up and took a quick shower and she remembered her dream. She knew what she had to do. The one person that would get her back on track; she had to talk to Pastor Peterson. He would listen and he would tell her how to fix things and if he couldn't, she would surely lose her mind.

Tina poured the bubble bath under the running water and the mist had created a relaxing atmosphere. She released the belt from around her waist letting her robe fall to the floor. Her body needed this, but that wasn't all that it was in need of. Reaching over the counter, Tina retrieved her glass of wine and slowly stepped into the tub; the water felt amazing as she leaned back and let her body rest up against the tub.

The sit down with Pastor Peterson was the remedy that she needed. She held nothing back; she had told him everything. From the diaries to Mack, the nightmares of Macy, losing the love of her life, and the road of revenge that she had choose to take; he listened. She felt that her soul was becoming more and more satisfied as she pulled out her inner secrets, her hurts, and heartaches; it wasn't easy but it felt good to release all of the stuff that she had allowed to build up inside her. The weight had been lifted and she believed that everything would be alright. She loved Pastor Peterson. He made her realize that the tugging at her heart every time that she did something to her family was her conscience and that's why she wasn't truly happy. It satisfied her flesh but, in her heart, she knew it was wrong. Her mission now was to try to repair some of the damage that she had done. She could make things a little easier for her family as far as what money could do but the rest had to run its course. She loved her daughter and her heart ached for her but Macy was gone and it was nothing that she could do to bring her back. She had to get on with her life and start taking care of herself for the sake of her own sanity. Her bitterness and implacable ways had caused enough hurt and she would just have to leave the situation in the hands of the man upstairs.

As Tina took a sip of her wine, she knew that it wasn't going to be easy but the hardest part was now over. She realized that it was imperative for her to accept the fact that what she had done was wrong no matter how much she may have thought that her family deserved it, she had to ask God for forgiveness, she had to forgive those that she felt wronged her and her daughter and she had to forgive herself. Forgiveness was a powerful thing. Tina took a deep breath and let out a sigh of relief. For once, her mind, body and spirit felt free.

Mommy said, "Vengeance is mine, thus saith the Lord, I will repay".

Yes Mommy, I hear you loud and clear. Tina smiled.

CHAPTER FIFTY-EIGHT

Tina tried not to stare but Robert looked so pitiful and so vulnerable. It was obvious that he had not shaved in quite a while and his clothes hung on his body; a far cry from what he used to look like. Robert stepped aside letting Tina through the door and as she glanced around the room, Diane had been right. Robert was doing worse than what she thought. The place was a mess and it smelled like the trash had not been taken out in weeks.

They sat and he talked. Tina thought that he was going to bawl right in front of her and the more that she listened to him, the more she felt like she wanted to bawl too. So, she held onto her strong persona showing her brother that he was indeed the weakest link or was he, she thought. In all the years that she had known him, he never bowed down to anybody; He had too much pride for that so the load had to be extreme for him to even get up the nerve to ask her for anything.

"Well, I don't think that I can do it, so I can't make any promises." Tina said sarcastically but she had every intention of giving Robert what he needed. She was giving him back his money. She had to take into consideration that she was the reason why his life was in such a mess in the first place; it was the least that she could do. Before she had intervened, Robert had made a good life for himself. His business was taking him to heights that he probably had never imagined so she felt like she had to give him his life back in spite of his harsh behavior toward her daughter. Now he was sitting before her as humble as he could be. I guess sometimes being knocked down is the only way to get you to come back up with some sense and a better way of treating people, Tina thought. His whole attitude had changed. Tina got up to leave.

"Tina" Robert said, and Tina turned to face him. "Thank you for whatever you decide to trust me with." He told her.

"Ok" she said.

Tina walked quickly to her car with mixed emotions. Yes, she was trying to change and it was going to take some time but in no way did she feel sorry for her brother. She felt some kind of way for being put into a situation whereas she felt like she had to retaliate against him and all of the rest of them. The whole situation was so sad for her. A knot had formed in her throat and Tina was glad that she had worn her sunglasses which helped hide the tears that were now running down her face.

***

A couple of weeks later, Robert stood in his kitchen holding a cashier's check for three hundred and fifty thousand dollars that he had received from his baby sister Tina. In his dire desperation, he had finally gotten the nerve to ask her for help not believing that she would even consider it.

While in a drunken stupor, Robert had lost track of time and had forgotten about the mail that was delivered federal express and he threw it on the kitchen table not realizing what was in it. He didn't care anymore and besides, all the mail that he was getting were bills that he couldn't pay. He looked at the check again to make sure that his eyes were not playing tricks on him and noticed the date on the note, two weeks had already passed. Tears began to swell in his eyes, he was feeling the guilt. It was he who had Tina's car rigged which caused the accident that put her in a coma; it was he who turned his back on her, refusing to even acknowledge that she was his sister and it was he who had taken his wrath out on an innocent child, his own niece who was the next best thing to getting back at her. He would never know what had actually changed Tina's mind but he damn sure would never forget it.

Robert sat down on the sofa and began to cry. He had taken a long look at himself and he didn't like what he saw nor was he proud of the things that he had done. Mommy used to say that money wasn't the root of all evil it was the love of it and he had done a whole lot of wrong for just that. My God he thought, he was seeing it up close and personal. Robert put his head down. He had not prayed in years but this had brought him to his knees.

Robert got up and went into the bathroom. He took a towel and wiped the tears from his face. He opened up the medicine cabinet and took out his shaving cream and his shaver. This was the end of his first beginning and now his second beginning had begun.

Mommy said, *"If you get knocked down just get your behind back up and make it work."*

Robert was thinking, *"Mommy you were right about everything!"*

CHAPTER FIFTY-NINE

Diane was hysterical and all Tina could make of it was that it was something wrong with Brook and she needed to get to the hospital as soon as possible.

"Ok Diane I'm on my way." Tina said over the phone.

Twenty minutes later, Tina was pulling up in the parking lot near the emergency entrance. She grabbed her pocketbook sending some of her things falling to the floor of the car, but with no time to waste, Tina left them there and hurried to the receptionist desk where she was directed to the intensive care unit.

Tina pulled the curtain back and shock overtook her. Her eyes were drawn to the figure lying on the bed and she quickly held onto the railing to keep her balance. Diane sat next to the bed, with her eyes closed and her body in a position to pray.

"My God this can't be" Tina whispered.

Brook had been beaten severely; the left side of her face smashed in and unrecognizable. Dry blood smeared the pillow under her head and her right eye was so swollen, that Tina didn't think it was possible for a human eye to look like that.

"Who did this, Diane" Tina whispered.

Diane lifted her head up and reached out for Tina and Tina took hold of her hand.

"Antoine, his name is Antoine." Diane answered her. "Look what he did to my baby." Diane said crying and caressing Brook's hand.

"I don't know any of the details yet but the police told me that he didn't even try to resist arrest; he waited for the cops to get there." "Look what he did to her." Diane said.

Tina felt a sickness to her stomach and both were startled at the sound of the officer's voice.

"Diane Casey?" The officer said in a low voice.

"Yes" Diane said between sobs.

Diane got up from the chair and she and Tina held on to each other and followed the officer out into the corridor.

"Ma'am your daughter's ex-boyfriend, Antoine White, will be officially charged with attempted murder." The officer explained.

"Boyfriend, my daughter wasn't seeing him." Diane explained with a confused look on her face.

"That's in the statement that he gave us." "Apparently, after he had broken off the relationship, your daughter went to his apartment and an argument started." "Witnesses said that he told her to leave and when she refused, he began hitting her." The officer stated.

"This doesn't make any sense." "Antoine used to date my nie." Diane said as her voice dropped to a mere whisper.

"Was she about to say niece," Tina thought.

"Oh, Dear God" Diane said and she managed to walk away.

"Sorry Sir" Tina said to the officer and she went to console her sister.

Tina didn't know what to do or what to think. Seeing Emanuel in the mall with his woman, and now seeing Brook beaten to a pulp by this Antoine White was taken a toll on her emotional state. She knew that she had to be strong for her sister even though she felt like she was losing the battle herself. Her thoughts were wandering all over the place; and one place was focused on Antoine White so while family and friends were gathering at the hospital with Diane, Tina found the opportunity to slip away and go home to get some sleep but that was not her only motive. She had some very important calls to make and she wanted to make them first thing in the morning.

After tossing and turning most of the night, Tina found herself awakened to the sound of heavy rain and was surprised to see that it was already morning. Still feeling exhausted, she had to find a way to push through her exhaustion in order to see this, Antoine White. Having good friends in the DA's office had made it possible so now she was preparing to see him in the early afternoon which give her plenty of time to get back to the hospital with Diane. Tina hoped that maybe Antoine White could shed some light on Macy and maybe he knew what could have set her off and snatched her will to live.

Diane lifted her head up and thought that she heard Brook say something. Again, Brook mumbled some words and Diane gently rubbed the side of her face. Brook had finally come to and Diane was so relieved to finally hear her baby's voice.

"It wasn't my fault." Brook whispered to her mother.

Diane listened carefully as Brook tried to explain what had happened. As Diane listened, tears streamed down Brooks face and Diane tried to console her with words of comfort.

"Baby just try to rest; we can talk about it later ok." Diane said to her.

"I didn't go there to cause trouble Mother I went to apologize to him, I did." "For once I wanted to do something right." Brook said. "He wouldn't listen to me Mother." "He just kept hitting me over and over." Brook explained.

Diane believed that Brook was on the road to turning her life around to become the person that she knew she could be. Brook had gotten up early two Sundays ago and surprised her by going to church. Diane could definitely see the change in her; a change that convinced Diane that what her daughter was telling her was the truth. What Diane couldn't understand was the rage that had caused Antoine to do something like this.

Mommy said, "Sometimes a person can bring out the worse in you, if you let them."

And Diane put her head down and began to pray again.

CHAPTER SIXTY

Emanuel sat down to enjoy his cup of coffee as he read the morning newspaper. It wasn't long before his mind drifted to Tina and he wondered where she could have been the night he had waited patiently outside her house. He had called her a thousand times and she still had not returned his calls. Was she seeing someone? Did seeing him with Pat push her in the arms of someone else? As fine as Tina was, he knew that it wasn't going to take long for some dude to push up on her and the thought only made him feel even more uptight. He put the paper down with an attitude. He felt like such an idiot for reaching out to her and the couple of days off only added to his misery. He had to get back to work; at least it would give him less time to sit around and wonder about what she was doing and who she was doing it with.

***

Tina tried to relax. The story that Antoine had told her was overwhelming and she didn't like what was building up inside of her again. He went into details about how he had met Macy, their relationship together and what he believed caused Macy to relapse. He cried like a baby when he described the hurt on Macy's face when she realized that he had slept with Brook and Brook making matters worse by rubbing it in and giving Macy explicit details of their night of simple lust. He told Tina how Brook hated Macy and how she purposely set out to hurt her by using him and he hated her for it. He told her how he left home to get away from Brook and how she attacked him at the gas station that day. So, when she showed up at his place unannounced insisting that they talk he snapped under pressure. As he told his story, Antoine was so remorseful and very apologetic for what he had done. Sharing how he was raised and even he couldn't believe what he had done. Tina believed that his story was authentic and there was no reason to reprimand him for his actions for fifteen minutes of being out of control, was going to cost him dearly.

Tina didn't know what to think of her niece. Brook was a very vindictive person but no human being deserved to be beaten like that not even her. Once again Tina found herself in a place where she had tried so hard to get out of. Depression was creeping in, leaving her with a feeling of such hopelessness. Dwelling on it wasn't going to change anything so she managed to make it upstairs, got in her bed and went to sleep.

She sat in the church waiting for the bride to make her grand entrance. She thought it funny that no one was in the church but her. As she stood to greet the bride, Tina's smile turned to a grimly frown for the bride that walked down the aisle was a grown woman in nature with a little girl's face. Tina stood there crippled with fear; she screamed; for the face that she seen was the face of Macy.

Tina jumped up out of her sleep; breathe she told herself. Startled, she reached for her phone but remembered that it had been days since she had used it; she could not find it. She wanted desperately to call Emanuel but remembered that she and he were no more. Her emotions overtook her and Tina held her head in her hands and wept. She wept for her daughter, for Brook, and for the love of her life.

***

Cynthia pulled up just in time to see Tina getting in her car. She knew that her best friend was going through some things and the news that she was about to tell her wasn't going to make matters any better. This was a bad time for everyone.

"Oh God I don't feel like being bothered with no one," Tina thought when she seen Cynthia walking toward her. Still feeling depressed, Tina had not talked to anyone in days but she had finally managed to get herself up and dressed so that she could pick up some things from the store.

"Hey Cyn, what's up girl?" Tina asked after rolling down the window.

"Ting I'll drive move over." "Everyone's been trying to get in touch with you, why haven't you answered your phone?" Cynthia asked.

"I can't find it." Tina responded.

"Here dial your number." Cynthia suggested handing Tina her phone. Tina took the phone and dialed her number and a faint sound came from under the seat. Tina stuck her hand under the seat and retrieved her phone, glasses and some change that had obviously fallen out of her purse.

"Got it" Tina said.

"Ting" Cynthia said.

"Yes" Tina said still looking at her phone.

"Brook died last night."

Tina closed her eyes and thought of the dream that she had a couple of nights before.

Mommy said, "If you dream of a wedding it's going to be a funeral."

"You ok?" Cynthia asked.

"I will be." Tina responded.

The ride to Diane's house seemed to take forever and as Tina and Cynthia approached the house, people had parked their cars along both sides of the street when word had spread about Brook's passing. Tina made her way into the house and Diane broke down and cried after seeing her. The two were once again united like back in the day; tragedy bringing them together again.

"I'm so sorry," Tina said and she held Diane tight.

"I'm sorry too." Diane said between sobs.

They comforted each other and now the grieving process had begun.

Diane cried confessing that she had done some things and begged Tina for her forgiveness. Tina never questioned these things and never acknowledged what she already knew because in her opinion, Diane was already living in her own private hell so there was no need to. She seen her pain, and felt her hurt so she took Diane in her arms and rocked her as if she was a baby, reassuring her that everything would be ok. Tina felt numb. Love again, hate again. It was an emotional rollercoaster.

Tina pulled the quilt over Diane who was finally resting quietly. She had assured her sister that she would help with making the arrangements for Brook's home going service and now Tina was left alone to ponder with her thoughts. Brook's confession to her mother had taken Tina by surprise and she found it mind boggling to think that after all the years that had passed, she was blamed for something that Brook had done. She was the one who had told Thomas's wife about his affair. Years of animosity held against her, destroying a bind between brother and sister; wasted years.

Tina wanted so much to call Emanuel. She wanted him to console her and hold her and tell her that everything would be alright. Tina put her head down on the table and began to cry. This was becoming a daily ritual for her.

Robert, Thomas and Cynthia had arrived almost at the same time and Tina was relieved to see them. Robert had given her a hug so tight that she thought that she would stop breathing and Thomas was a little friendlier than usual. Cynthia was nice enough to go and get some chicken from Popeye's but no one seemed to have an appetite. Cynthia like always, managed to change the mood by bringing up something funny that Robert had done when they were younger. She always had a crush on him but after high school, she had gone off to college and both became involved with other people. Cynthia's personality had a way of bringing out the light in any dark situation and Tina wondered how she would have reacted, if she had told her about everything that had happened. Tina wouldn't find out until later that while in college, Cynthia had lost her virginity to Robert and he had lost his heart to her and his trust in women because of her; Cynthia had broken his heart. They talked and laughed at childhood memories and it felt like the good old times before life had changed their course. Tina wondered how different things would have been if Mommy was still alive.

Diane had awakened and was feeling a little better but still not in the mood to talk funeral so they sat in the living room and watched tv. As Tina looked at her sister, they definitely had something in common. Both had lost their only child. One had lost her life and the other had taken her life. What a tragedy, a lost.

Mommy said, "This is not our permanent home, so we're all on borrowed time."

CHAPTER SIXTY-ONE

Mommy was the real character in the family. Sweet Annie Lee, Tina's grandmother on her mother's side. She was the best thing since apple pie and Tina's mother resembled her a lot but they were nothing alike. Tina and her siblings loved their parents but Mommy provided them with the outward love and affection that they needed emotionally. They loved her like their mother and they also learned a lot from her. It was her stories and some good sound advice that got them through some tough times and she always had an answer for you know matter how difficult the situation presented itself. She had a strong will and a close relationship with the Lord and was always saying quotes.

Mommy spoiled her grandbabies every chance she got and those chances came on birthdays and holidays. Oh, how they loved her. After the accident, Tina would often see images of a woman's face but could never put a name to it until everything came back to her the night at the hotel. It was Mommy's face that Tina seen and Mommy's voice that she heard. When Mommy died, the kids were never the same. She lived a ripe old age of 87 and went peacefully in her sleep.

Precious memories do the soul good and Tina thought of her parents too. They were strict and they expected the best from their children and God help you if you fell short of their expectations; you practically caught hell as a victim to their constant reminders of your shortcomings.

Elaina Monroe was the one who passed on her good looks to her children. She was a beautiful woman and Tina resembled her the most. She was medium height with long light brown hair and caramel color skin; she was basically of Creole descent. She was strong willed and didn't take any shit from nobody except her husband whom she married at a young age. When she was right about something, and most of the time she thought that she was, she would go to the extreme to rub it in your face especially with her mouth. She did not work but chose to stay at home and take care of her children.

Elaina met Thomas Sr. in a field picking blueberries one morning. Her family would get up early, before the sun came up, and would take a half hour ride to Jim's farm. As usual, Elaina had said something that her sister Ruthie didn't like the night before and the fussing had started up again this particular morning. They were always at it and Elaina could make Ruthie cry at the drop of a hat.

"You are so rude Elaina why do you have to talk like that?" Ruthie asked her.

"What I said I can say it again and besides it is the damn truth"! Elaina shouted. "Isn't that what Mommy says to tell the truth and the truth will set you the hell free"! "Having all of them babies and not a husband in sight and probably don't even know who the daddies are"! Elaina argued concerning a young lady that her sister baby-sitted for.

Elaina didn't see him walking up behind her. She was facing the opposite direction.

"You're right, I guess you're talking about Maryann Williams huh?" He said to Elaina. "Hi I'm Thomas Lewis from across the way.

"Hi I'm Ruthie and this is my sister Elaina."

Elaina was speechless and that's the affect that he would always have on her. Their eyes met and they married six months later.

Tina could recall several incidents in which her mother would get in heated arguments with people; from the neighbors to people at the grocery store, it didn't matter. She would use that mouth of hers like a weapon but she never used it when her children were being verbally abused by their father. She never came to their defense not because she feared her husband, but because she thought that kind of discipline was acceptable. Tina knew all too well that habits and personality traits are sometimes passed down from generation to generation and Brook had inherited the sailors' tongue from her grandmother. Elaina died from a cerebral hemorrhage at the age of 60.

Their dad, Thomas E. Lewis Sr., was African American and Indian. He was a very handsome man and had passed his intelligence on to his children. He was very tall in statue, brown complexion with curly black hair. He was a very proud man who worked as an airplane carrier and he worked hard for his money and provided well for his family. He didn't want his wife to work and felt that she didn't have to because he was making a pretty decent income.

Him and his wife believed in not spoiling their children and only providing them with the things that they needed and very seldom did they get what they wanted. They were stern with strict discipline and Thomas Sr. would often verbally abuse his children. They believed that this would set the path for good, hard working, successful children but they failed to see that it was doing them more harm than good especially Diane who seemed to suffer the most; but Mommy seen it. They would often tell their children that no one was going to give them anything and if they did it was sure to cost them one way or another and that's why you had to work hard to get what you wanted. They hated handouts. They provided the best education for their children and they had high expectations for all of them but Tina made them the proudest. Everything she did she exceeded in.

Thomas Sr. was determined to make his own way in life even if it killed him and it did. He died five years after his wife from a massive heart attack. He was 65 years old.

CHAPTER SIXTY-TWO

Tina sat on the sofa sipping on some wine. Christmas had come and gone and folks were preparing for the New Year. She had decided to stay at home and have a quiet evening alone in spite of Diane insisting that she come to the Watch Night service at the church. Diane was adjusting as best as she could. She had her moments when she would break down but she always found the strength to get back up again and she could thank Steve for that. He was a major support system for her.

The home going service for Brook was beautiful but difficult to deal with and the family said their farewells through teary eyes and heavy hearts. Diane held up pretty good at the service but fell apart at the burial which Tina always thought was the worst part.

Tina was feeling lonely yet she wanted to be alone. The long bath had made her sleepy but yet she couldn't fall asleep. She was anxious to do something but she didn't know what that something was. Just maybe she should have gone to church and the doorbell snapped her back to reality and she got up to answer the door.

"Oh no you're not, girl get dress and come on with us" Cynthia said looking at Tina in her pajamas.

"Hey I made plans to stay at home girl; I'm going to bring in the New Year in my bed alone unfortunately." Tina said laughing.

"Are you sure, you're ok?" Cynthia asked.

"I'm fine, don't worry about me." Tina added waving her hand.

"Ok I tried and oh and by the way, clear your voicemail it's full." Cynthia told her.

"Oh, I will and tell that brother of mine I said Happy New Year." Tina said and she watched Cynthia walk back to the car.

Cynthia and Robert had started seeing each other right after the funeral. Did they have what it took to make the relationship work Tina didn't know but her brother seemed to be a completely different person these days and just maybe they could pull it off. Cynthia had told her about their little fling back in the day and how they managed to keep it a secret from her was nuts. Tina grinned; she was happy for them. She had also heard through the grapevine that Thomas and his wife were talking again and she was glad to hear that so the New Year was looking promising after all.

As Tina closed the door, she was able to say good-bye to all the stuff that once held her captive but it was one thing that was left for her to do before the New Year came in. She walked to the closet and retrieved the two diaries, thinking that this was the best thing to do. After she got the diaries, she walked to the fire place and placed the two books into the flames; such a bitter sweet moment. The two diaries were the only things that connected her to her daughter but at the same time it held so much hurt and pain that Tina thought of them as a curse instead of a blessing. Pastor Peterson would be proud of her for he had said that no one can bring you peace but yourself. The diaries kept her going back to a place where she didn't want to be.

Watching the flames turn colors, Tina thought of Malone. Getting into a fight didn't make matters any better for him and Tina prayed that by her talking to a couple of people, would get him an early release before his mouth got him killed. That was a great concern for her. As for everyone else, if the truths were told, it seemed like the worse had brought out the best in each one of them. It was a rude awakening and she was thankful that no one had suspected her of doing anything; Destiny did but she couldn't prove anything. Fortunately, everything had worked itself out.

As the flames died down, Tina cried softly. Not because she was sad but because she was finally letting go of the very thing that was controlling her life. It was over now and done with. Tina wiped her face and started to look for her phone. She just couldn't keep up with the thing anymore. She looked on the sides of the cushions of the sofa and on the table and then she remembered using it in the bedroom. So much had happened that she had forgotten to clear her messages. The phone was on her night table and Tina sat down on the bed and started to check and clear them one by one. Messages from her hair dresser, a client, her brother, her sister and then she noticed not one call but numerous calls from Emanuel.

"What? Oh God!" She said pulling her voice messages up as fast as she could.

Tina listened intensely to Emanuel explaining the night at the mall with Patricia and that she was just a friend and nothing more. It was like he felt obligated to explain. Tina jumped up from the bed.

"I can't believe this thank you Lord, thank you." Tina said over and over again. "Emanuel, I hope I'm not too late." She whispered.

***

Emanuel was just finishing up at the hospital and was trying to make it home to get something to eat. Being on call for the Holiday prevented him from making any plans to go out so he had kindly turned down an invitation from Patty to spend the evening together with her and the kids. Emanuel couldn't remember a time when he was alone on New Year's Eve and it felt pretty damn lonely. He was missing the hell out of Tina and was angry at himself for missing her.

He had seen Tina at Brook's Home Going Service and felt bad for not extending his condolences but seeing her on the arm of another man had pissed him off so he slipped out the door before Tina got the chance to see him. She could have given him the common courtesy of returning his phone calls even if she was seeing someone but at least he finally got the closure that he needed to go on with his life. He just hoped that he could find someone that he could love just as much as he loved her. That was his New Year's Resolution.

Emanuel had just got out the car when he heard his phone ring and when he answered it, her voice made him come to a complete halt. He didn't know what to expect so he let her do the talking. He listened as she went into details about just getting around to checking her messages, and seeing him that night with Patricia and how she felt when she left the mall that night and he could hear it in her voice that she was on the verge of crying.

"I'm saying all of this because I hope that I'm not too late Emanuel?" Tina told him.

Emanuel was silent and then he let out a sigh of relief.

"No baby, you're not," he told her.

"Really," she asked?

"Really," he answered.

"Ok so you were smiling at that heifer and I'm saying to myself, oh know he didn't," Tina said laughing and crying at the same time.

"Damn woman, so who was the dude at the funeral?" Emanuel asked curiously. "I thought that was your man so I slipped out the church to keep from whipping his ass." Emanuel said jokingly.

Tina explained and the two talked and talked sharing and realizing their love for each other. A lesson learned for both of them that things are not always what they seem to be.

"Listen I really don't want to spend the evening alone so how about some company?" "I can bring a change of clothing and if I don't get called back to the hospital I'll just stay there if that's ok with you?" Emanuel asked.

"That's a good idea." Tina said. "I can't wait to see you Emanuel." She told him.

"I can't wait either," he said.

The New Year came in with a calm serenity and Tina was happier than she had ever been. She watched Emanuel as he slept and she vowed to never again allow anything to put a wedge between her and the one that she loved. Emanuel listened attentively caressing her shoulders as she told him her story. His eyes saying, I love you and I'll go through it with you if you let me in. He never questioned anything that she had done, only saying, I'm so sorry. *How could she not trust him,* was in her thoughts? Tina came to realize that trust had nothing to do with it. She didn't tell him out of fearing that he would have talked her out of doing what her mind was already made up to do.

Tina finished her story and the New Year came in finding them holding on to each other both saying Happy New Year added with a gentle, passionate kiss; no words could describe the depth of their intimacy.

Mommy said, "If someone or something comes back to you, it was meant to be," and Tina smiled and gently kissed Emanuel on his nose awaking him and he pulled her to him and they both fell asleep in each other's arms.

Happy New Year!

CHAPTER SIXTY-THREE

The cottage was located in a little town surrounded by a forest of trees. She was elated when her husband had come home and said that he had found the perfect place. His description of the cottage had made her fall in love with it even before she had seen it and when she had seen it for the first time she never wanted to leave. It was exactly what they had been looking for; a place to start a family. One, two or maybe three babies and she smiled to herself. She admired the beautiful scenery of spring flowers that were just beginning to bloom.

Sitting down at the vanity, she had already sent her seven guests several gifts throughout the month and the purple tulips were the last to be delivered. They were her favorite flower and purple was her favorite color too. The gifts were hints of what was to come. Glancing up at the mirror, she is a picture of extreme beauty. The resemblance of her mother is astonishing; hair, skin color, and yes, those beautiful eyes. The eyes that her husband had fallen in love with. You must have robbed a cat; he would tease her. She had to chuckle at the comment.

She closed her eyes and thought of how she almost missed out on such happiness; for she had chosen the road of destruction as her path and had given up all hope of what life had to offer. Something she always wondered. How a person could reach that point of no return and unfortunately, she knew the answer. Day after day she had to convince her self that there was a reason why things happened the way that they did and she strongly believed in the saying, "What doesn't kill you will make you stronger." She could testify to that.

Then the image that stood before her that dreadful day, the one that she truly believed God had sent to her. To give her back everything that she had lost and a whole lot more. God had overlooked her flaws and had given her a second chance to live a life full of love with no room for hate. He had forgiven her, so she had forgiven them and most importantly, she had forgiven herself. She felt like the happiest person on the planet and soon very soon another prayer would be answered and things would change for the better; at least for some. She smiled with sweet thoughts; she could barely contain herself so she hummed to her favorite hymn "When I Came to You."

He stood there staring and listening to her with great admiration. Life was finally good for them but it had not been easy. A face that had once showed the countenance of pain and sorrow was restored with such peace and serenity. He would do anything for her even kill for her if he had to. That's how deep his love was for her. He felt so fortunate to have her in his life yet she insisted that she was the fortunate one. He remembered holding her at night trying to reassure her that everything would be alright even when he wasn't sure himself. She was his miracle and while he was trying to save her, she had already saved him. For he was following the footsteps of those who met him no good but his love for her had kept him from making foolish decisions.

"Hey Babe, what are you doing?" He asked.

She jumped at the sound of his voice and looked up at him and smiled.

"Oh, just thinking about some things" she said.

"You know it's almost time to make that move." He said to her as he bends down to kiss her.

"Yes, I know and everything looks like it's falling into place."

"Good" he said.

***

She was just finishing up the laundry and went upstairs to put the linings away. There she saw the two talking and laughing and couldn't help but think what a wonderful couple. They seem to be so much in love and she was happy to be part of their family. She had known her from a little girl and couldn't help but think how proud her parents would be and she was proud of her too. Funny how life turns out never exactly how you think it will. She was the best thing that ever happened to her son. God had his hands on both of them.

"Ok that's enough you two." She said to them and they couldn't help but laugh.

"Ok ladies on that note, I have to make a quick run so I'll be back in about an hour ok babe" he said to her.

"Ok dinner will be ready by the time you get back." She said to him.

He kissed her cheek and his mother's too and left out the room. He had some unfinished business to take care of and was meeting with Mack at the café. The money had been good and he would miss the excitement but he had made a decision to go down another road once the cat was out of the bag. Besides, he had saved enough money and had invested in a couple of deals that set him and his wife up for life. They were more than able to live whatever life style they choose and they were also eager to start a family soon.

An hour had passed and he was back on the highway heading home. The meeting went well with Mack and they had kindly shook hands and embraced like two brothers would. Even though they were not blood related, they had a bond between them that no one could shake and they vowed to stay in touch with each other. The stuff that they had gone through was lessons learned and looking back over the years, he wouldn't change a thing. He had one more meeting for tomorrow evening and it was sure to be a mind blower for all but it was necessary and there was no way around it. The drive home was relaxing and he turned on the radio for company even though she never stayed out of his mind for long. He smiled just thinking about her.

The two women worked together to get dinner ready. The older one prepared the meal while the younger one sat the table. As she breathed in the smell of fresh flowers, it reminded her of the yesteryears when the one who borne her graced her table with the same. One day soon it wouldn't be just a thought but an actual moment taken out of the past and brought to the present. What a joy it will be.

Dinner was ready and the timing was perfect. The lights shone through the windows indicating that the man of the house was home. The three sat and ate like one happy family; sharing in casual conversation and anxiously waiting for the day when their lives would forever be changed.

Mommy said, "Life is not perfect, and that's what makes it beautiful."

CHAPTER SIXTY-FOUR

Pastor Peterson had just finished counseling a young couple whose wedding was to take place in a couple of weeks. As he finished the paper work, he was very happy that he would be able to give the young couple his blessings. His thoughts of them were prematurely interrupted by a knock at the door.

"Come in," Pastor Peterson said.

"Hi, I'm looking for Pastor Peterson" he said.

"That would be me, how can I help you son?"

Pastor Peterson noticed that the young man looked unfamiliar to him and questioned him about his membership.

"Are you a member here?" He asked him.

"No," he responded, "But my wife was," he said.

Sometime had passed and the gentleman exited from Pastor Peterson's office. He knew that it wasn't going to be easy so how do you really prepare someone for something like this? He thought. A reality check, you can't. He had done his part so now everything was ready to fall into place.

Pastor Peterson sat at his desk and could hardly believe what had just transpired in his office. Usually nothing shocked him but this was the most startling news that he had ever received. He thought it had been a bad joke until a phone call confirmed it.

"My God," Pastor Peterson said as he thought about all who would be involved. He had always felt that something was off about the whole situation, but no one was saying anything and no one knew anything so he had no choice but to accept things for what they were. Now he realized that it wasn't his imagination and he was right.

The meeting would be in three days and he prayed for strength as this was a very delicate situation to deal with. This will surely change their lives forever, he thought.

"My God, my God" he said as he got up to leave the office and still wasn't quite sure how he was going to break the news to his wife.

Tony's flight had arrived in Atlanta at 12 o'clock in the afternoon. Sheila practically demanded that she accompany him on this trip and any other trip and he didn't argue with her either. Sheila wasn't going to let him out of her sight and that was something that he could live with. He was just happy that she had given their marriage another chance and since everything was out in the open, it had given him the opportunity to tell her about his ex-wife and the story about his daughter. He couldn't stand to have that over his head any longer. Sheila wasn't happy about it but she appreciated his honesty; so far so good.

Tony couldn't imagine what was going on. It was obvious that Pastor Peterson sound upset over the phone and that was very unusual for him. Nothing seemed to bother that man but something had definitely shaken him up and Tony couldn't wait to find out. As him and Sheila pulled in the church's parking lot, curiosity took over him and he wondered what in the world it could be.

Emanuel and Tina arrived next. Pastor Peterson had stressed the importance of being at the church on time and they were relieved that they were a little early than expected being that Emanuel had run into an emergency at the hospital but was able to get everything in order before leaving.

Tina didn't know what to think after Pastor Peterson expressed his urgency to meet with her. She knew something was going on when she came home one night to find Emanuel on the phone talking with him. She could see Emanuel through the window and his facial expression was that of a person receiving some disturbing news. When she questioned him about it, he brushed her off and told her it was nothing and handed her the phone. Look whose keeping secrets now, she thought at the time. The rest of that evening, Emanuel wasn't his usual self. He wanted to hold her; he told her that he loved her and it was like he couldn't express it enough. Late at night when they had gone to bed, she rolled over to find him staring at her with a look that she couldn't explain. As they got out the car, Tina wondered if that conversation had anything to do with the meeting that they were about to have.

Emanuel took Tina's hand and they walked into the church. He had done everything he could to avoid telling Tina anything about what was about to take place and he felt bad because they had promised that they would never keep anything from each other again but Emanuel knew that this was a rare instance and he had to keep his mouth shut. All would be revealed soon enough and the only thing that he would be able to do is stand by her and love her.

CHAPTER SIXTY-FIVE

The ride had been long and the anxiety was building up. Her husband noticed and held her hand to reassure her. A life changing event was about to happen and the closer they got to their destination, the more she felt like she was about to lose it. This is not the way she thought she was going to feel; frightened and unsure if she was even doing it the right way. She had played it over and over in her head what she wanted to say and what she wanted to do and now that it was almost time, she was starting to panic. This was supposed to be a happy occasion so why was she feeling this way. She closed her eyes and prayed.

Tina and Emanuel entered the Pastor's office and were surprised to see Tony and a female already seated. Tina was also offended when she got a nasty look me down from the female that Tony introduced as his wife Shelia. Handshakes and hugs were given and Tina and Emanuel took a seat on the sofa on the right side of the room.

Thomas and Robert arrived and both were curious as to why Pastor Peterson wanted to see them. With no clue to go on, they greeted each other with a hand shake and entered the church. Five minutes later, Diane pulled up humming, "This Little Light of Mine." She was under the impression that she was wanted to participate in some kind of church event. She was good at organizing things and was delighted that the Pastor had called on her.

"Does anyone know what's going on?" Tony asked looking at Tina.

"No, we don't but I'm quite sure we will find out soon." She said.

Just as Tina finished her sentence, the door opened and Cynthia entered the room and Thomas, Robert and Diane were right behind her. Emanuel could tell that Cynthia knew what was going on by the quick glance that she had given him when she came into the room.

"Hey everybody" she said and the two men got up to welcome her and the introductions were started up again.

Cynthia took a seat on the opposite side of the room but not before giving Tina a slight kiss on the cheek. Thomas, Robert and Diane had now joined the group and sat next to Cynthia with Diane closest to the door. Everyone was speculating as to what was going on and two minutes later Pastor Peterson along with his wife Rebecca, entered the room and closed the door behind them.

After greeting everyone with handshakes, and gentle embraces, Pastor Peterson took a chair from the corner of the room and placed it near Tina. Tina thought that he didn't look like himself. He looked tired; like he had been deprived of sleep.

"Ok everyone is here so we can get started." Pastor Peterson said looking around the room.

"Tony if you don't mind can you switch seats with your wife, please" Pastor Peterson asked so that Tony was next to Tina. He was than able to take a hold of Tony and Tina's hand. Rebecca sat at her husband's desk.

"I must say that in all my years as a Pastor this is the most complicated situation that I have ever had to deal with and I am certain that the news will come as a shock to everyone. "With God's help we will all get through this." "Let's pray." Pastor Peterson said.

Tina's heart began to race. The words that Pastor Peterson had just spoken had given her the impression that something major was about to happen. *What in the world is going on,* she thought; and then with no time to prepare her brain for the words that came next. Tina doubted that she had even heard him correctly.

"What did you say?" Tina asked.

Everything is going in slow motion; Tina can't seem to pull herself out of it. She wants to speak again but this time she can't. Tina glances at Emanuel than back to Pastor Peterson. She glances around the room and everyone seems to be as shocked as she is. Emanuel takes Tina's hand and with the other he rubs her back assuring her that everything was going to be ok. Tina's eyes follow Rebecca as she gets up and goes to the door and opens it. The two enter the room and all eyes are on them. Tina squeezes Emanuel's hand. The guy looks familiar and Tina tries hard to remember where she had seen him. Then she looks at her and it's like looking in a mirror at herself. Tina remembers her dreams; the dreams which haunted her and gave her false hope in believing that her daughter was alive but she was too afraid to tell anyone not even Emanuel, for fear that he along with everyone else would think that she was crazy. Tina's breathing becomes unsteady and tears are streaming down her face as the young lady walks toward her. She kneels down.

"Mommy and daddy, it's me, Macy."

Tina opens her mouth but still nothing comes out. She begins to shake uncontrollably; her color turns pale; she faints and Emanuel grabs a hold of her.

"Tina, baby talk to me," Emanuel says while patting the side of her face but Tina doesn't respond. Macy backs away holding her hand to her mouth and her husband stands next to her to console her.

"Will she be, ok?" Macy asked out of concern and Emanuel gives her a quick glance.

"She should be" he answered.

"I'll go get a wet cloth." Cynthia said and she left the room.

Pastor Peterson and his wife are looking after Tony who apparently is in shock also. With tears running down his face, his breathing is heavy and his eyes are on his daughter. Sheila puts her arm around him and tries to comfort him. The pain and the shame are too much. It was all coming back.

"My God" he says loudly.

Diane held so tight to the sides of the chair that her hands were becoming numb. She couldn't say anything and she couldn't move. Once again, what should have been a celebrated occasion was becoming a nightmare for some. The guilt was overwhelming. Thomas sat in the chair holding his head in his hands as Robert paced the floor as if he was waiting to hear the outcome of a major business deal; each feeling the guilt and shame of it all and unable to utter a word.

Mommy said, "When you take hold of the silence in you, you can make sense of the stuff going on around you".

CHAPTER SIXTY-SIX

D*on't you wish life was like an edit-movie? Take out the bad parts, speed up the slow parts, fast-forward to the good and exciting, being the main character; to be, to do, and to do without; Possessing the strength and accepting the suffering and efforts that life implies and realizing that you don't have to run away because this isn't your final cut.*

Tina stood at the grave site and exhaled. She had so much to be thankful for.

"Life can be so unpredictable," she could hear Mommy say.

Tina kneeled down to place the bouquet of flowers on Brook's grave; something she had promised Diane she would do on Brook's birthday and on Christmas. As Tina watched Diane pull off that day, she knew in her heart that it was for the best. Did Diane want to get away or run away like Macy said? Macy would ask. Run away from the truth because it hurt too much. Tina would never see her sister again, not even on her wedding day. I guess Macy was a constant reminder of a past that she wanted so desperately to forget but sometimes it's not so easy to forget and you allow yourself to become enslaved to your own inner demons. They all could relate to that.

Mommy said, "We are our own worst enemy." Truth there, Tina thought.

The family did come together for holidays and special occasions but it wasn't like it was back in the day, nothing was. It was always a feeling in the air that something just wasn't right or the stare on one's face that let you know that their thoughts had entered that time zone that was so dark and unpleasant. Accepting or not, it was a part of their family history. Tina stood up after placing the flowers on the grave. She thought of Tony and how he had really taken advantage of his second chance at being a real father to Macy; Giving her not only his time, but his never-ending love. It was a good thing to see them together.

My beautiful baby girl, Tina thought with a smile. Not the little girl with the ponytails, but the beautiful young woman who was so full of life and love that could melt your heart away. Tina knew God had his hand in this by sending Jessie and her son Jolan, whom they called Duces. The tall handsome guy who she had bumped into that day at the mall. He was sent to save her daughter when she had given up on life and was going to prove it by swinging at the end of a noose. She told her story, filling in the answers to questions that Tina did not know. She was a true example of not looking like what she had been through. A light shone on her face and through her heart. Macy was an incredible young woman and Tiny admired her strength. She and her husband loved each other unconditionally and that love created the grandchild that she and Tony were so anxiously waiting to meet in just a couple of months.

And then there's Emanuel Tina thought feeling really fortunate. God had not only given her the man that she needed but also the man that she wanted. A man that truly loved her; her Knight and Shining Armor whom she would be marrying a week from the day. Everything that she thought she had lost was giving back to her. God was truly amazing. Tina blew a kiss at the grave of her niece and walked away.

Mommy said, "Deal only with the present don't step back into yesterday; for yesterday is gone; and the future is not ours to know, just give me today."

Made in the USA
Middletown, DE
04 October 2024

62038310R00179